AWAY FROM KEYBOARD COLLECTION

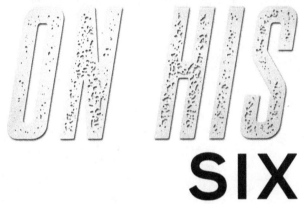

SIX

PATRICIA D. EDDY

Editing by The Novel Fixer and Jayne Frost

Proofreading by Darcy Jayne

Formatting by The Novel Fixer

Cover by Deranged Doctor Design

If you love sexy vampires and demons, I'd love to send you the prequel to the upcoming Immortal Protectors series. FOR FREE! Sign up for my Unstoppable Newsletter on my website and tell me where to send your free book!
http://patriciadeddy.com.

1

—————

Ryker

The worst part of Hell? Hard to choose. The isolation? The screams of my men echoing off the walls? The ever-changing schedule designed to keep us all off balance, never knowing whether it was day or night? The God-awful scraps of food infected with maggots or dotted with mold? The smell?

Not the pain.

Pain can be controlled. I've learned to ignore the physical blows. The blades. The cigarettes. The troughs of dirty, parasite-infested water they shove my head into until I'm seconds from passing out. Electricity and fire are the hardest, but most times, I can at least dampen the agony of ten thousand volts shooting through my body or flames charring my skin by sending my mind somewhere else. Somewhere quiet and warm with no walls, where nothing is out of my control. My safe space. I'm there now. On the beach, in the sun. Waves lap softly at the shore, and birds fly overhead, their white and gray bodies graceful as they arc through the sky.

Until I'm yanked back into the depths of the dark, cold caves under the mountains. Blindfolded, I hold my breath, listening for footsteps. For the jingle of keys or the scrape of a boot against stone.

On my knees, my hands tied behind my back, I fight the dizziness. I don't remember the last time I ate, and the only water I've had in the past twenty-four hours was licked off the walls of the hole in the ground they just pulled me out of.

"Tell us what we need to know, Ryker. Then we can treat your wounds, send you back to your family." The head interrogator, Kahlid, leans close enough I can smell the garlic on his breath. "We do not want to hurt you, my friend. But you must understand. We have no choice."

The punch to my liver sends pain exploding across my back. I start to fall, but the noose around my neck stops my descent, choking me, and I gasp for breath, wheezing until Kahlid grabs my chin and forces me back up to my knees.

"Tell us, Ryker. Why were you in the mountains? What were you searching for?"

In fifteen months, I haven't said a thing beyond my name, rank, and every curse word I've ever heard—and some I invented just for this place. Pretending I don't know anything...I gave that up after the first week. One of my men was so delirious before he died, he told them we were all Special Forces. Sepsis had a hold of him, and he didn't know what he was saying. Hell, he thought he was talking to me. But I was gagged and bound a few feet away, watching as Kahlid ripped out his fingernails one at a time.

"Go fuck yourself," I manage, my throat raw and my tongue so dry it sticks to the roof of my mouth. "Quit wasting my goddam time."

The tip of the knife slices just under the blindfold, a scant millimeter from my eye. Blood drips down my cheek, splashing my chest and soaking into my threadbare t-shirt. What's one more scar? I already look like Quasimodo.

The door opens with a screech of metal, and I hear Dax breathing. He's getting worse every day. Weaker. He can't walk. Fuckers broke his leg two weeks ago, and though I set it—sort of —with a makeshift splint and some dirty rags, it's infected, and the forced inactivity has driven him half-insane.

"Watch...the leg...asshole," he growls. Good. At least he's still got his wits about him today.

"Over there," Kahlid says.

I hold my breath and listen, trying to get a sense of where they're taking him, what they're doing. The last book I read before we found ourselves guests in the worst accommodations Yelp has ever seen was all about tricking your brain into remembering a shit-ton of information.

I catalog everything. How Kahlid's footsteps sound different from Basheert's. The limp that marks Hamid's walk. The sweet odor on the guards' breaths after breakfast and how it differs from the scent of garlic they eat with dinner.

Despite being blindfolded anytime they pull me out of my cell or the hole, I have a map of this place burned into my brain. The room we're in...it's twenty feet by thirty feet. Along one wall, there are hasps sunk into the rock they can tie or lock us to. The ceiling is low. The door, lower. If I don't duck, I hit my head every time.

I never duck. Can't let them know what I know.

Two sets of hands grab my arms and haul me to the center of the room. I'm a big guy—close to seven feet tall. Before...fifteen months ago...I was close to two-ninety. But now...I've lost at least fifty pounds.

Kahlid pulls the noose over my head, and I swallow hard. I can't stand the sensation of anything around my neck anymore. Not after the hundreds of times they've choked me until I've passed out.

"Take off the blindfolds," Kahlid orders.

Fuck.

I blink against the dim lights.

Dax hangs from his wrists against the far wall, trying to balance on his one good leg. The left half of his face is bruised and bloody. Fuckers beat the shit out of him yesterday.

"Sergeant Holloway. Welcome."

"Fuck you." Dax spits in Kahlid's general direction.

"We want to offer you medical care, Sergeant. Dash."

Dash. Shitstain hasn't once called him by the right name.

"Life is full of disappointment. Get used to it."

I wait for one of the guards to kick Dax's leg or punch him in the gut or something. Instead, Kahlid jerks his head in my direction. The closest asshole pulls a leather strap out of his pocket as the two goons holding me tighten their grip.

After a quick jab to my jaw, the leather is pulled between my teeth and the strap bound tightly around my head. One of Kahlid's favorite games. Torture one of us to make the other talk.

We're the only two left. Hab only lasted a week here. Ripper... he vanished three months ago. And Gose...Kahlid gutted him right in front of me.

But me and Dax...we always were the strongest. The meanest. The closest. Came up together. Trained together. Had our first kills within days of one another. There's a bond you can't break after seven years serving side-by-side in some of the worst conditions on this earth.

The look that passes between us speaks whole paragraphs. And at the same time nothing at all. A mutual understanding. No one talks. No one breaks. No matter what.

We signed up for this. Knew the risks. Left our goodbye notes in our footlockers back at Bagram. The final farewells to our families.

A guard rips open my shirt. Damn thing tears like tissue paper. I don't look down. The entire right side of my body resembles a map drawn by a second grader. Scars on top of scars on top

On His Six

of scars. These pathetic excuses for men have carved me up like a Thanksgiving turkey.

"Tell us why you and your team were in the mountains. What were you looking for, Dash? That is all we want to know. Help me to help you."

"Fuck off."

The hiss of a blowtorch makes us both flinch. As the flames lick across my chest, I bite down—hard—on the leather and try to hold Dax's gaze.

"Don't," I try to say, but I can only manage a guttural moan as the edges of my vision darken. I shake my head, and the agony of burning flesh becomes my entire existence. With my next breath, I let the blackness claim me.

I come to with a jerk and a shout—back in my bed in Seattle, the caves buried under several tons of rocks and six years. My captors are dead. The familiar scent of my apartment surrounds me, and my legs are tangled in the thin sheet.

Sweat chills on my skin as I fumble for my water bottle next to my bed. The damn thing bounces to the floor with a clang, and water dribbles over the cement.

"Fuck."

The bullet wound in my side throbs. Two weeks after the disaster that almost killed my whole team, I still can't move like I want to. This forced inactivity is...taking me places I can't go. Hab's broken body. Naz begging me to kill him. One of my guards pleading for his life, then shooting me in the back five seconds later.

The hell with Doc Reynolds' advice. I need to hit something. Do something. Anything but stay here another fucking minute.

I throw open the blackout drapes to reveal the Seattle skyline. When I bought this place, I gutted it down to the studs. It's a fucking Faraday Cage in here. No electronic signals in or out—except the hardline and the cell repeater. No Wi-Fi. The windows aren't bulletproof—I couldn't afford that shit. But the special glazing ensures no one can see in. Not even when it's pitch dark outside and I have all the lights on.

Refilling the water bottle, I try to soothe my raw throat. Doesn't matter that the stitches came out four days ago. I can still feel the blood soaking into my shirt. The white-hot pain as Doc fished a bullet fragment out of the wound, the iodine he poured over my skin.

No hospital.

No anesthetic.

No trace.

I've suffered through worse. In my line of work, injuries aren't an "if," they're a "when."

Five times, I've been shot. Leg, back, shoulder, side, and arm. You never get used to the sensation. The pop as the bullet enters the body. The distinct lack of pain at first. After a few seconds, you feel like someone just lit a match inside you.

Leaning against the counter, I close my eyes and take a couple of deep breaths. Images of West bleeding out in a veterinarian's office in Colombia flicker until I shove them away.

Too much blood in my life.

On my hands.

How could I choose this? *Twice?* I should have gone into private security with a cushy office like Dax, but no. I had to pick K&R. My hands curl into fists when I think about others rotting in the same type of hell I escaped from.

Forcing my fingers to relax, I examine the scars and know, deep in my gut, this was my only option. Doesn't matter how risky. If there's a chance—and there's always a chance—I consider the case.

"Fuck." I cradle my head in my hands, trying to ease the pressure building behind my eyes. "Since when did I become a liability?"

I'm slipping. Losing my edge. Misjudging Coop. Ignoring my

instincts. Believing my leadership could keep him in line. My mistake could have cost West, Inara, and Royce their lives.

Flipping on the coffee maker, I catch sight of the crumpled postcard on the counter. The damn thing showed up last night.

We hope you'll join us at Libations at 2:00 p.m. Sunday, April 25th as
we say our vows. Appetizers will be served.
No gifts.
Cam and West

I should go, but I can't bring myself to RSVP. The idea of spending an afternoon celebrating love—an emotion I'll never understand—leaves me cold. I don't know how to face them. West and Inara—my team. Not after my fuck-ups. And I don't mingle. Don't do casual conversation.

The night West and I cleaned up Coop's mess, we talked more in six hours than we had in months. And in the two weeks since, I haven't spoken a word to a soul other than the doc.

The rich scent of coffee fills the open kitchen. Leaning against the counter in only a pair of briefs, I run my callused fingers over the new scar on my side and scowl. In a few weeks, it'll blend in with all the rest. The stripes across my back. The burns along my chest. The rough, pebbled flesh down my right arm.

I flex my hands, trying to work out the customary aches that always accompany morning—or the rain. If I didn't love Seattle so much, I'd move somewhere warmer. The fuckers who ran Hell broke all of my fingers more than once, along with a lot of other bones, and I'll never be pain free.

Once my coffee mug's full, I wander over to my laptop. Plugging in the internet cable, I wake up the machine and check my email.

Great. Another message from Inara.

Ry,

West and I are meeting Graham at the warehouse for some drills tonight at seven. Come join us. We're all going a little stir crazy.

Inara

I can't. Fuck. I'm a piece of work. One hundred percent asshole. I tried. After cleaning up the mess in the rail yard after our last mission and seeing the doc, I came back here, showered, and then forced myself to head to University Village. My worst nightmare. Buying Royce a new phone and watch nearly killed me. All those people. And then I walked into H&M and asked the clerk for two casual women's outfits in size six. Pretty sure the girl thought I had someone tied up in my basement. I don't know what possessed me, but Inara lost everything in the fire that burned down her house and almost killed her and Royce. And since Coop targeting her was my fault to begin with, I had to do something.

After I click reply, I stare at the blank screen for a full five minutes before I figure out what to say—and do.

I'm headed out of town for a few days. Need to clear my head. After West gets back from his honeymoon, we'll start regular training sessions again. Use the warehouse whenever you want. Expense a couple of cases of water and energy drinks. I'll reimburse you. Don't get soft.

No pleasantries. No emotion. Just the facts. That's all I can give her. The coffee goes down too quickly, and before I know it, I'm on my third cup and looking at flights to Boston. Dax, the only other member of my squad who made it through fifteen months of Hell, lives in Back Bay. He'll understand.

At least...I think he will. We haven't talked in...longer than I want to admit. But shit like we endured bonds you for life. And if he doesn't, at least I won't be here where ghosts haunt me at every turn.

Though the sun's only been up for an hour, the three-hour time difference means Dax answers on the second ring.

"Ry? Seriously? You've got some nerve calling here."

The anger in his voice sets me on edge, and I stare up at the ceiling, fighting against the instinct to hang up on the asshole. "Yeah. Seriously. You gonna cut me some fucking slack, or do I hang up right now?"

"I'm not the one who went dark for six years. Half a dozen calls, unanswered. Twice as many emails. I figured you were either dead or...fuck. I don't know."

My heart pounds hard enough I feel the beat in my ears and behind my eyes. I'm a solid guy—muscular—two hundred and eighty pounds. And right now, I feel like I'm about to crumble into a million pieces. "Been busy," I snap. "Hidden Agenda doesn't run itself. If you'd joined me, you'd know that."

"Well, maybe if you'd...goddammit. I don't have time for this shit. What do you want?"

"Nothing, apparently. Take care of yourself, Dax." Jabbing the phone screen, I sever the last, thin thread that bound us together.

Wren

The hard knot in my chest makes breathing difficult, and I fumble for the little plastic container in my messenger bag. My monitor's glow casts the office in an eerie blueish light, and I scan the lines of text that scroll by as my thumb flicks the little catch on the box.

Before I can fish out one of the little pills, an alert pops up on my screen.

MATCHING RECORDS DETECTED

"About damn time," I mutter as my fingers fly over the keyboard. Two entries, four hours apart. ATM receipts. "Stupid, Billy. Really stupid."

Five minutes later, I head for Dax's office. My boss sits with his back to me, staring out the window—or pretending to. "He's in Burlington," I say after I knock twice. "Or was, three hours ago. I caught him withdrawing three hundred from an ATM on the corner of Wilson and Fourth."

Turning, Dax runs a hand through his dark locks. "Good work. Any sign of the kid?"

"No." I shove my hands into my pockets and lower my gaze to my well-worn Vans. "And he's changed vehicles. The ATM camera's black and white, but it looks like he's driving a dark-colored sedan. Pattern matching should let me narrow it down, but I can only do so much."

"Keep trying. The hospital called. His wife is going to live. She'll be awake in a few hours, and I want to be able to tell her that we found her daughter by then." With a hiss, Dax pulls off his tinted glasses and pinches the bridge of his nose. "Get back to work, Wren. And...thanks."

There's no mistaking his dismissal, and I hurry away as he mutters, "Goddamn migraine. Not now."

Anxiety tightens in my chest again, and I force down one of my pills with a swig of cold coffee before I turn to my second screen. What I'm about to do...so illegal. But before our client, Misty, went into surgery, she told Dax and Ford that she'd found email messages between her estranged husband and a known sex-trafficking ring operating out of Portland, Maine. If we don't find the deadbeat soon, he'll sell their daughter, and none of us will be able to forgive ourselves.

The traffic camera network security in Burlington is a joke, and before the anxiety pill even takes effect, I have a partial plate and footage of the pervert heading north out of town on Route 2.

"Come on, come on. Where's the girl?" I advance and rewind the footage a dozen times, until finally, I see a shadow moving in the back seat. Not confirmation, but I'll take any possibility she might be alive as a good sign.

I follow the car—a late model Ford Taurus—until it leaves the city and run some quick calculations in my little notebook. Faster that way, leaving my computers free to try to break in to the state's EZ Pass system.

It'll only take the scumbag another two hours to get to the outskirts of Portland—if that's even where he's going. After that, we could lose the kid forever.

"Yes!" Pumping my fist as the Turnpike's network firewall crumbles in the face of my code, I run the partial plate, triumph welling in my chest as it comes back with a match.

"Dax!" I yell and jump up, then curse as I bang my knee on the leg of the desk, snag my ankle, and fall to the floor with a bone-jarring *thud*. "*Dang it*. I found him. He got onto the highway at Exit 87B five minutes ago heading east. Average highway speed of sixty-three miles an hour!"

By the time I extricate myself from the tangled mess of wires under my desk, Dax is relaying my info to his friends at the New York FBI office. I hover at the door until he's done, fiddling with my green pendant—a gift from my brother and one of the ways I deal with my anxiety. The emerald glass warms in my hand, and having something to do with my fingers helps calm my racing heart and eases the tightness in my chest.

"Wren?" Dax raises his head, his brows furrowed as he ends the call.

Taking two steps into his office, I shift from foot to foot. "How long until we know?"

"Not long." With a sweep of his hand, he invites me to sink into his guest chair, then swivels to his file cabinet. When he sets two glasses and a bottle of scotch on the desk between us, I blow out a breath. I should keep pounding the coffee—just in case, but Dax doesn't share often, and we've been on thin ice since Zion disappeared.

I pour, nudge one of the glasses towards Dax, and flop back

against the soft leather. "I think the daughter's still in the car. But I can't be sure."

"If she's not..."

The scotch burns a trail down my throat, roughening my voice. "I know. We'll never find her."

We sit in silence for the next ten minutes until Dax's phone buzzes on his desk, making both of us jump. The pretty British voice announces, "Ridge calling." His FBI contact.

He fumbles for the phone, nearly knocking over the bottle of scotch in the process. "Dammit," he snaps as he closes his fingers around the lump of plastic and glass.

"Ridge," he says. "Tell me you got him."

After a brief pause, Dax drops his head against the high back of his ergonomic chair. "Thank God. She's unharmed?" Another pause. "I'll be at the hospital in an hour. Bring her there. Her mother will want to see her. There's an aunt she can stay with until Misty's recovered enough to go home."

My fingers find their way to my pendant again, and I stroke the smooth surface until Dax ends the call. "You did it, Wren," he says. "They pulled him over just north of exit 95. The kid was asleep in the back seat. He'd given her a sedative, but the agents were able to wake her up and confirm she's not injured. Good job."

I shudder as the anxiety seeps out of me, almost like a deflating balloon. The meds, scotch, and relief at saving the girl all combine to leave me exhausted. "Th-thanks. I'll...uh...see you tomorrow."

For a brief moment, a frown curves Dax's lips, but then he nods. "I know it's late. If you want a day off..."

"No. I need to work. I'll be here." I rise so fast, I almost knock over the chair. "You need anything before I—"

"No." His curt dismissal makes me flinch, and I kick myself for offering. The man hates letting anyone help him. Hell, if he could code the way I can, he'd have found the perp himself.

As I lock up my laptop and sling my messenger bag over my shoulder, I catch sight of the single photo on my desk, half-obscured by coffee mugs and granola bar wrappers.

I can't leave like this. Sweeping the trash into the bin and gathering up the mugs, I trudge into the small office kitchen, load the dishwasher, and make sure there's nothing out of place. Only then do I return to my office and brush my fingers over the silver frame.

"I miss you, Zion." My baby brother smiles in the photo…his arms around me, full of promise with his basketball team crowding around us, celebrating their championship. Before everything went to hell. Before he discovered heroin. Before he disappeared. Before…

Tears burn my eyes, but I don't let them fall. I've cried so much for him these past few years. If I start again, a part of me fears I'll never stop. And tonight…tonight is a good night. I did my job. Stopped a bad man from hurting a little girl. "You'd be impressed, Z," I say as I straighten the frame. "Big sis did good."

2

Wren

A bouquet of daisies sits on my desk when I trudge into the office the next day, with an effusive note from our client thanking me—us—for finding her daughter. Her husband is in jail now, and by some small miracle, he didn't do more than scare the kid a little.

"S'up, Wren?" Ford says as I stop at the coffee machine. "Nectar of the gods?"

I stare longingly at the pot and inhale deeply. The rich brew beckons, but between the late night and the fitful dreams that plagued me during the few hours I managed to sleep...I'm already on the edge of an anxiety attack. Instead, I reach for a bag of herbal tea. "Trying to cut back."

"You?" He snorts. "Pretty sure you went through four pots last night." His hazel eyes crinkle around the edges, a lopsided grin curving his full lips. "I heard all about how you saved the day. Good job."

"Thanks." My cheeks flush, the all-too-familiar deflection coiling on my tongue. "I got lucky."

"Hardly. You're a badass." Ford's our resident weapons specialist and the vice president of Second Sight. He's also pushing fifty but has more in common with a body-builder than someone who's not too far away from getting an AARP card.

With a congratulatory slap to my shoulder, he lumbers back to his office, and I fill my mug with hot water. I hate tea. But my therapist insists giving up caffeine will help. Of course, she doesn't have to pull fifteen-hour days tracking down the worst of humanity. Or live with the aftermath when we fail.

Once I'm at my desk, I close my eyes and let the light, floral scent fill the small space. I don't have a window. The walls are bare. Somewhere between cream and white. I could paint. Hang art. Bring in a plant. But when I'm here, my entire focus is on my screens. And the criminals I track down for Dax and his crew.

I flop back in my chair. My eyes burn after so little sleep, and I regret not taking Dax up on his offer of a day off.

Three times in the middle of the night, I woke up crying, dreaming of Zion as I saw him exactly six weeks ago. His bright blue eyes clear, hair washed and combed, clean-shaven, with an excited edge to his voice as he told me all about his new job—janitor at the Presbyterian Church down in Somerville.

"I know it's a shit gig, Wren, but when I told them about the drug charge, they didn't even blink. Asked me if I was clean, and as soon as I said they could drug test me every fucking day if they wanted—" his cheeks flush pink, *"—I apologized for the swearing. Anyway, they hired me on the spot. Even gave me the day off for court next week. I start tomorrow."*

"That's great, kiddo. I'm really proud of you." I ruffle his hair, despite knowing how much he hates it. *"And you're going to keep attending meetings, right?"*

"Every day." His eyes darken, and he takes my hands. When did he get so tall? So...adult? I half-raised him after our mom split when I was

twenty-one and Zion only thirteen. I still think he should be this wiry, athletic kid, but he has a foot on me now, and though his recovery left him painfully thin, his hands dwarf mine. "I'm never going back to that life, Wren. I promise."

Tears line my eyes as I pull him into a tight embrace. "I'm going to hold you to that. I need you around, Z."

"I'm not going anywhere."

Except...a week later, when I went to pick him up for his court date, he was gone.

"Wren." Dax raps sharply on my door, and I jerk, spilling the tea all over my jeans.

"Cracker Jacks," I swear. Mom would be proud. Three years working for former SEALs, Special Forces, and Rangers, and I still haven't given up my...*unique* spin on profanity. Courtesy of her job as a preschool teacher and her off-beat sense of humor. At least with all the time I spent lost in my memories, the chamomile had time to cool.

I fumble for a stack of napkins in my top drawer as Dax takes a step forward, his brows knitting together. "Wren?"

Times like these, he looks a little like a lost puppy. "Sorry," I say. "I'm...edgy today. Spilled my tea. What's up?"

Reaching into his back pocket, he offers me a handkerchief, and the expression on his face makes me shudder as our fingers brush. "What is it, boss?"

"You...uh...got a call a few minutes ago. They couldn't reach you on your cell, so they rang the office. Marjorie didn't think you were in." His voice roughens as I try to mop up the spilled tea, and he takes a step forward, fumbling for the edge of my desk chair. "Wren...the city's knocking down a bunch of buildings on the edge of the waterfront. The cops got tired of raiding the drug dens a few years ago and just let them be until...yesterday. Down in the basement of the old cannery...they found a body."

I can't breathe. My entire world slows, then slams to a halt as a dull roar in my ears competes with Dax's deep voice.

"It's Zion."

♥

TWO HOURS LATER, Dax sits next to me in a small office at the South Boston police department. With my hands clasped in my lap, I stare straight ahead, keeping my emotions locked away where they can't hurt me.

I wanted to come alone. But Dax...for all of his faults, he cares about everyone in the office like we're his family. And I guess...we are. But after he put up Zion's bail—and lost ten grand when Z never showed for his trial—we've been...distant.

"Miss Kane? I'm Detective Raskins." The rumpled, skinny man sits across from us and opens a Manilla folder. I fixate on a shock of his straw-colored hair sticking straight up on the side of his head. Anything to avoid the inevitable. "You *are* Wren Kane, aren't you?"

At my side, Dax clears his throat and covers my hand with his. "Wren."

The contact shatters the little bubble with only me and the detective's cowlick, and I nod. "Yes. You...f-found my brother?"

Raskins slides a photograph towards me, face down, but doesn't take his hand away. "The cold weather this spring...probably the only reason we got an ID at all. Dental records gave us a partial match, and between that, his driver's license, and this..."

When he flips the photo, a dull roar fills my ears. Someone's squeezing my heart. Hard enough that I wonder if it's about to burst. The purple, green, and gray fluorite beads aren't anything unique, but in the middle of the bracelet, a shiny silver sphere bears the inscription I special ordered when Zion got his one-month chip from NA.

Courage

"That's...his," I manage. I run my fingers over the picture, feeling the undulations in the crystals, seeing Zion fiddle with them as we sat in a Nar-Anon meeting together for the first time. "How...long ago did he...die? And...how?"

"A month, give or take. Kind of hard to tell after a few weeks. But the basement of the cannery never got much above sixty degrees. He was found behind a stack of old pallets...which was probably why the body wasn't picked clean." Raskins takes another picture out of the folder.

"Cause of death was ruled an overdose. We pulled all the usual paraphernalia out of his pockets, found the needle underneath him."

I can't make sense of what I'm seeing. Choking back a sob, I shake my head and shove the picture back at the detective. "No. Not Zion. He was *clean*. He went to meetings every day. He had a job. He was making amends. He *promised* me."

The detective watches me with jaded eyes, then tucks the photo back into the folder. "His stash was gone, but some other junkie probably took that off him pretty quick."

"Zion...someone did this to him. Did something to him. Look again. Look *harder!*" I know I sound hysterical, though my eyes are dry. There's no way he started using again. I don't care about the needle, matches, spoon, and rubber tube in the picture. I don't care he was in a known drug den. "My brother never broke a promise to me. Never."

"Wren."

Dax's overly patient tone grates on my last nerve. "Don't. You do *not* get to say 'I told you so.' Because you're wrong. You're both wrong." Grasping my necklace to try to stop myself from landing in a full-blown panic attack, I tug on it so hard the chain snaps. A single tear burns my eye, and I blink it away, clutching the pendant in my palm until the edges bruise my skin.

"There's no evidence of foul play, Ms. Kane. And one of your brother's drug buddies told us he used to hang out at the cannery when he wanted to get high. Addicts...when they relapse...it's easy to OD."

Standing up so quickly the metal chair almost topples over, I shake my head. "Not Z." I have to get out of here. I can't...breathe. "I'll...be...outside," I wheeze, and with my bag clutched to my chest, I race for the door.

DAX and I don't speak on our way back to the office. He managed to convince Detective Raskins to turn over my brother's bracelet, and I'm twirling it around my wrist like it's the only thing keeping me sane. My heart still feels like it's about to come out of my chest, but the worst of the panic is fading now that my meds are taking effect.

As we climb the steps up from the T station, his hand around my elbow, I stare up at the bright blue sky. Rain and clouds have dominated the weather for weeks, and today...when I left my apartment, the day held such promise. Now...

"Do you have anyone to stay with you?" Dax stops once we enter the lobby of the six-story office building Second Sight calls home.

"I want to be alone." I slip out of his grasp, but three steps from the door, I turn. "I'm sorry, Dax. I'll...pay you back. Every penny."

"Wren, you don't..."

I'm out the door before he can finish his sentence. I don't want sympathy. I want my brother back.

CANDLES BURN all around the living room, though from my position on the kitchen floor I can't see any of the flames. Just the gently flickering light painting my walls with shadows.

I don't know what possessed me to try to eat something— going through the motions, I guess—but the pizza has gone cold on the counter, and I can't get up off the floor. Pixel, my little Bichon Poodle mix, crawls into my lap and starts licking my chin.

I curl my arms around her solid body, twenty-five pounds of love with a white fur coat, tiny black nose, and brown eyes. For a long time, she doesn't move—just snuggles closer. When my anxiety started interfering with my day-to-day life three years ago, Zion gave her to me.

Of course, I didn't realize at the time, but he used the money he earned from selling drugs to set me up with dog food, a plush bed, crate, leash, and license for the furball.

Now, she's all I have left of him. My little dog and the bracelet he wore every day for two months.

I don't know how to cry. If I start, I have this irrational fear I won't ever stop. So now, I just sit with Pixel, burying my face in her fur, with this lump in my throat I can't seem to force away.

The image of the drug paraphernalia haunts me. After Mom disappeared, Z and I made one vow to each other.

Never break a promise.

Our only rule. When he was using, strung out, working for some Russian kingpin selling drugs to school kids all across St. Petersburg and lying about where he was, he kept telling me he'd get clean. But he never used those two little words.

"I promise."

I begged him every time he called me—not that he reached out very often. *"Promise me, Z."*

But he never did.

Until he came home. Escaped. Saved up enough for a flight back to the United States and showed up at my apartment at 3:00 a.m., shaking, sweating, and almost passing out at my door.

"Z. Holy Fudgsicles. What—?"

"Help me."

And then...our last conversation. *"I'm never going back to that life, Wren. I promise."*

I promise.

"So much for promises, Z." I swallow my sob and press a quick kiss to the top of Pixel's furry head. "It's just us now, baby girl."

She whines, and I think, maybe...just maybe she understands my pain.

AFTER I SEND Dax a quick email, letting him know I won't be in today because I need to start packing up Zion's apartment, I bundle Pixel into her harness and head for the outskirts of Back Bay. I don't want to go. Heck, in the past two hours, I've cleaned my bathroom, gone through a whole pile of junk mail, and dusted the top of the fridge.

But I can't put this off any longer. When he didn't show up at his trial, the police issued a warrant for his arrest and searched his place. No drugs. No indication he was backsliding at all.

I kept up with the rent. Always hoping he'd come back to me. But now... The prospect of talking to his landlord fills me with dread. As we exit the T, Pixel yips at me, sitting up on her haunches and begging as she catches the scent of barbecue from the shop on the corner. "You ate this morning, little miss."

Though...I didn't. And the sweet and spicy scent calls to me. *"You should try the brisket, sis. It's just like Mom used to make."*

Probably why Zion picked this apartment building. That and the reduced rent they offered to halfway house graduates. "Fine. But you only get one piece," I say as I urge Pixel down the street. Once she's tied up outside, I venture into a tiny, hole-in-the-wall space jam-packed with tables. And no customers. Of course, it's only a little after eleven.

"Can I get a brisket plate to go? And a side of burnt ends?" I ask when a tired looking young man stifles a yawn behind the register.

"Sure. That'll be ten minutes."

As I turn over my credit card, the cashier stares at my name. "Wren Kane? Are you Z's sister?"

"Y-yes. You know—?" The lump in my throat threatens to choke me before I can correct myself. No one *knows* Zion anymore. We all…knew him.

"I haven't seen him around in a few weeks. Is he okay?"

My legs start to feel like wet noodles, and I brace myself against the counter. "No," I whisper. "He's…he's gone."

The kid—he can't be much older than twenty-three—skirts the counter and takes my arm to help me into a chair. "You don't look so good."

For some reason, that strikes me as the funniest thing I've heard in two days. I can't help laughing until a rough sob escapes my throat. Still…no tears. God, I wish I could cry. "I'm sorry. I haven't slept. I'm not…*dang it.*" Bracing my elbows on my knees, I drop my head into my hands as the kid shifts from foot to foot next to me. When I finally manage to rein in my emotions, I wipe my cheeks, amazed they're dry.

"Zion OD'd. The police found his body yesterday. Or…maybe the day before. I don't…I didn't ask."

"He wouldn't." The kid sinks down into the chair across from me. "Wren—Miss Kane—Z came in here every weekend and washed dishes in exchange for a brisket plate. My pop owns this place, and when he found out Z was an addict, he made him a deal. Stay clean, work the weekends when we're slammed, and he could eat here any time he wanted."

"Really?" Pixel yips from outside, and I glance at the sidewalk, seeing her wagging her tail as she stands up and sticks her little black nose through the open door. "Sit," I say as I hold up a finger.

"Aw, man. Is that the puppy? Z talked about her all the time. And you. Can I…go say hi?" The kid practically bounces out of his chair when I nod, and he drops to his knees next to Pixel and scratches her belly until her back leg starts to thump on the ground with delight.

Z gave me the dog because when I'm in the throes of an anxiety attack, having something else to focus on can help me forget about the tightness in my chest, the shaking hands, the nausea. Grief and anxiety—they're not altogether different at times.

When he returns, he holds out his hand. "I'm Brennan."

"Wren. I mean…I guess you know that." My cheeks heat and the band around my heart warns me grief is hovering, ready to drown me at a moment's notice. "Did you…know Z well? Were you…friends?"

"Yeah. I mean…we didn't hang out much, but we talked whenever he worked." Brennan's gaze falls to my wrist. "Shit, man. He really is gone, isn't he?" Gesturing to the beads, he says, "Dude never took that off. Said it reminded him why he couldn't ever use again."

My eyes burn, and I fiddle with the bracelet.

"I can't believe he OD'd. He wouldn't even have a beer with me at the end of the night. Said even though he'd never had a problem with alcohol, he didn't want anything that might make him feel…not himself again." Brennan shakes his head as a bell dings from the kitchen. After he washes his hands, he bags up two brown cardboard containers.

"They found him with all the paraphernalia," I say quietly as I accept the bag. "In a known drug den. He promised me…"

"Pop always said Z had demons." With a shake of his head as I try to offer my credit card, Brennan stares back out at Pixel. "But he also said if anyone could beat them…Z could. No charge for the food, Wren. You come in here anytime, and I'll take care of you."

"Can I…" I'm not a hugger. Hell, I don't even like touching people most of the time. But this kid and his dad might have been the closest things Zion had to real friends. "I mean…never mind."

But Brennan seems to understand. He trudges out from behind the counter again and gives me a quick, tight embrace. "He always said you saved him."

I barely manage to make it out the door before finally, my tears fall.

Zion's apartment looks exactly the same as it did the last time I was here—right after he disappeared and I met the police officers to let them in. Pristine. Well, other than the thin layer of dust that covers everything. It smells faintly of him, and as Pixel races around the small space, searching for her favorite uncle, I hover at Z's bedroom door.

My cheeks are still wet, though by the time I'd reached the rickety elevator, I'd lost all will to cry. With a loud sniffle, I give in to the pull of his bed and lie down, burying my face in his pillow.

I remember that newborn smell he had when Mom brought him home from the hospital. How he tried aftershave for the first time when he went to prom and used so much, he had to take a second shower as his date waited in our living room. The scent of vomit that clung to him when he showed up at my apartment after traveling for two solid days on six different flights to get home from Russia.

"You promised." Hugging his pillow, I give serious thought to claiming a fraction of the sleep that eluded me last night, but Pixel yips from the front room—the little happy noise that generally signifies an impending meal, and I remember my barbecue.

We eat on the couch, the dog getting her own plate next to me —sans sauce. Z wasn't kidding. The food tastes just like the slow cooked brisket Mom used to make, and I let myself sink into memories of happier times. Before Dad died, before Mom abandoned us, before Zion's first taste of heroin.

Lost, eating on autopilot, I finish the whole container before a knock on the door makes me yelp, and the dish clatters to the floor.

Snatching up my phone, I swear under my breath as I see five missed texts.

"Wren," a familiar voice calls from outside, "you in there?"

I don't speak as I unlock the door—I can't. I'm too shocked. "What are you doing here?"

Ford, Ella, and Trevor—my closest friends from the office—stand in the hall, holding boxes, packing tape, and beer. "You shouldn't do this alone," Ford says as he slips by me. "We should be able to get everything done in an hour or so. Maybe two tops."

"I..." I don't want them here. But...I don't want them to go either. Ella wraps her arms around me, and I squeeze her back. "Thank you."

LATE THAT NIGHT, I crawl into bed with a mug of tea and Zion's copy of *Harry Potter and the Sorcerer's Stone*. He must have read the damn thing a hundred times—the cover's worn, the spine broken and floppy. On the title page, he left me a little note, which nearly sent me into tears again. So the book came home with me, rather than end up in a box I might never open again.

Wren, this book is like me. Used up, tattered, and kind of a mess. But that's why it's perfect. Because on every page, there's a story. All for you, Firefly.

His nickname for me. Silly. But I'm paler than a sheet, and with my red locks...he used to say my hair lit up the whole room.

Flipping to his favorite part—when Hagrid shows up at the hut on the rock to tell Harry he's a wizard—I try to focus on the words, but the strain of the day weighs me down. The citrusy scent of chamomile infuses the room, and I sip my tea as I stare at the framed photo Zion had on his dresser—the one that now graces my nightstand.

A month before he disappeared, I took him to a Red Sox game. We binged on hot dogs and nachos, and even though it started pouring in the ninth inning, we stayed until the end—a Sox walk off home run in the tenth.

Exhaustion has my head bobbing, and a few drops of tea splash onto one of the pages as I almost drop my mug.

"*Snack cakes!*" Scrambling up, I grab a handful of Kleenex and blot the liquid. The action forces the spine to bend further, and I catch sight of Z's writing. Tiny, cursive letters almost hidden in the crease between the pages.

Four sets of numbers, separated by periods. Followed by a slash, then the word "firefly."

"What in the whole of the universe, Z?"

When I took computer programming classes in college, Z wanted to learn too. So we studied together every night. The kid had so much natural talent...and zero motivation beyond impressing his big sister. But he could have aced that class. The numbers...they're an IP address or I'll eat my mug...handle and all.

Once my computer wakes up, I enter the numbers and the directory name.

She who stands up for herself..._____.

Anxiety wells in my chest as I type the password: *rules her own heart.*

A quote our father scribbled on Post-It notes all over the house after I broke up with my one and only high school boyfriend. I punched the little weasel when he pulled up my dress in the school hallway after prom.

When the screen fills with text, I gasp. "Oh, Zion. What did you do?"

3

Ryker

*P*ressing my thumb to the biometric lock, I wait for the beep, then enter my ten-digit passcode. As I step inside the warehouse, I breathe deep. Sweat, coffee, bleach, and the lingering scent of laundry detergent fill my nose. Home. Or as close as I'll ever get to one.

Despite my condo's comforts—and security measures—the warehouse is the only place I've found any peace since I left the military.

Dim lights along the ceiling illuminate the wide-open room. The boxing ring almost glows, the light blue surface clean and shiny. The clock on the microwave flashes. Power must have gone out sometime in the past two weeks.

Heading for the lockers, I let the backpack fall from my shoulder. I can't go to Cam and West's wedding, but that doesn't mean I'm a total dick. I slide the card out of my bag and slip it between the slats of West's locker. It doesn't say much—then again, neither do I. Not anymore.

Inara gets a note too, though hers... I open the letter, wishing I could talk myself out of this, but knowing I can't.

I'm going dark while I'm away. You and Royce need to focus on healing. Cam and West should have a proper honeymoon. I'll be back when I figure my shit out. Until then, you're in charge. Run drills. Keep the new guy on his toes. But no jobs. Stay safe. I'll make contact when I get back. - R

She wants me to "open up." Hell, she even offered to make me an appointment with her shrink after the mess that almost got us all killed. But I've had enough people in my head. After I escaped Hell, I spent a year in therapy. Talking about my feelings. Recounting every single day. Every fear. Every time I prayed for death. Didn't do a damn thing. I still have nightmares every night.

So I'm taking the coward's way out. At least until I get my head on straight again. This isn't who I am. I'm the guy who took down ten Taliban guards while bleeding from a dozen different wounds. The guy who crawled over rocks and through the Afghan underbrush for two miles in pitch blackness before he found West and his SEAL team. The guy who couldn't wait more than ten days to go back in and try to save the only member of his squad left.

I'm not a fucking coward. But as I pull my go bag from my locker and rifle through the contents, shame warms the back of my neck.

The overhead lights come on with a crackle, and I whirl around, pulling my gun as I move.

"Ry?" Inara holds up her hands twenty feet away, wariness edging her tone. "I didn't think you were coming back for a while."

I blow out a breath and holster my gun. "It's not even five in the morning. What the hell are you doing here?"

"Royce and I have an early flight." She glances back towards the kitchen, where Royce leans against the counter with his arms crossed. "We're...um...going to meet his parents. I needed to lock up my guns. We have a new safe on order, but it won't be in for another couple of weeks."

I should apologize...to both of them...for the hurt in her eyes I put there. But I don't know what to say. "That's...I'm happy for you."

Closing the distance between us, Inara touches my arm. "I'm worried about you, Ry."

"I'm fine." *Always am.* "Just need a few days away. I'm going to catch up with a buddy from my army days. Blow off some steam in Boston."

"Blow off steam? You?" Her fingers tighten around my wrist. "Talk to me," she whispers. "Please."

I want to. For a few seconds, the urge to confess everything wells up, almost choking me. But I can't. She'd never trust me again. "Nothing to talk about. I fucked up with Coop, and I need to get my head on straight before we go out on another mission."

Pulling away, I snag one of the many ID packets from my go bag and shove it into my backpack. "I've got some shit to take care of before I head to the airport."

"Fine." Her tone says she's anything but fine. "Have a safe trip."

Her eyes glisten, but she turns away to punch in her locker code. Unable to stand the awkward silence any longer, I throw the backpack over my shoulder and head for the kitchen.

Royce holds out his hand as I approach, and I force myself to shake. "You solid?" I ask.

"Good as broken." He offers me a lopsided smile, the left corner of his mouth a little lower than the right. "Sorry. Stroke humor. D-didn't sleep well last night. And...seeing you draw down on Inara—"

"I'm sorry." Shoving my hands into my pockets, I force myself to hold his gaze. "For everything."

"You didn't put the gun in Coop's hand. Or knock the screw out of his head. The People's Army did that." Royce stares at the lockers, and I can almost *feel* his need to go check on Inara. But he shakes his head and focuses on me again. "You don't need to apologize to me. She's the one you're hurting now."

Regrets crawl up my spine, and I turn, watching one of my only friends fumble through securing her guns, pausing every few seconds to run a hand over her cheeks.

Give me a compound full of armed hostiles and I know exactly what to do. This... My fingers curl around the key to my bike, and I turn on my heel and stride towards the door.

"Ryker," Royce calls, and I slow for a beat until my demons grab hold, and I burst into the cool, dark morning. "Don't—"

As the door slams behind me, I wonder if I'll ever feel at home here again.

Logan Airport never changes. The white walls of baggage claim are scuffed and dirty, devoid of all decoration beyond the rental car posters and the occasional pay phone.

Striding past the throngs of grumpy passengers—an hour delay outbound, turbulence over the Rockies, and a busted toilet don't make for a happy flight—I sling my backpack over my shoulder and stride towards the T-station. I want a beer and some privacy.

An hour later, the room at the Fairmont has every luxury I could ever want, but I chose this hotel because the insulation is the best in the city, and from my corner room, I won't hear another soul the whole time I'm here. Cracking open the mini-bar, I pull out a Sam Adams. When in Rome...or Back Bay, I guess.

Before my deployment, I lived five miles from this spot. I grew up in San Diego but did four years at Boston College and a year in the Boston Public School System before 9/11. Now, memories of my former life haunt me in the dark corners of the room.

The kids playing at recess. The smell of pencil lead. Finger paints. The heat of a June afternoon as the last bell rings, signifying freedom...

The beer goes down too easy and doesn't do a damn thing to silence the voices in my head. So I switch to vodka. When that's gone too, I strip down to my briefs, set the desk chair against the door, wrap a length of wire around the window crank, close the blackout shades, unplug the clock, and fall face down on top of the sheets, wondering why the fuck I came back here.

Wren

Trudging into the office a little after ten—this is becoming a habit —I drop my messenger bag at my desk and head directly for Dax's office. After my customary two raps, he motions me in.

"You shouldn't be here, Wren." His gentle tone threatens to send me over the edge. I don't know if I want to cry, curl up in a ball in the corner, or hit something. Though, with my luck, I'd break my fingers and still wouldn't feel any better.

Shutting the door behind me, I rest my back against the smooth wood. "Zion didn't OD."

"Not this again," he says under his breath. "Wren—"

"No. This is the part where I talk, and you listen." I slap my hand over my mouth before I add insult to injury by calling him a self-righteous jerk. Blowing out a breath, I pull the USB thumb drive from my pocket, stumble forward a few steps, and press the small piece of metal and circuitry into Dax's hand.

"What's this?" His brows knit together as he turns the drive over in his palm.

"Evidence. Can I...?"

"Do I have a choice?" Pushing back from his desk, he waves his hand at his computer. "Go for it."

Once I have the drive ready, I touch his arm. "Zion died for this. I need you to promise me you won't show this to anyone without talking to me first."

Dax groans. "Jesus, Wren. I know betrayal better than anyone in this office, including you. Get to the point and tell me what's on the fucking drive."

Shame heats my cheeks. Dax spent fifteen months in a Taliban prison. Beaten, tortured, and interrogated for information he refused to give up because someone didn't do their job. "I'm sorry, boss. I...didn't think."

"You're allowed a couple of those. Especially when you're mourning. But this better be damn good." He leans back in his chair as I double-click the video, and a blond giant with tattoos covering his forearms sits at a desk with his hands folded in front of him.

"Hello, Zion," the man says, his Russian accent thick. "You were expecting someone else, I think. I will fix that." On screen, the man snaps his fingers, and a second man, larger, meaner, drags a woman into the frame. She's crying, her face bruised and bloodied, her eyes swollen so badly, she can barely see.

"Wren?" Dax asks. "What is this?"

"Just...listen. I'll explain when it's over." I don't want to watch it again, but Zion left it for me so I could help. So I could fix his mistakes, and so I clench my hands into fists and wait for the brute on screen to continue.

"Elena paid dearly for helping you," the man says, and the woman whimpers as he grabs her chin and squeezes—hard. "Take her away, Misha."

The other goon drags the woman from the room, and she calls out, "Kolya, please baby. I love you. Do not do this—" A door slams, and the blond behemoth on screen smiles.

"I am going to find you, Zion. I own your pitiful existence. You have one chance. Come back to me. Pledge your loyalty. If you burn your passport in front of me, pass my...initiation test, I might let Elena stay. Otherwise…" The blond Russian shrugs. "Maybe I let her make me some money."

The video cuts out, and I yank the USB drive from Dax's computer. There's so much more I want to show him, but I need assurances. Or…at least…I need him to believe me. I lean forward, my hands braced on his desk. "That was Nikolay—Kolya —Yegorovich. He runs the *Nevsky Bratva*. One of the largest drug cartels in Western Russia. He's the man who stopped Zion from calling me for almost two years. The woman…her name is Elena. And I think…I think Zion loved her."

Dax rubs the back of his neck as he sighs. "Wren, I don't know where the hell you got this, but what do you expect me to do about it? I'm not up to speed on the big cartels in Russia, but if this guy is who you say he is, only the Russian authorities are going to be able to take him down—if they even want to—and there wasn't anything on that video they could use to do it. Hell, he probably has half of the city officials in his pocket as it is. And you have no proof *he's* the one who kept Zion away from you for two years. I know Z is—was—your brother. And he was a good kid. But heroin can make devils out of angels."

I sputter, the words tumbling over one another and catching in my throat as my anxiety edges towards panic. "He was m-more than a g-good kid. Z…he was smart. Too smart for his own good. He *knew* Kolya might come after him, and he made sure if he died…he wanted me to find this."

"Explain."

Forcing myself to calm down, I blow out a breath and start at the beginning. "Z's favorite book was *Harry Potter and the Sorcerer's Stone.*"

FORTY-FIVE MINUTES LATER, I realize how ridiculous my story sounds. To his credit, Dax listened to every word. Or…pretended to. But now, as I beg him for the resources to fulfill Z's last promise—a week off, Ford, and Trevor—hope withers away. My brother was brilliant. But even after the drugs, after escaping the Russian mafia, after getting clean...he was still so naive. And I'm afraid I am too.

Dax slides a hip on the edge of his desk and offers me his hands. When our fingers link, he holds on tight as his voice softens. "Wren, I hired you because you're the best hacker on the east coast. And in three years, you've saved more people than I can count. Including almost every member of this team at least once. I know you wanted to save your brother too. And you tried. Over and over again. But he made the choice to shoot up again. You read the police report. No evidence of foul play."

"But he promised..." I hate the whiny edge to my voice, and as I hear my words, I shake my head. "I know how stupid that sounds. But he never would have broken a promise to me. Not a *promise*."

As Dax sighs, I know I've lost. And the glimmer of hope that maybe I could do one last thing for my baby brother dies.

"Firefly! Stop. You're walking too fast!"

The echoes of his voice haunt me. I always stopped. Always waited. Always helped. Always smiled at his silly nickname for me.

Pushing to my feet, I trip on the chair in my haste to reach the door and slam my shoulder into the wood. "Dammit. I...I need to go. I'm sorry, Dax. I...didn't mean to waste your morning. I'll let you know when I'm ready to come back to work. A couple days. Maybe three. I...I'm sorry."

And before I can lose myself to a full-blown panic attack, I run.

4

Ryker

a woman sprints around the corner and crashes into me before I can get out of the way. Snaking an arm around her as her legs buckle, I look into a pair of pale green eyes wild with panic. "Whoa. You okay?"

"L-let g-go."

"Take a deep breath for me, sweetheart." I don't know where the term of endearment comes from, but she looks like she needs to hear it. "I won't hurt you."

She shoves against me with more strength than a little thing like her should have, and I release her, catching sight of the ropes of old burns winding around my right forearm. Yeah. No wonder she's terrified. Sometimes I forget. Just for a minute. Most people don't see anything but a monster when they look at me. Hell, that's all I see half the time.

The woman flees without another word, leaving behind the subtle scent of honeysuckle. With a shake of my head, I take a seat in the little waiting area the receptionist directs me to.

Wiping my hands on my jeans, I try to talk myself into leaving. After we got out...I only saw Dax once in the hospital. I couldn't face him. Kept tabs on him through West and a couple of the other SEALs who went back with me to obliterate Hell for good, but every time I tried to pick up the phone...I'd see him in his cell. Hear him screaming. Imagine what he went through after I escaped.

"You can go back now, Mr. McCabe," the receptionist says with a bright smile and a gesture towards the hallway. "All the way down the hall to the last office on the right."

My heartbeat thuds in my ears. I don't know why the hell I'm here. Except...Dax is in every one of my nightmares, and I need to find a way to exorcise those demons for good. Or stop fighting.

Conversations float around me from some of the other offices, and three guys gather around a break area, falling silent and giving me hard stares as I pass.

At Dax's door, I pause with my fist raised, ready to knock. He's standing at the window, his back to me, sunlight cutting a slash across the far corner of the office and hitting his shoulder and left arm.

"You never were very good at taking hints," he says, his voice devoid of all emotion. "Say your piece and get out."

Stepping inside, I close the door behind me. "I deserve that."

"No shit."

I'm not having this conversation with the man's back, so I take two steps forward and reach for his arm. But Dax whirls around, grabs my hand, and twists, sending me to a knee. "You want to get your ass kicked? Happy to oblige."

A hint of a southern accent colors his words, and I stare up at him in shock. Sweeping my other leg around, I catch him behind the ankles and send him to the ground with a loud *oof*. Once my hand's free, I grab his arm again and haul him to his feet. "I'm not doing this with you, Dax. Not now, not ever."

The door swings open with a loud bang, and a big, burly

dude with a few strands of gray at his temples bursts in. "You okay, boss?"

"Fine. Ryker was just leaving, Ford."

With a quick glance at Ford, I weigh the odds of taking him down. Fair. Not great. But if I run now, I'm not going to resolve a damn thing with the man I know better than anyone else in this world. "No. I'm not." In my periphery, Ford takes a step closer, but I raise my hands in surrender. "I came here to apologize. Not fight. Five minutes. Give me five minutes, and you'll never see me again."

Dax rubs the back of his neck, eyes closed, and sighs.

"Please." I'm close to begging, and the memories roughen my voice.

"Please. I've told you everything I know. I'm just a grunt. A mechanic. I follow orders. I was only on the chopper as a precaution," Dax says as two men kick him and spit on him.

"Five minutes. Ford, shut the door."

Once we're alone again, I stare down at my best friend's shoes. "I broke the only promise that mattered."

"Yeah. You did. You deserted me."

Despite knowing he's right, I flinch at the words. "If I'd stuck to the plan, maybe..."

"If you'd stuck to the plan, maybe I'd know what my own fucking office looks like." He takes off his tinted glasses and throws them down on the desk. "Maybe those bastards wouldn't have held me down and blinded me with acid. Maybe you wouldn't be so much of a coward that you can't even look me in the eyes."

I draw in a sharp breath, because...how the hell does he know?

"I can hear the echo of your voice off the floor, dumbass."

Raising my head, I blow out a breath. "I'm sorry."

"You should be." He shoves his hands into his pockets, the movement highlighting the muscle he's put on in the past six years. His hair's longer. The black strands are tousled, partially covering the long, narrow scar across his forehead. "Why did you come? Why now?"

"Something happened."

"A lot of things happened. Lucy couldn't handle being married to a blind, scarred, ex-soldier suffering from PTSD and bolted. I lost my house, my in-laws, half my civvie friends... And the one person on earth who knew the shit I was going through wouldn't return my calls."

I wince and rub my hand over my scalp. My hair never grew back right after we got out of Hell, and I feel the half-dozen divots where our captors slammed my head into the edge of a table over and over again. "I had my own demons."

"Like I didn't know that. We were twenty feet from one another for fifteen fucking months, Ry. I heard every punch. Every scream. Every time they dragged you back to your cell barely alive. And we vowed to get out. Planned every single day we had the strength to speak. Every day we could move well enough to tap out cryptic messages during shift change. We were brothers. In all the ways that counted. And then—"

"You couldn't walk," I snap. "The infection in your calf? You were half-out of your mind with the fever, and we had—I had—one shot. One night without a moon. And how many times did they let us suffer when our wounds got infected? How was I supposed to know they were going to force a couple amoxicillin down your throat? I went through with the plan because I was fucking terrified I was going to lose you too!"

Dax's silence threatens to choke me. Without the glasses, the shiny, mottled skin around his eyes is obvious. The deep azure irises have faded to a pale, arctic blue. I know he can't see me, but his stare bores into me, as if he's trying to figure out if I'm full of shit or regrets.

When he pinches the bridge of his nose, pain deepening the lines around his mouth, I take step closer. "For a year, I picked up the phone every damn day. Trying to find a way to tell you how sorry I was. And every day, I failed. I failed you in Hell. I failed all of them."

"You didn't fail me in Hell, Ry. You failed me after we got out. *That's* when I needed you. Your five minutes are up. Go back to wherever the fuck you came from."

If he'd shot me in the heart, I'd be in less pain than I am at this moment. But he's right. And nothing will give us those six years back.

"If you ever need—"

He growls an oath and lunges for me, grabbing my arms hard enough to leave bruises. "Get gone. Now. Or I won't be responsible for what happens next."

When he releases me, I do the only thing I can. Double-time it out of the office and into the elevator.

5

Ryker

The elevator doors snick open, and I pull out my phone as I shoulder my way through a small crowd milling around the building's information desk. The device clatters to the ground as something slams into me, and I see only red curls and a heart-shaped face with big, pale green eyes.

"This is becoming a habit." I'm done with Boston—and with this day—and a rough edge creeps into my tone. But I steady her with my hands wrapped gently around her upper arms. "Are you all right?"

"Wh-what...are y-you...doing?" Honeysuckle twists out of my grasp, her hands balled into fists at her sides.

"Just making sure you're not going down." I bend to scoop up my phone, taking a quick glance at the screen to verify it's still intact. When I return my gaze to her, she's backing away warily, glancing at the revolving door to the street like it's a fucking lifeline.

"Hey. It's okay. I'm not following you. Stalking you. Whatever. I was just leaving."

Her brow scrunches, and as she processes my words, those eyes darken with streaks of amber. "Get over yourself." She shakes her head, bringing another whiff of her sweet scent to my nose. "Men. Not everything's about *you*."

Shock steals my continued apology, and instead, I frown. "Then what's got you so worked up that you run into me twice in fifteen minutes? Because where I'm from, we watch where we're going."

"You seriously expect me to tell you?" A little feminine snort wrinkles her nose. "It's none of your business, jerk." She starts to stalk towards the elevator, but then turns back to me. "Wait. You're not...like...a new client, are you? Second Sight?"

"No," I say bitterly. "Look at me, sweetheart. Do I look like I need help? I fix problems for other people. Even if I *was* searching for someone to fix my problems, Dax wouldn't give me the time of day. Not anymore." She flinches, and I've hit a nerve with something. Dax, probably. "I take it you know the guy?"

"He's...my boss."

"Lucky you. I used to be *his* boss. He was a lot nicer back then." I run a hand over my bald head. "Sorry. I shouldn't...I don't know him at all these days. He's probably the boss of the year."

She takes a step forward, those eyes no longer wary, but curious, and I can't look away. "You...fix problems?"

"Yeah. Sometimes." Studying her, I notice the dark circles and swollen lids. The tiny lines of strain and exhaustion around her mouth. She wears no make-up, and she toys with a green pendant hanging low between her breasts. Short, unpainted nails. No rings. Just a single purple and green beaded bracelet around a slender wrist. "You have a problem?"

A single nod, and she takes another step closer. "I...I'm Wren. Wren Kane."

"Ryker McCabe." I offer a hand, and her cool fingers curl

around mine. "You want to get a cup of coffee and tell me about your problem, Wren?"

At her nod, I gesture towards the lobby door. "Pretty sure I saw a shop on the corner. They any good?"

"Passable. And quiet." Wren pulls her jacket tighter around her shoulders and meets my gaze. Uncertainty swims in her eyes, and her chest stutters as her respiration rate hitches up.

"I won't force you, sweetheart. You can change your mind."

There's that term again. *Sweetheart.* Why can't I stop with it?

With a shake of her head, she looks at the revolving door. "I promised him. And I can't...it's the last thing he ever asked. Dax won't help me. You shouldn't either. But—"

"Dax won't help?" I snort. "Then I'm in. Come on, Wren Kane. Coffee's on me."

Wren

The giant across from me cups his black coffee like it's liquid gold, while I take one sip of my cappuccino before my stomach protests.

"So...want to tell me why you ran into me? Twice?" He arches his brows, which highlights the differences in his eyes. A vertical scar bisects his left lid, and the eye doesn't fully open. Ropes of damaged skin—burns, I think—cover his left cheek and down his neck. When I saw him the first time, I only focused on his strong arm holding me up and his gravelly voice. Now, I take in the rest of him.

Large hands. Ink peeking out from the cuff of his sweatshirt. He's almost as big as Ford, but younger. Mid-thirties, if I had to guess. Curiosity lends a gleam to his eyes, and their multitude of colors—part green, part blue, part hazel—mesmerizes me.

"Um, my phone...died. And my car won't start. I was coming

back into the office to call for a tow." My chest tightens, and I skim my fingers over my necklace, needing the familiar comfort of the smooth edges. I'm running on caffeine and adrenaline, and that's a sure-fire recipe for a panic attack—which I've only barely avoided twice this morning. "The first time..." Can I really share this with a stranger? I release the pendant and reach for my cappuccino. But my hands aren't steady, and I almost drop the cup, a bit of foam landing on the table between us.

"Wren, stop." Ryker reaches out, the lightest stroke of his fingers over mine. "Take a deep breath. Count to ten."

I jerk back, digging in my bag for my pill case. "Just...a minute."

Ryker's gaze never leaves my face as he waits for me to take my meds. "Anxiety or panic attacks?"

"Both." My voice cracks, and I clear my throat. "I...don't do well with new people."

His deep chuckle brings a smile to his face, and he looks surprised at the expression for a moment before shaking his head. "I don't do well with people in general. So you've got a leg up on me."

"I don't...I don't know you. I shouldn't—"

"I'm Special Forces. Or, I was. Now, I run a K&R firm in Seattle. Kidnap and Ransom. I get people out of trouble. Most of the time. You don't have any reason to believe me, but..." He digs his hand into the pocket of his jeans, coming away with his wallet. Behind a credit card and hotel room key, he finds a picture, stares at it for a moment, and then passes it across the small table. "Recognize anyone?"

The photo's wrinkled and faded, well-worn around the edges. Six men. All in full gear. Ryker's easy to spot. He's the biggest guy there. Except...he has a full head of blond hair. I slide my gaze back and forth between the photo and Ryker, trying to reconcile the man across from me with the man in the photograph. He could have been a model. Next to him, laughing, a younger Dax stares back at me.

"Oh God. You were with him. In..."

"Hell." Ryker's eyes dim, and his lips press together for a breath. "Dax was my second. The only other member of my squad to survive."

What do you say to that? *I'm sorry? That's awful?* I settle for a nod. "Dax doesn't talk about it. He gave me the tl;dr version when he hired me, but—"

"Tl; dr?"

A wrinkle appears between Ryker's brows, and I manage a smile. "Sorry. I forget not everyone speaks geek. It means 'too long; didn't read.' Basically, the two-sentence summary."

"Tl;dr. I like that." Another long sip of coffee, and he frowns. "Whatever this is...are you sure you don't want to go to Dax with it? He's a good guy, despite kicking me out of his office."

I snort into my mug. "I already did. He won't help. The first time I ran into you, I'd just left him. He thinks I'm insane for wanting to go up against the Russian mob."

A low whistle escapes Ryker's lips. "You sure he's not right?"

"No."

"Then why...?"

I twirl the bracelet around my wrist. I don't know how much to share. How much I can even get through without breaking down. The anxiety pill dulls my senses, but at least my heart isn't pounding half out of my chest. Still...I hate making decisions when I feel like this. Exhausted. A little fuzzy. Alone.

Unable to share Z with this guy I just met, I hedge. "Personal reasons."

With those two words, Ryker's entire demeanor changes. Gone is the gentle giant offering a sympathetic shoulder. His multi-color eyes harden, and he runs a hand over his bald head. "If you want my help, you have to give me more than 'personal reasons.' I've been in this business a long time, Wren. Five years is an eternity in K&R work. I tried to save a guy from the Russians once. Out of forty-seven targets, I've only lost two, and the *bratva* killed one of them."

I can't do this. Can't tell him about the letter Zion left me. About the other recording I *didn't* play for Dax. "I'm sorry, Mr. McCabe. This was a mistake. I...I should go."

Grabbing my messenger bag, I rise, a little too quickly, and teeter for a moment as Ryker's hand shoots to my hip to steady me. "Wait."

"No, I can't ask you to get involved in this. It's...too dangerous. Dax is right. This is...suicide."

"You're probably right, but—" he holds up his phone, "—at least let me call you a tow."

"I'll take the T home. I can deal with the car tomorrow. Th-thanks for the coffee." Leaving said coffee still almost full on the table, I rush out of the shop, ignoring the deep voice calling my name.

Ryker

$\mathcal{M}$y room smells like honeysuckle. Or...maybe I do. Stripping off my shirt, I hold it to my nose. Yep. Wren. I should change. But instead, I shrug back into the black cotton blend and sink down onto the desk chair.

Ten minutes with her and I can't get her out of my head. Probably because she's the second person today to tell me to take a hike.

Being a loner never bothered me. My brother and I didn't get along. Until it was almost too late. I spent a lot of time in my own head. Never knew what it was like to have a close-knit group of friends until I joined the 10th Special Forces Regiment in 2004. I had nine years with a group of the best men in the world. Until Hell destroyed us. Destroyed me.

My phone buzzes on the desk, and I glance down at the screen and snort. Inara's blunt when she texts.

Worried about you. Check in.

I should answer, but what am I going to say? I'm worried about me too? I don't know how to get my head back on straight?

"Fuck it." I unlock the phone and send her a quick reply.

Doing fine. Enjoying Boston for a few days. Be back next week.

It's all I've got. Maybe if I say it enough—that I'm fine—it'll be true.

With nothing to do, I grab my laptop to check my email. But I find myself Googling "Wren Kane."

Only a handful of results. A Facebook profile—heavily locked down—shows her smiling, her red hair on fire in the sun. A mention in a computer science journal lists her as a graduate of MIT, and I whistle. Smart little bird.

Why would she be going up against the Russian mob? And why the fuck would Dax refuse to help her?

I try my best to ignore the sinking feeling in the pit of my stomach half the day. Even manage to leave the hotel and walk down to the Public Garden, but everywhere I go, the scent of honeysuckle follows me.

Finding a spot on a bench by the lagoon, I dial one of the few people I trust in this world.

"You're the last person I expected to call," West says. "Hang on a sec." His voice lowers, and he tells someone—his fiancé, I assume from the tone—he'll be back in a few minutes. "You want to explain why you're not coming to our wedding?"

"I don't do weddings." Rubbing the back of my neck, I try to wipe away the shame crawling down my spine and settling in my gut. "You don't want me there, man."

"You saved my life in Colombia. Half-carried me through the jungle when I was bleeding out all over the damn place. Hell, you even found a back-alley veterinarian to dig the bullet out of my gut. Why wouldn't I want you there?"

I can still feel his blood dripping over my hands. See his unfocused eyes as I wrapped duct tape around his waist to seal the wound—or try to. Hear myself as I ordered him to buck up and run.

"You're a goddamned SEAL, Sampson. If you can't run five hundred yards while bleeding from a stomach wound, you don't deserve to wear the uniform."

"Because I almost got you killed two weeks ago?"

West snorts. "That fucking shitstain didn't land a shot anywhere near me. You on the other hand...need to work on your evasion skills."

I let the dig slide because he's right. "Look, I have some shit I need to take care of, okay? You and Cam don't need me there bringing everyone down."

Defeat tinges his next words. "Whatever. Why'd you call? I have a class to teach in an hour."

"I need your opinion—and Cam's tech skills."

"You taking on a job?" He's wary, but interest piques his tone. "Angel? Can you come in here?"

A few quiet words pass between the two, and then there's a click over the line. "You're on speaker, Ry."

"Cam, I need some intel on a Wren Kane. She's...I don't know what she is. But she went to MIT for computer science engineering, and—"

"She's a hacker," Cam says. "I met her once. She came out for an interview. Royce tried to tempt her away from wherever she's working with a hell of a job offer, but something happened, and she told him she had to stay in Boston."

"And the *Nevsky Bratva?*"

"Ry..." West blows out a breath. "Why are you asking about the Russian mob?"

"Because Wren Kane is wrapped up with them somehow. And she asked for my help. And then decided she didn't trust me with the details and bolted." Those pale green eyes haunt me, and I don't know why I can't let this go.

West clears his throat. "If they're after her, she's in deep shit.

PATRICIA EDDY

The *Nevsky Bratva* is the largest heroin operation in eastern Russia. They have bases in St. Petersburg and Moscow, and they've recently expanded to the United States. Miami and New Jersey. One of the guys from BUDS works for the CIA now. He told me some stories..."

"I was afraid of that. No wonder Dax turned her down."

"Dax...Holloway?" West asks. From the tone in his voice, I can imagine what he looks like right now. Brows arched, hands on his hips. Blue eyes dark. "Ry, is that why you went to Boston?"

I don't want to admit my failings, don't want to have to explain how Dax kicked me out and told me he never wanted to see me again.

"Um..." Cam says. "Who's Dax Holloway?"

"The only other survivor of Hell. My best friend before I fucked everything up. And Wren's boss."

West whistles. "So, let me get this straight. You went to Boston to try to fix things with Dax. And somehow, you meet one of his employees who has a problem with the Russian mob—and her boss—and *you're* going to help her out?"

"No." I start to pace, digging my fingers into my palm, using the pain in my joints to help me focus. "Maybe."

The call switches off of speaker, and it's just West on the line with me now. "Listen, Ry. I know shooting Coop left you with some new demons. I'm not going to pretend to know why or how to help. But if you're going to tangle with the Russian mob, don't do it halfway. And don't even think about doing it alone. You need us, we're there."

No way in hell I'll call West or Inara for this. Not after everything I've put them through. But since admitting that will only lead to a fight—one he'll never win—I sigh. "If I make a move, I'll let you know. Thanks, West. And...congratulations. Beers are on me when I get back."

"Just come back alive," he says.

"Hooah."

AFTER A SOLITARY LOBSTER roll on the waterfront, I take a walk to try to clear my head. But though I set out with no destination in mind, I find myself outside Dax's office, staring up at the sixth-floor windows.

Until the front doors open, and a white cane emerges, followed by the man who spent fifteen months on the other side of a stone wall, tapping out messages to try to keep me sane.

Dax strides with purpose, a man who knows exactly where he's going and probably doesn't need the cane any more than he needs me in his life. I fall into step a dozen yards back, staying behind him as he weaves through a throng of people, pauses at a stoplight, and then sets off across the street.

Outside one of a dozen identical buildings in the North End, Dax does a one-eighty, leans against a tree, and stares right at me. "If you think I can't hear you, Ry, you're a damn fool. You've been on my six since I left the office."

Fuck.

I shove my hands into my pockets as I approach. "What gave me away?"

"You've worn the same aftershave for fifteen years. Caught a whiff of it when I left the office. And you apologized twice when you almost ran into people three blocks back."

When I'm on mission, I never miss a beat. But here...I'm out of my element. "Instructor Taylor would've had my ass."

"Damn straight. You want to talk more, you follow me inside. You can borrow some gloves."

TWENTY MINUTES LATER, still wearing my jeans and t-shirt, but barefoot, I step into the boxing ring. Dax, dressed in basketball shorts, his chest bare, ducks under the ropes. Without his glasses, his eyes reflect the overhead lights, milky pupils and pale irises trying to track my movements as I circle him. But he's slow, a step behind me as I keep my footfalls quick and soft.

"I had coffee with Wren Kane today."

Dax sends a jab in my direction, coming within an inch of my chin. Weaving to the side, I catch him in the gut with a quick right cross. "Want to tell me why you refused to help her?"

"None of your business," he says as he throws a hook that sends me spinning into the ropes. "You trying to spy on me now?"

"No." My jaw throbs, but I use the momentum from the ropes to right myself and reset. "I don't give a fuck who she works for. But she's scared. And desperate enough to confess some of her troubles to a stranger. So...want to tell me why the most decent guy I've ever met—who happens to own a security firm—would refuse to help one of his own?"

"Because she's grasping at straws to make sense of her brother's death. When the truth is," grabbing hold of my shoulders, Dax pulls me closer and knees me in the gut, "the guy was a drug addict."

My uppercut sends him sprawling back onto his ass. "Shit." Extending a gloved hand, I tap his arm, but he bats me away and rolls to his feet.

"I can handle my own," Dax mutters. "Now fight, dammit."

Half an hour later, I'm wheezing. Flat on my back. Staring up into Dax's triumphant face.

"You done proving you can still get it up?" I ask as I push to my feet. "Or do you need to take a few more shots at me before we can have a goddamned conversation?"

"You lost. To a blind man. Of the two of us, I'd wager you're the one who needs the little blue pills."

"Never have, never will." I hold out my hands to the attendant so he can remove my gloves. Ducking out of the ring, I grab a bottle of water from a cooler and drop onto a bench. "But I know when I've been beat."

"Care to repeat that?" He joins me, feeling his way carefully along the wall until he finds the seat next to me.

I punch him in the arm. "You heard me the first time."

We sit, the bruises aching, until Dax sighs. "Wren is the most logical woman I know. If she's determined to go after the *bratva*, no one's going to stop her."

"Then why won't you help?"

Dropping his head back against the wall, Dax swears under his breath. "I'll meet you out front in ten minutes. We'll go see her together."

7
_____

Wren

*M*y cold pizza sits untouched as I watch the second
video—the one I didn't get a chance to show Dax
—for the fifth time. On the screen, a pretty young woman with
sad blue eyes sniffles and holds an ice pack to her cheek.

"I am scared, Zion. Kolya is not himself. He is convinced
everyone is spying on him. And...the money...most of it is gone."
She dabs her eyes with a tissue, then pauses with a whispered
curse and sets the phone down.

Clipped footsteps race across the floor, a door opens, closes,
and then she lowers her voice. "I must be quick. He will be back
soon, and he will want to fuck." The girl—Elena—chokes back a
sob. "Ana is gone. Kolya...*sold* her. He made so much money.
Now...he talks about selling more. I do not want him to sell me. If
he finds out what I did...he threatened me many times after you
escaped. Me and Semyon. And the way he looks at Semyon now
—I am afraid Kolya will sell him too. The man who took Ana...he
hurt her badly before he paid. There was so much blood."

PATRICIA EDDY

Elena presses her lips together and glances over her shoulder. "Can you help me, Zion? Please? I am foolish, I think. Asking a boy to rescue me. You are safe in America. But you are my only hope. You once said you could get me and Semyon out. Your sister would help. Is that still true? I hope it is." A loud crash sounds from the next room, and Elena gasps. "Please hurry."

The video ends, and I close my eyes. What am I missing? Rewinding, I mute the sound, focusing on Elena and the room around her. There has to be some sort of clue who she is beyond her first name.

Two piercings in each ear. Dirty blond hair. Wait. As she moves the ice pack around on her cheek, a tattoo peeks out from her sleeve. Except...it's a freakin' butterfly. Only the most common tattoo ever.

Unable to stifle my frustrated moan, I run my fingers along Zion's bracelet over and over again, needing the repetition and the comfort of the warm beads to distract from the utter defeat enveloping me.

Two quick raps on my front door make me squeak, and I leap off the couch. Taking a deep breath, I try to calm my racing heart.

"Wren? Open up."

Dax? I'm so confused—and angry he won't help me—I forget my momentary panic and throw the door open. Only to stare directly into a black t-shirt stretched over the broadest chest I've ever seen.

My gaze trails up, and shock strangles the words in my throat. "Wh-what are *you* doing here?"

"Nice to see you too, sweetheart," Ryker drawls. "Mind if we come in?"

I step back, and Pixel barrels in from the bedroom. My feeble attempts to stop my dog from welcoming the unexpected guests fail miserably, and I barely manage not to step on her. Off balance, I stumble, and Ryker reaches out to steady me.

"Three times in one day?" He arches a brow, and I step back.

"I was doing just fine," I mutter and snap my fingers so Pixel stops yipping and jumping around Dax's legs. Despite not being able to see her antics, he manages to expertly avoid her little paws as he follows Ryker into my apartment and shuts the door.

"Um. Can I get you...I have beer and uh...red wine and Diet Coke." Entertaining isn't...me. I can hang with the guys all night long after a hard job. Drink half of them under the table if I really want to, but only when we're in a big group. Me alone with my boss and the tank I ran away from this afternoon? Not my comfort zone.

Ryker glances at Dax, then shrugs. "Stick-Up-His-Ass will take a Diet Coke. But I'll have a beer."

"Fuck you," Dax says. "I need a beer for this conversation."

I can't move, my mouth hanging open slightly at the venom— and something else—I hear in my boss's voice. He's always been a little lost, but watching him with Ryker is eerie. Like he's a ghost of his real self. After seeing the photo Ryker carries in his wallet, I think maybe the Dax I know is a ghost of who he used to be.

"Wren? Sit down. Ry, get the beers." Dax reaches for my arm, coming up just short, and I clear my throat to let him know where I am.

Ryker strides into my kitchen and rummages in the fridge while I take Dax's arm and lead him to an overstuffed chair across from the couch. "Chair," I whisper, and he nods, though his movements are stiff as he takes a seat.

Shutting my laptop, I clutch it to my chest when Ryker swaggers over with three beers clutched in his beefy hands. Despite his size, he moves with a grace I've rarely seen in men—only Dax and Ford can glide soundlessly across the floor like that. Training, Ford once told me.

"Mind if I sit?" Ryker asks, gesturing to the cushion next to me.

"Uh…sure."

Once everyone has a beer, Ryker lifts his bottle. "Hooah." Dax frowns, and silence hangs in the air. "Fine. See if I care," Ryker mutters. Turning to me, he arches a brow. "So…tell us about the *Nevsky Bratva*."

"No." I take a long pull on my beer as the two men stare at me like I've grown a second head. "You didn't change your mind about Z in the past eight hours, Dax."

"No. I didn't. I've known way too many guys pulled under by addiction. Zion had the same demons. The need. The craving. The desperation to just…escape. To feel good—or maybe nothing at all. To *not hurt* anymore."

"You didn't know him." The lump in my throat roughens my voice, and I suck down another swallow of beer. "Zion was clean. Going to meetings every day. He got a job. He *promised* me he'd never go back to that life."

"Can we start from the beginning?" Ryker settles back on the couch and stretches his long legs under my coffee table. "You did a hell of a lot of dancing in that coffee shop, sweetheart. Tell me what we're dealing with. All of it."

NINETY MINUTES, another round of beers, and the leftover pizza later, I'm worried I've said too much. Or not enough. "This girl's in trouble. So's her brother. And Zion promised to get them out of Russia."

"And how the hell did he think he was going to do that?" Dax asks.

"Me." I risk a glance at Dax, see his expression, and can't help the small, frustrated sound that catches in my throat. "Fine. You. Us. Second Sight. Remember when Z called me at work? A month before he showed up at my door?"

"You said he was high as a kite."

"He was. Kept talking about getting passports for all of them." Flopping back on the couch, I play with my bracelet. "The next day, Kolya told Elena he was going to kill Zion. She...she convinced one of Kolya's generals to fake Zion's death." I open my laptop and pull up Z's last message to me.

Firefly, I'm so sorry. When Elena told me what Kolya was going to do, I had to leave her and Semyon behind. I hated it. But...she made me promise I'd never go back to Russia. She begged Misha to give me an overdose—but not enough to kill me. Just...make me look like I'd died. I don't know why he agreed. He dumped me in a little town a couple hours away, and when I came to...I couldn't think straight. I took a bunch of pills—I don't even know what they were—and puked my guts out all over a car. And then this grandma comes out of the house next door and starts yelling at me. I was so messed up, I told her everything. She's the reason I came home.

When I saw Elena's video, I wanted to tell you. But...then I got Kolya's message, and I knew I had to get out of town. He never lets anyone go, and I can't put you in danger. I'm uploading all this from a little internet cafe in Quincy. I'm going to get as far away from Boston as I can, and then I'll call you. If he doesn't find me first. I'm sorry I won't be there for court. I know I'm letting you down. But this might be my only chance to stay alive. I love you. -Z

<hr />

Ryker

Glancing at Dax, I try to get a read on him. But after so many years, I'm lost. So I swallow my pride and ask. "Dax? Tell me what you're thinking."

He snorts. "There's no proof this girl is even still alive. I know you want to believe the best about your brother, Wren, but without any evidence Zion was murdered...what the hell do you expect us to do about this?"

Us. The word gives me pause until I realize he's talking about his company. Not me. Sitting across from him, it's easy to fool myself into thinking no time's passed, and we're still on the same team.

Wren meets my gaze for only a second, but the fire in her green eyes shocks me. "Help me find her. I'm close. I have enough for facial recognition. I just need to get to St. Petersburg. Traffic cameras, government surveillance systems, identification cards... plus Z's notes...I can find her. Then we can get her out."

"Why?" I ask. "This girl's nothing to you. A drug lord's punching bag of the week." As I say the words, I try not to cringe. I don't like the idea of abandoning Elena there, and I don't even know the kid. *Never leave a man behind.* It's our code. It's why I got into K&R. Because Dax and I got left behind and look where it got us.

"My brother loved her." Wren fiddles with her bracelet, staring down at the purple and green beads. "And he promised her."

"You're willing to risk your life—the lives of your coworkers— because of a promise?" I ask. "Do you have a death wish?"

Wren blows out a breath and turns to me. "No. I don't. But promises mean something to me. Our mother ran out on us when Zion was thirteen. The day she left, Z was sick. Pneumonia. I came over to spend time with him, and as soon as I walked in the door, Mom took off. Z was crying, and the last thing Mom said to him was, 'I'll be back in a few hours. I promise.'"

Draining the last of her beer, she starts peeling off the label in long, narrow strips. "After three days, the police in Atlantic City called and told us she'd been arrested for vehicular homicide. She was drunk off her ass and killed three people." Wren's voice cracks, and she slams the bottle down. "She died in prison eighteen months after her sentencing."

"I'm sorry," I say and fight the urge to take her hand. I don't do comforting. But something about this woman calls to me. Begs me to be...better. Someone I'm not.

"Don't apologize." Wren gives me a sidelong glance and shakes her head. "She never contacted us or responded to any of my repeated attempts to see her. That's not the point." Clenching her fists for a moment and squeezing her eyes shut, she forces out a breath. "When I got the call about the arrest and looked up the charge, I knew she was never coming home. *I* had to tell Zion. And the two of us agreed we'd never use the words 'I promise' unless we were sure we meant them. In ten years, Z never went back on a promise. Not even when he was at his lowest. He'd say, 'I swear' or 'Scout's honor' or 'You know it.' Not 'I promise.' But he said the words to her...and he said them to me. He promised he was clean. That he was never going back to drugs. Ever."

"I promise I'll come back for you, Dax. But if I don't go now, we'll both die."

"Ry...don't leave me..."

I look over at Dax and wonder if he's reliving the same memory. "I'll get Elena out," I say before common sense can over-rule me. "Give me all the info you have on her and keep working from here. I'll go to St. Petersburg and find her."

"You won't find her without me." Wren straightens her shoulders. "It'll be a heck of a lot easier for me to hack the systems I need if I'm on-site."

"No. You're staying in Boston. I can't protect you in Russia."

"Unless you're prepared to lock me away somewhere by force, you can't stop me. And I'm pretty sure the two of you aren't *that* stupid." Wren pushes to her feet, and her little dog leaps up and runs to the door, rearing up on her hind legs and begging. "I have to take Pixel out. You can stay here and we can talk more when I get back, or you can leave. The door is self-locking," she says as she jingles her keys in one hand and holds the dog's leash in the other.

When she slips into the hall, I stare up at the ceiling. "You know how to pick 'em, Dax. She's..."

"Headstrong? Loyal? Altruistic?" He chuckles. "Fucking stubborn?"

"All of the above." Wandering over to her second-floor window, I peer out into the April evening. Wren lets the dog scamper from tree to tree, the little thing sniffing and occasionally looking back at her. The street's deserted, the neighborhood quiet well past nine at night.

I'm about to turn back when I catch movement out of the corner of my eye. A shadow darts out from between the buildings, too fast to be anything good, and instinct kicks in. "Hostile!" I shout as I sprint for her door. Curling my hand around the stairwell railing, I use my momentum to carry me halfway down, then jump the last four stairs, hitting the building's door at full speed. Pixel growls, then there's a muffled scream, a male curse, and a smack.

"Dose her and get it over with," a tense voice snaps.

I'm almost to the corner of the building when I hear Wren moan. "Nnnooo..."

Shit. They're taking her. I press my back to the wall. Plan. Assess. Act.

"Fucking bitch bit me." This from someone older. Or bigger. The tone deeper.

"Get the dog. Take it back into her apartment and grab her computer," the first voice orders, jingling keys. "Meet me at the car."

Angling a quick glance around the corner of the building, I make out two men. One hefts Wren over his shoulder in a fireman's carry, and the other reaches for the dog. But Pixel has a little fight in her and latches on to the man's hand. Perfect distraction.

In three steps, I lay the dog's new chew toy out with one hard uppercut, then move on to the asshole holding Wren. "Let her go, or you won't walk again for a very long time."

Wren slides to the ground, unconscious, as he reaches behind his back. But I'm too well-trained to be intimidated by a kid who can't be more than twenty-one. Ducking my shoulder, I ram into his gut, sending the gun clattering to the cobblestones as we hit the ground.

"Big mistake." Grabbing him by his skinny arms, I lift him and then slam him back down again, driving the air from his lungs. "Who sent you?"

A metallic tapping sounds from the front of the building. "Call the dog," I shout.

"Pixel. Come." Dax whistles, and the ball of fur takes off for the door.

The kid spits in my face, and I roll my eyes. "You see me, right? I could rip you in half and not even break a sweat. Who. Sent. You?"

"You're dead, big man. You and the girl. I won't tell you shit."

"Suit yourself." One more punch and he's unconscious, and I pat down his pockets, hoping...yes. Zip ties. No good—or bad—kidnapper ever leaves home without them. When the two men are secured, I move to Wren.

A goose egg swells on her cheek, but her heartbeat is steady. "Wren? How deep are you under, sweetheart?" She doesn't answer when I brush her hair off her forehead. After a sigh, I mutter, "Pretty deep, then."

"Ry. Sit rep," Dax calls.

"Two hostiles. Restrained. Wren's unconscious. Get your ass over here."

Tap, tap, tap. Dax's cane skitters over the cobbles as he slowly makes his way down the alley. "Pixel's tied up inside," he says. "Cops are on the way."

Gently, I lift Wren into my arms. "I'm getting her out of here. These idiots wanted both her and her laptop."

"Fuck. Go. Call me when you're secure. I'll get her computer and call Ford to take the dog for a few days."

"Any chance you can keep her name out of this?" I ask as I settle her against my chest and dig for the keys to my rental.

"Not likely, but I'll try." Dax claps his hand on my shoulder as I start to move past him. "I don't know how to forgive you for ghosting, Ry. But I'm damn glad you're here. Keep her safe."

I nod before I remember he can't see me. "I will."

8

Wren

I'm floating. Why am I floating? Something firm and warm moves under me, and I try to force my eyes open, but they don't want to obey. A little moan coils in my throat, and the thing under me moves again.

"Shhh, sweetheart. We're almost to the room."

The room? I don't understand. "Mmmy...head."

"I know. I'll get you some ice in a couple of minutes." There's a beep and a click, and then I'm not floating anymore. A warm hand cups my cheek, and I finally manage to pry my lids open. "Ryker?"

"Good. Do you know what day it is?"

"Of course I know what day it is," I snap as I push myself up to sitting. And fall over when I'm suddenly on a tilt-a-whirl. "Crap on a cracker."

"That's not a day of the week." Ryker takes my wrist, and as the room comes into focus again, he checks his watch. "Who's the President?"

"I don't have a concussion. I got punched in the face."

I got punched in the face.

As the words register, and the memories come flooding back, I start shaking. "I got punched in the face. And drugged. And—" I swallow a sob. "Where's Pixel?"

"She's fine. Dax is taking her to Ford's for a couple of days."

"What did they give me?" I rear up again and grab his muscular forearm as his brows furrow. "Ryker, tell me. What did they give me?"

"I don't know. Some sort of sedative. Why? Are you allergic to —" His eyes darken, the colors shifting to a deeper hue as he searches my face.

"No. I just...Zion. My mom had an addictive personality. So does—did—Z. I don't...I can't..." I start to hyperventilate, and my heart hammers against my chest so hard I think the thing from *Alien* is about to burst forth and kill both of us.

"Look at me, Wren." His voice turns rougher, demanding, and he presses my palm to his chest. "Breathe with me. In. Out. Match my pace." I try, but I can't stop wheezing. "Slower. Listen to my voice. In. Good. Out." He covers my hand with his until the world slows and rights itself again.

"Flippin' flapjacks. Fudgsicles. Cracker Jacks."

"Oh fuck. I knew it. You do have a concussion." Ryker slides his arms under me as I choke out a laugh. "What?"

"I don't really...swear." That doesn't clear anything up, and he carries me halfway to the door before I manage to stop him by squeezing the back of his neck. "Those...are my curse words."

"Seriously? Are you religious or—"

"No. But Mom was a pre-school teacher...before." I swallow hard as memories threaten. "Anyone can say fuck. Flippin' flapjacks? Now *that's* unique."

His laugh seems to surprise him, and he sets me back on the bed. "This is not the night I thought I'd be having."

Without thinking, I try to rub my right eye. It's hot and itchy, but when I touch my cheek, the pain blooms across my whole face. "Oh God. That...ow."

"I'll get you some ice. Stay there." He points at me, his eyes narrowing. "I mean it. Do not move. And don't touch the phone."

"I'm not an idiot. Two guys just tried to kidnap me off the street." I regret my words as worry tightens tiny lines around his eyes, but after a heartbeat, he nods and heads for the door. Letting myself sink back against the pillows, I try not to relive those terrifying few seconds. The rough hands. The scent of cigarettes. The salty taste of the guy's palm as I bit down.

Dammit. My laptop. If Ryker and Dax left my apartment unprotected, everything Zion sent me is probably...well, no. The guys who tried to take me might have it, but they can't access it. Not without a hell of a lot of work and a hacker as good as I am.

Closing my eyes, I try to recall as much about them as I can. I don't hear the door open and close, and gasp as Ryker slides a hip onto the mattress. "Here."

The bath towel ice pack he holds to my cheek feels like heaven and hell at the same time. Cool and comforting, but the pressure is almost too much. "Is...what if it's broken?"

Ryker sits back. "Follow my finger. Don't move your head. Any more dizziness? Nausea?"

"No. How the hell did they find me?" My voice cracks, and I pull my knees up to my chest. "What...happened to them?"

"I knocked them out. Dax called 911 and stayed on-scene. I need to contact him now that we're...as safe as I can make us for the moment. This hotel room isn't in my name—and even if it was, there's nothing linking the two of us...together." Ryker probes the edge of the bruise, his fingers gentle. Scars wind their way up his forearms, intertwined with tattoos of skulls and barbed wire. "You're okay. Nothing's broken."

"You're sure?" The headache currently splitting my skull disagrees with his assessment, but I've never had a broken bone before.

Shadows dance across his face, dimming the light in his eyes. "Fifty-four."

"Huh?"

"I've had fifty-four bones in my body broken. I'm pretty sure." He shakes his head and stands.

"Oh my God. How?"

"Don't ask me that." Ryker heads for the window as his fingers dance over his phone screen. He parts the curtains, angles a glance down at the street, and his shoulders visibly relax. Taking a seat in the desk chair a few feet away, he leans back and crosses his legs at the ankles. "Tell me everything you remember about the fuckers who tried to take you."

Shivering, I wrap my arms around myself and draw my knees up to my chest. Now that I'm safe, the adrenaline's wearing off and my anxiety starts to creep back in. "I...you don't have my bag, do you?"

Ryker frowns. "No. My priority was getting you out of there. What do you need?"

"Meds. I'll be...okay. Just need a minute."

My teeth start to chatter, and with a curse, Ryker crosses the room in two steps, pulls back the blankets and orders me under them. "You're in shock. Sort of. I'll get you another blanket and what—coffee? Tea?"

"T-t-tea."

I can't get warm, even under the blankets, fully clothed. The little electric tea kettle on the desk starts to whistle, and Ryker pours the water over a bag of chamomile, adds honey, then presses the mug into my hands. And proceeds to position himself with his back against the headboard. "Come here."

"I just m-met you!"

"I'm not asking you to sleep with me, sweetheart. You need to get warm. You see anything else in this room as big as me?" His sharp tone helps me focus, and I meet his frosty gaze. "Until you can manage to get through a sentence without those teeth clicking like a pair of castanets, you'll...snuggle."

He says it like it's the worst possible activity in the entire world, and I wriggle closer and let him drape his arm around me. I do it to spite him, but he's right. He's warm. And massive.

"Drink your tea and then we'll talk."

"Are you always this...prickly?" I chance a peek up at him as I take a sip. "And how'd you know I wanted the tea sweetened?"

"You put honey in your coffee this morning. And yes. This is my warm and fuzzy side. Don't get used to it."

Ryker doesn't speak again as I let the tea soothe me. His slow, rhythmic breathing against my back helps tamp down my anxiety, and when I set the mug down, I lean my head against his shoulder. "Thank you. I never leave home without my meds. But walking Pixel...I just didn't think..."

"Why would you? It's a safe neighborhood."

"It is, but how'd you know that?"

"Used to live here. A long time ago." His tone warns me he doesn't like talking about himself, and I close my eyes.

"Pixel wasn't happy. She kept whining. I guess I should have listened to her." With a shrug, I nestle a little deeper into the crook of his arm. I'm so tired. And he feels warm. And...safe. "She wouldn't pick a spot, and I was about ready to just take her back inside. But then she growled, and it shocked me. Before I could turn around, someone grabbed me from behind."

I can still feel the hand over my mouth, and I scrub at my lips with my sleeve. "I...I tried to—"

"You're safe, Wren." Ryker tightens his arm around me, and with his free hand, takes my wrist and checks my pulse. "No one's going to find you here."

Nodding, I try to ignore what feels like clog dancers inside my skull. "I screamed, but he had his hand over my mouth. Pretty sure I kicked the other one in the shins. But the guy holding me dragged me between the buildings, and I bit him."

"Good." Ryker's thumb traces lazy patterns over the inside of my wrist, and the slow back and forth helps calm me.

"That's when the other one punched me. After that, I don't remember anything else."

"What did they say to you?" He switches to circles, then triangles, then squares, and the constant variation helps keep me focused.

Except when I close my eyes, I hear the gravelly voice of my attacker, and I can't get the words out. I reach for my bracelet, dislodging Ryker's hand. The smooth beads click as I run my fingers over them, tugging at the elastic.

Breathe in. Two. Three. Four. Out. Two. Three. Four. Five. Six.

"Wren. Tell me."

After another round of breathing, I manage, "You're going to join your brother, bitch. But the boss wants to talk to you first."

Ryker

Stretching out as close to the edge of the bed as I can, I stare at the clock, willing Dax to get his ass over here. But talking to the cops always takes a lot longer than it should—all that fucking paperwork.

At least he confirmed he has Wren's laptop and messenger bag. She needs her meds, and though she's finally asleep, little whimpers escape her lips every few minutes.

I can't get comfortable. Turning to face the slight woman in my bed, I study her delicate features. Freckles dot her cheeks, and her auburn lashes flutter as she dreams. She clutches my pillow to her chest, and as she shifts, her sweatshirt slides up, revealing a deep bruise on her left wrist. Dammit. She should have told me about the injury.

Carefully, I ease my phone from the pocket of my jeans and send Dax another text.

Pick up an ACE bandage and an extra ice pack. And where the hell are you anyway?

"No." Wren moans and tenses, and her legs twitch under the blankets. A tear shines in the corner of her eye.

"Shhh, sweetheart. You're fine." For some reason, I can't stop with the "sweetheart" bit. Reaching out, I brush a silky lock of hair away from her face.

My phone vibrates, and I jerk my hand away, rolling off the bed.

I'm blind, you piece of shit. Cut me some fucking slack.

Shame has me cracking my knuckles as I move back to the window. This is why I left Boston six years ago. What the hell am I supposed to say? Sorry? Sorry I abandoned you? Sorry those fuckers poured acid in your eyes? Sorry I couldn't deal with my own shit and yours too?

I roll an apology around in my head. Or hell. A hundred of them. All the things I wish I'd said rather than walking out of the rehab facility without a backwards glance. Leaning against the wall, I scan the street, the lights of Boston Public Garden blurring as I sink into my memories.

"Ry. You still alive, man?"

"Debatable."

"Where this time?"

"Left side of my face."

I run my hand over the jagged scar that trails from my brow all the way to the corner of my mouth.

"Ryker?" Cool fingers curl over my arm, and I whirl around and grab Wren's wrist.

"Don't *ever* sneak up on me," I growl before I register the fear in her eyes. Neither of us breathe, and I blink hard. Her bruises peek out from under my fingers.

Step away, you fucking ape. You're not back there, and she's not the enemy.

"Shit. Wren..."

"Let go." Her voice is barely a whisper, but she doesn't back down. "You were talking to yourself." I stare at her, trying to remember what the hell I might have been saying, and her brows furrow. "You sounded...angry."

Her sweet scent pulls me closer, and I fight to relax my fingers, cupping her forearm so I can bring her wrist to my lips and ghost a kiss over the bruises. "How bad?"

"F-fine," she whispers as she meets my gaze, confusion darkening her jade green eyes.

I search her face for the truth, finding it in the way she ducks her head. "Wren."

"Hurts less than my cheek."

Her hair covers most of the swelling around her eye, and I brush the auburn curls away. "I should have been faster."

"This isn't your fault," she says. "If it's anyone's fault...it's mine."

"No, sweetheart. No." Leaning down, I trace her jaw with the backs of my knuckles. Wren tips her head up, her eyes fluttering closed, and I feather a kiss to her lips. She tastes like honey, and fear tightens in my gut. I want more, and that's a dangerous game I can't play. Because she's the one who'll lose.

Two knocks, followed by three more force us apart. "Dax," I say when she darts behind me. "Maybe now we'll get some answers."

⬥

SHOVING a bag in my general direction as he crosses the threshold, Dax tests the area in front of him with his cane. "Next time you need supplies after midnight, do what I usually do. Call someone who can see."

"James Joyce on a pogo-stick. Both of you to your separate corners. Now," Wren says as we both swivel our heads in her general direction.

"James Joyce on a pogo-stick? Where do you come up with this shit?" I ask.

She takes Dax's arm and leads him across the room. "Desk. Right in front of you." Guiding his hand to the back of the office chair, she glares at me. "I told you. My mom was a teacher for years. At a Catholic school. Some things stick."

I dig into the plastic pharmacy bag and come away with the ACE bandage. "Let me see your wrist, sweetheart."

"In a minute." Wren slings the messenger bag over her shoulder and disappears into the bathroom, leaving a trail of honeysuckle behind.

"Sweetheart?" Dax asks, arching a brow. "Last I checked, Ryker McCabe didn't do relationships. Any relationships."

"The girl's been through some shit. It slipped out."

Half a dozen times.

"I'm not a girl," she snaps from behind the bathroom door. "And I can hear every word."

For a few seconds, I don't recognize the sound filling the room, until I look over at Dax to see him laughing. Fuck. I haven't seen him laugh since...before Hell.

We used to be the two practical jokers in our unit. Pine tar on the toilet seat. Lube on the plastic tub of powdered coffee creamer. A footlocker full of dildos whenever we got a newbie in our ranks. And then...we both stopped laughing.

"Shut up," I mutter, but there's no venom in my tone. "About earlier...I'm—"

The apology dies in my throat as Wren emerges from the bathroom with a pill case clutched in her hand and her well-worn pink sweatshirt in the other. A black tank clings to her slight curves. "What?" She looks between the two of us, but Dax just shrugs.

"Nothing." My jeans feel a little snug, and I turn back to the bed—the bed she was *just* sleeping in, dammit—and rip open the ACE bandage. "Wrist."

"We're back to the single-word answers?" She sighs as she lowers herself carefully onto the edge of the mattress. "It's not broken. I don't need—"

My glare cuts her off, and she holds out her arm. "So...what did the cops say?" I ask as I gently probe the swelling, checking for any hot spots or areas of acute pain. Wren grimaces, but otherwise remains silent.

"Being blind has its advantages once in a while," Dax says and runs a hand through his dark hair. "No one pays attention to the guy with the cane. The men who attacked you haven't said a word, but when the detective was done with me, I had to wait for someone to help me get back out of the building, and I eaves-dropped a little. Those two are repeat offenders. Mostly intimida-tion, but they've also been written up on drug charges half a dozen times. Minor possession with intent to sell."

"Any ties to—"

"I'm getting to that. You have coffee in this hotel room?"

"Yeah. Just a minute." I press Wren's thumb against her palm, holding the end of the bandage in place.

As I wrap her wrist, she stares down at my fingers curled around hers. This girl—woman—does something to me I don't like. I can't get enough of her. She's innocent, but not. Sweet, but not. All contradictions and mysteries I'd love to solve. Except, if I tried, I'd drag her down into the dark pit I exist in, and no one deserves that.

"There you go." Squeezing the cold pack to activate it, I press it gently to her cheek. "Better?"

She nods, then curls her legs under her as she settles back against the pillows.

"You still take your coffee black?" I ask Dax as I fill the little pod machine with water.

Dax snorts. "Is there any other way?"

"Men. Lattes are delicious," Wren says, her words a little slurred.

"What's wrong?" I freeze with my hand on the brew button, but she just smiles.

"Meds kicking in." Her eyelids flutter closed. "Plus... exhausted. Prolly gonna sleep a while. Sorry."

Once I start the coffee, I return to her side, pull back the blankets, and tuck her in. "Sleep as long as you want. I'll be here." I punctuate my whisper with a kiss to her forehead, and she settles.

Why didn't I spring for a suite?

Dax sits quietly, flopped back in the chair with annoyance etched all over his face. When I press the mug of coffee into his hand, he tips his head up. "Nice of you to remember I was here, dickwad."

"I'm not...good with people."

"No shit." He takes a sip, then grimaces. "And your hotel has crappy coffee."

"Every hotel has crappy coffee. You want a good brew, come out to Seattle. Sampson can tell you the origin of every fucking bean he grinds."

"The SEAL?" With a low whistle, Dax sets his mug aside. "I heard he quit after some overzealous colonel sent in the drones early and decimated his team."

"He did. And now he works for me. K&R." Needing something to do with all this energy thrumming through my body, I head for the window again. I can't stand staring at four walls. Can't stand being cooped up with no way out. If the window in this room opened more than an inch, I'd have my head half out of it by now.

"Always knew that's where you were headed." After a sigh, he turns in my general direction. "Listen, Ry. I meant what I said back at Wren's. I don't know how to forgive you. But...it doesn't matter now. Because Wren's in trouble, and I can't protect her. Not like this." He gestures to his tinted glasses. "Those two assholes have been linked to the Solensky drug ring operating out of Roxbury."

"And the Solensky drug ring..."

"Has ties to the *Nevsky Bratva*." He nods, winces, and removes his glasses to pinch the bridge of his nose. "Fucking migraines. I need to crash. I called in a few favors, and if I'm lucky, I'll know more when the sun comes up."

"Go home." I glance back at Wren. "She's safe here. At least for tonight."

Pushing to his feet with a groan, Dax unfolds his cane. "Good. She matters, Ry. And if I'm right, I owe her one hell of an apology. Because her brother mattered too, and my prejudices may have killed him." He reaches back to his hip and withdraws a belt holster and a 9mm. "You didn't get this from me. But unless you flew across the country armed..."

"I didn't." As I take the gun, I clasp his hand for an extra beat. "Thanks."

Dax slips through the hotel room door, and I wish I could have my friend back for one day. Just long enough to tell him he matters too.

9

Wren

*R*olling over, I catch my wrist in the sheets and wince. The pain forces me fully awake, and I barely stop myself from rubbing my eyes. My headache's mostly gone, and the hard knot of anxiety lodged in my chest lessened overnight. My eye still feels hot and swollen though, and I really don't want to look in the mirror.

Squinting as the beside clock comes into focus, I'm shocked. It's after nine. And...where the hell is Ryker? As I push up to sitting, I see him—stretched out in front of the door. On his side. One hand resting on a pistol. He looks...almost peaceful, and I have a feeling Ryker McCabe doesn't do peaceful very often.

"Where did you get a gun?"

He's instantly awake, the gun held firmly, but his finger off the trigger. "Dax."

"Is there some reason you felt the need to sleep on the floor?" I ask as I swing my legs over the side of the bed. My body aches, but no new injuries make themselves known—I'm just sore from being grabbed and dropped by guys who didn't care if I was comfortable.

"Safer." Lumbering to his feet, he checks the gun's safety and then tucks it into a holster.

"In case housekeeping decides to raid the place?"

The look he gives me is one part "isn't she cute?" and two parts "how did I get stuck babysitting this idiot?"

"In case anyone followed Dax from the police station last night. Not like he could have seen them." Touching both the deadbolt and the safety lock, almost automatically, he nods towards the bathroom. "Go on. I'll order us some breakfast and then I'll take you to your office. What do you want?"

Rolling my eyes, I trudge towards the small, marbled bathroom with fancier toiletries than I've ever seen. "I don't need anything."

"Well, you're getting something."

I stick my tongue out at him. "Fine. Eggs. Scrambled." Shutting the bathroom door with a little more force than necessary, I sink down onto the edge of the tub, rubbing my sore shoulder absently. There's dirt in my hair from the alley, and...ugh. Blood under my fingernails. Dax kept my name out of the police report, but do I need to worry about DNA?

Peeking back into the room to ask Ryker, I gawk. He's doing one-armed pushups, alternating arms every five rounds. He's shirtless, his back a mountain of sculpted muscle and scars, with a massive tattoo running between his shoulder blades. A skull with an evil grin and glowing red eyes looks out from a shield, bolts of lightning forming an *X* behind the image. A green beret sits atop the skull, with a black and orange patch on one side.

"*De oppresso liber?*" I ask, unable to look away—or get control of my mouth, apparently.

Faster than a man his size should be able to move, he scrambles up and clutches his black t-shirt to his chest. "You need something?"

The strain in his voice warns me he's not going to answer my question—or lower that shirt anytime soon. "Um, there's blood under my nails. I scratched one of the guys who tried to take me. Do I need to...the police...?"

He takes my hand, staring down at my dirty nails as his warmth seeps into my fingers. "No. The police have enough evidence to put them away without you getting involved."

My gaze roves over his arms, over the burns winding down his entire left shoulder, over more ink, bright colors, bold lines. Releasing my fingers, Ryker nudges me towards the bathroom. "Use any of my stuff you need."

Dismissed, I trudge off to the shower, hoping I can find some way to wash away the feeling my life is never going to be the same again.

WHEN I EMERGE from the bathroom smelling of Ryker's deodorant and shampoo, my hair still damp, he's pouring a second cup of coffee from a porcelain teapot. A massive spread graces a rolling cart: scrambled eggs, bacon, toast, orange juice, and fresh fruit.

"How much do you think I eat?" I ask as I continue to use one of the hand towels to blot at my hair.

"I have no idea." He says it like it's the most obvious thing in the world. "If this isn't enough—"

"This would feed me for a week." I sink down onto the bed. "Can we go to my place before we head to the office? I'd really like to get a change of clothes and my brother's book."

"Not a good idea." Ryker takes his mug of coffee and a small duffel bag and beelines for the bathroom. Before I can reply, he shuts the door.

Ten minutes later, I've done nothing more than push the eggs around on my plate and force down two slices of bacon. Well, nothing more than planning the verbal assault I'm going to unleash on him for dismissing me like that.

"We leave in ten minutes," he says when he emerges.

I point to the desk chair I've pulled to the other side of the breakfast cart. "No. Sit your butt down."

"Excuse me?"

"Sit. Down." A knot of anxiety starts to tighten in my chest, but I force myself to look him in the eye. "Someone's after me. I don't know why. I don't know how they found me. But they're after *me*. I'm so out of my element, I don't know which way is up. But I do know you were really sweet last night. And now...you're being a jerk."

His ruddy cheeks darken slightly as he swipes a piece of toast from a stack thicker than my laptop. "Sorry."

"You can do better than that." I try to arch a brow, but my swollen cheek and eye don't like that motion, and I stifle a wince. "You saved my life. You slept in front of the door in case anyone tried to break in. You're like...Rambo or something."

He snorts and rubs a meaty palm over the back of his head. "I'm not Rambo, sweetheart. Sylvester Stallone's seventy years old."

"And you are...?" To keep him talking, I shove a forkful of eggs into my mouth. He was so concerned about my dietary habits, maybe he'll stay put as long as I'm eating.

"Thirty-five."

I pick up another slice of bacon. "What's the tattoo on your back?" When he stares at me, almost unblinking, I add, "It's beautiful."

"I'm not interested in 'chatting,' Wren. I was distracted at your apartment last night and you paid the price. Take your time eating. I'm going to scout from here to the lobby. You don't open the door for anyone. Got it?"

I nod, but as he rises, his hands find his hips and he pins me with a hard stare until I sigh. "I got it."

❤

"How quickly can you get her papers?" Ryker asks as he paces Second Sight's conference room.

"Two days." Clive—our relocation specialist—scribbles on a legal pad.

"Not fast enough."

Clive drops his pen. "Listen, dude. I don't know who the fuck you are, but it takes time to build a profile that won't crumble under scrutiny."

"Dude? You better watch yourself, punk."

"Enough!" Dax slams his fist down on the table and everyone falls silent. "Ry, I swear to God, if you don't pull that stick out of your ass soon, I'm going to do it for you. Then beat you bloody with it. Clive, take it down a notch and work faster. We don't need this to be ironclad. Just enough to get her into the country and hold up to the basic searches the Russian police might run if things go FUBAR."

Ryker mutters something under his breath, and Dax swivels his head around. It's spooky how accurate he is. Even though he can't see Ryker at all, he's staring right at him. "This is *my* company. Not yours. You want to run things, go back to Seattle."

Clive slinks from the room while I hack into the traffic cameras around my apartment building. The ride to Second Sight in Ryker's rental car was utterly silent. He wrapped his arm around me when we exited his hotel room and kept me tucked to his side the entire time we were outside. I miss his warmth, the gentle way he eased my messenger bag from my shoulder outside the car, his strong hand helping me to my feet after we parked downstairs.

So now, I ignore him—and everyone else in the room. I need to pack a bag for Russia. Check on Pixel. And I need a few minutes alone.

"Wren?" Ryker sinks down next to me. "Did you hear me?"

His dark brows furrow when I shake my head, and I swear he looks worried. "Please stay here."

"No. We had this discussion last night. You need me." I leave the rest of the sentence unspoken. I need him too. This man exudes danger, and I know, without a doubt, he'll do just about anything to keep me safe. While I trust the men and women I work with, I'd pick Ryker in a fight every time.

"I need to be able to move around without worrying about you," he snaps.

"I won't leave the hotel." At his frown, I roll my eyes. "Or wherever you want us to hole up. I need a hardline or a strong Wi-Fi signal, power, and to be left alone. You get me that, I'll find Elena and her brother."

Dax clears his throat. "You don't know her like I do, Ry. Accept it. She's going with you."

When Ryker curses under his breath and flops against the back of his chair, I can't hide my smile. "So...when do we leave?"

10

Ryker

*T*wo days. We've been stuck in this hotel room for two
fucking days. At least I was able to upgrade us to a
suite. I don't need the second bedroom—a hell of a lot safer to
sleep in front of the door—but at least this way, I don't smell
honeysuckle constantly.

Only every time I pass by her room. Which is probably more
often than I should.

Slowly, I let my gaze rove over the large bath towels spread
out on the floor in front of me. Two pistols, a rifle with a
collapsible stock, half a dozen magazines, five boxes of bullets, a
tactical knife, fully stocked med kit, two coils of rope, black
greasepaint, a compass, two batteries capable of charging any of
the four burner phones, cables, two IDs for me, two for Wren,
and two for Elena and Semyon—if they're even still alive.

I still feel like I'm missing something. Or many things.

Dax and his team came through—in a big way—but he made

a point to send Ford to deliver all this shit rather than come himself.

Why can't I settle? This mission isn't any more dangerous than Colombia. Except, West almost died on that trip. I can still feel his blood running over my hand. And he's a goddamned SEAL. Wren...she's not trained.

Her bedroom door is open a crack, and I can hear her talking to herself. Or maybe to the dog. Ford is going to keep the little fur ball while we're gone, but since the Fairmont allows dogs, I told him to bring Pixel here until we leave.

Wren's face when she saw the dog...I don't know that I'll ever forget it. The woman hasn't cried once in the four days I've known her, but her eyes watered and her lower lip wobbled when Pixel ran into the room.

Pushing to my feet, I wince as the gunshot wound twinges. I can fight—proved that laying the two assholes out the night Wren was attacked—but I'm not 100%. And damn. A hard knot tightens in my chest.

Creeping to the cracked door, I listen to Wren coo to the pup. "I'm going to miss you, baby girl," she says as she nuzzles Pixel's neck. "Ford will take good care of you. And when I get back, maybe we'll go up to Maine for a few days and you can play in the ocean."

Returning her focus to the well-worn copy of Harry Potter, she mouths a string of letters and numbers, then enters them into some decryption program on her laptop.

"What the hell are you trying to tell me, Z?" She twirls her wrist gently, and I hate seeing the bruises staining her pale skin.

"Does it still hurt?" I don't mean to disturb her, and she flinches as her entire body jerks.

"N-no. And sheesh. Have you ever heard of knocking?" Pixel jumps off the bed and pads over to me, sitting at my feet and thumping her tail on the carpet.

"The door was open." Turning my attention to the dog, I

crouch down and peer at her hopeful expression. "Trying to tell me something?"

She yips, runs back to her little bed in the corner of the room, and whines softly. Though I think we're safe here, I won't let Wren walk the dog. So now, the little thing comes to me every time she needs to go outside.

"All right, fluffball. Come on. Get your leash." I jerk my head towards the main room, and Pixel snags her leash between her teeth and drags it over to me.

"Can I come?" Wren slides off the bed, and I frown. "I haven't been outside in two days."

No. Stay inside. Stay in Boston. Stay alive.

Despite my fears, the look in her pale green eyes...I relent before I realize I've opened my mouth. "Fine. But cover up that hair."

She grabs the black knit cap I got for her yesterday and hides her curls as she hurries after me, but skids to a stop and gawks when she sees the weapons.

"Cracker Jacks," she whispers. "Do you really need all...that?"

"Maybe."

Cracker Jacks? Where does she come up with this shit?

After I drape the bedspread over my gear, I clip Pixel's leash to her collar and hold the door open for Wren. She eyes my hip, but I'm not about to reassure her. The pistol probably *is* overkill.

"How in the world did you teach her that leash trick?" Wren asks as I check the door locks.

After a shrug, I meet her gaze for a split second before returning my focus to our surroundings. "Didn't have to."

Down the back stairs, out the hotel's rear door, and around the block we walk, complete silence between us. Pixel is in heaven. Sniffing the sidewalks, stopping at each tree to give the dirt around it careful consideration before choosing one on the corner to deposit her scent.

Wren glares at me while the dog does her business, huffs out a little breath, and jams her hands on her hips. "You really don't know how to carry on a conversation, do you?"

I register her words as a group of guys—dressed for a night out on the town—amble down the sidewalk towards us. They don't look like threats, but I won't take a chance with her safety, and I put myself between her and the group, staring daggers into them as they come a little too close for comfort.

Behind me, Wren holds her breath, and dammit, why do I even notice?

Get out of your own head, Ry.

Clenching my free hand into a fist, I turn to her. "You want conversation? Or you want to stay alive?"

"Both. This is 'tourist central.' I don't think anyone's going to try to grab me right outside the hotel at nine o'clock at night." She rolls her eyes at me, then stalks back through the front door. Pixel paws at my leg, distracting me, and I scoop the little dog up in my arm and follow Wren back inside.

By the time we reach the stairs, Pixel starts to whine, as if she can sense how close I am to snapping.

"Ryker—"

"Wait," I hiss as I wave my key over the door lock. She wants to push me, she'll see the monster inside. But I won't let *him* out in public. "We're not doing this in the middle of the fucking hallway."

Easing the dog from my arms, she carries her into the bedroom, coos to her for a moment as she unclips the leash, and then stalks back into the main room. Pixel wisely stays away.

I don't know what to say to her. How to share space with her. How in hell I'm going to protect her once we get on that transport plane tomorrow.

"We're not in the hallway anymore."

Her biting tone has me snapping my gaze to hers, my hands balled into fists and my teeth grinding together so loudly she must be able to hear them. The challenge in her eyes surprises me, but I just take a step closer, forcing her to tip her head up to meet my eyes.

"Are you angling for a fight, sweetheart?"

Unlike the other day, the endearment falls bitterly from my lips. But something inside me cracks at my tone. Fuck. I can't decide if I want to hit something or gather Wren against my chest and kiss her until she can't remember her own name.

She cocks a reddish brow at me. "*You* sure are."

Forcing a deep breath, I uncurl my fingers. This was a terrible idea. I don't care how much she pushes me. I'm not unleashing my never-ending darkness on her. Not after she's lost her brother. "What do you want from me, Wren?"

Where did *that* come from?

She waves her hand at the weapons and gear under the bedspread. "Tell me why we need an arsenal. Stop grunting one-word answers. Sit down and eat a meal with me instead of carrying your plate into the other bedroom and shutting the door. *Anything* but this constant silent treatment."

"*I* need all that shit to keep you safe! You have no fucking clue what you've gotten yourself into with this. I've seen what the Russian mob does to their enemies. In the past five years, I've extracted two women from trafficking rings in Eastern Europe. Both strung out of their minds, covered in bruises, and too scared to even cry. How's *that* for an answer, sweetheart?"

"Ry..."

My hands shake as I shove them into the pockets of my jacket. Every time I close my eyes, I descend into my own personal hell. Dax, barely alive, burned and blistered skin all around his eyes. West bleeding out. Inara doing her best to keep Royce upright after Coop nearly killed all of us. Stalking over to the window, I angle my gaze to the sidewalk below. Situation normal on the street.

But when her fingers slide over my arm, my control snaps. I grab her and spin her until she's pressed against the wall, her well-worn MIT sweatshirt clinging to her small breasts as her breath heaves and then catches. "You want to know why I don't talk to you, little bird?"

"Yes." She holds my gaze, her eyes a dark jade now, with little copper flecks that sparkle in the lights. "Tell me." Her voice lowers, and she whispers, "Show me."

Sliding my fingers into her hair, I tip her head back and claim her mouth. After a soft moan, she molds herself to my body, and when I sweep my tongue against hers, she yields, opening to me.

Pure, raw need surges, my dick jutting painfully against my zipper. If I don't stop, don't walk away, I'll break her. Or...maybe I'll break myself.

Crawling through the Afghan desert bleeding from a dozen wounds was easier than releasing her, but after I memorize her taste, her scent, the way her ass feels cupped in my hands, I pull away.

Confusion paints her face in shadow, and she reaches up to touch her swollen lips as if she doesn't remember what it feels like to be kissed. I almost lose my resolve, but then I see the bruises around her wrist, and I turn, knowing I have to put some distance between us.

Shutting my bedroom door, I rest my back against the thick wood. This is for the best. I shattered into pieces six years ago, and I've never been able to put myself back together.

11

Ryker

Silence. Blessed silence. I hold my breath long enough to make sure Wren isn't about to push through the door. She's determined enough to try to "make" me talk. Of course, she has no idea how useless *that* endeavor would be.

I didn't break during fifteen months of Hell. A little wisp of a woman half my size isn't going to do what half a dozen Taliban couldn't.

My laptop screen flickers on, and I stride over to the desk. Despite our strained relationship, Dax tasked his people with finding out everything they can about the Nevsky Bratva.

Wren's facial recognition software just pinged with a hit. The girl is Elena Smolyskia. No proof of life, but no record of death either. If she's alive, she's buried deep. Ford will be there at 0700 to take you to the airfield. You need anything else?

Yeah. Someone to tie Wren up and stop her from coming with me. But since Dax actually thinks it's a good idea for her to go to

Russia, I know better than to ask. But there is one request I have to make.

Only one thing. If I don't come back, my letters will be in with Wren's civvies. Three of them. Inara Ruzgani. West Sampson. And you. But if you read yours and I'm still alive, I will tell your entire company how you couldn't hold your liquor that night in Mobile and paraded around the barracks naked for an hour.

I close the lid on my laptop two seconds after I send the message. I don't want to read his response. If he even sends one.

Unable to face the possibility Wren might be waiting in the main room for me, I rewind every moment from the time we returned to the suite in my head. Open the door. Let Wren go first. She takes the dog. I turn, lock the door, set the deadbolt, wedge the chair under the knob. Okay. I can risk sleeping in here. Or...trying to anyway.

Stretching out on the bed, fully clothed except for my boots, I stare at the ceiling, praying the sweet release of sleep finds me quickly—and that the nightmares don't follow.

"RYKER? RY?" Two quiet knocks rouse me what feels like minutes after I drift off.

"What's wrong?" Instantly awake, I'm up and have the door open before I finish speaking. Oh fuck.

Wren hugs herself tightly, wearing only a skimpy tank top and short shorts. The gesture emphasizes her breasts and the creamy skin at her throat. Thank God I'm still wearing my jeans. I'm half-hard already, and if I don't put some distance between us, the strongest denim in the world isn't going to hide my arousal.

"You're...not sleeping by the door. I worried..."

Fuck. *Think. Reassure her, you asshole.* "We're safe here, sweetheart. I just—" Scrambling for words, I take a step back to try to drive her scent from my nose. "I needed some space."

"Oh."

Kicking myself, I reach for her arm as she turns away. The hurt flickers over her delicate features for a brief second, but that's enough. I have to fix this. "Wait."

"Get some sleep, Ryker," she says as she ducks out from under my grasp and heads across the main room. "I need you at your best tomorrow."

"No." I rush forward to plant myself in front of her, and she drops her arms. Utterly defenseless—emotionally and physically. The raw need swimming in her eyes matches the emotions flooding me. "Wren, about earlier...I shouldn't have kissed you."

Except I had to. And I'd do it again.

"I'm right here. I've been right here for two days."

Shit. Did I say that out loud?

Wren steps forward and cups my cheek. "You don't realize it, Ryker...but you're easy to read. At least...for me. Why won't you talk to me?"

I don't have an answer. Not one I'm willing to share with her. But as her fingers trail over the scar that bisects my left eyelid, she levers up on her toes to kiss my jaw—the only part of my face she can reach. "What happened here?"

"Knife." The word scrapes over my dry throat, and the memories threaten to pull me under, but Wren's touch grounds me.

"And here?"

I barely feel her light touch over the angled lines on my left cheek—nerve damage left me with reduced sensation. "Razor blade."

"And this?" Down to my neck, where the burns start. Now, I don't feel her fingers at all. Yet, I'm hyper aware of her touch.

"Lighter. Cigarettes."

Her eyes glisten, and she trails her hand down my arm. "Keep going."

At the thick ropes of scars on my forearm, I say, "Blowtorch."

When she gets to my fingers—two of them not entirely straight anymore, "Boots."

I stop her when she reaches for the bottom of my t-shirt. "No, Wren. Don't."

"Have you ever shown anyone? Besides doctors?"

Shaking my head, I try to take a step back, but my legs won't obey. And this time, when she reaches for my shirt, I freeze, but don't try to stop her. My heart thunders in my chest, and I have to ball my hands into fists to stop them from trembling.

"You're too tall," she says with a small smile. "Help me."

Her soft words shatter my trance, and I snag the back of the shirt and yank it over my head. This is for the best. She'll see me —most of me—and she'll be so disgusted, she'll go back to her room and we'll go back to being...strangers. I can protect a stranger in Russia. Just not...someone I...need.

Except...she doesn't run. Her palms slide over my pecs, around to my shoulders, and she never stops touching me as she circles me. "Whoever put you back together did a Cracker Jack job, you know."

"Me."

"What?" Her eyes widen, and she links her fingers with mine. "You—"

"We didn't have medical care in Hell."

I expect pity, but instead, I see awe in her gaze. "Well, you're..."

"A monster."

Now, anger flashes across her face as she brings my hands to her waist. "I was going to say 'magnificent.' Don't put words in my mouth, Ryker. I can speak for myself."

I don't know how to reply, but she relieves me of the responsibility when she wraps her arms around me and rests her cheek against my chest. "Can I...stay with you tonight?"

Is she asking...? As I nod, I realize I don't care what she's asking for. A kiss, sex, or just someone to hold her while she sleeps...I'll give it to her.

12

Wren

*W*ell, I've done it. Demanded Ryker talk to me. *See* me. And now I'm in his bedroom. Staring at more muscles than I've ever seen. And more scars. The man's skin looks like a jigsaw puzzle. But there's beauty in his survival.

He keeps his arm around me as he leads me to the bed. I don't have any illusions as to what this is. Two lonely, needy people taking solace in one another. Despite my insistence that I go with him to Russia, I'm scared to death. Hell, the plane ride terrifies me. I'm a nervous flyer under the best circumstances. Let alone riding a transport plane into a foreign country where I don't speak the language and people probably want to kill me. Or worse.

"Do...you have a side?" I ask.

"No." The single word carries more uncertainty than should be possible, and I slip out from under his arm and dive under the covers on the far side of the bed. I don't know what I'm expecting.

Sex? Cuddling? A few more of those kisses that rocked me down to my core? All of the above? Or...just company?

Ryker sits stiffly, his back to me, and I reach out and stroke a hand over his shoulder blade. "I don't bite."

"Too bad." He jerks away from my touch, clears his throat, and then whispers a quick apology.

"Stop that." Sitting up, I try to turn him towards me, but the man's a mountain when he doesn't want to move, so I scramble over the bunched-up blankets until I'm kneeling at his side. "Did I say I was offended?"

He darts a quick glance at me. "No."

"You're allowed to joke, Ry. Err. Ryker."

"Ry's fine. My...uh...coworkers call me that."

"Not your friends?" In the brief flash of pain that darkens his eyes, I see the truth. He doesn't have any. Or...he doesn't think he does. "Tell me about them?"

With a sigh, he stretches his legs out, crossing them at the ankles, and lies back. I mirror his movements so he doesn't have to look me in the eyes, but he reaches for my hand and links our fingers.

"West and Inara. There's a new guy, Graham, but he's only been on two missions. I don't know him well enough to know if he'll stick around."

"West...you mentioned him at my apartment."

"Yeah. He's a former SEAL. Engaged to this computer genius. They're getting married next week."

"Oh sugar snacks. Are you missing the wedding because of me?" Guilt tangles the words in my throat, but he squeezes my fingers.

"No. I wasn't going anyway. Don't ask me why not."

Well, that was exactly what I was going to ask him, but fine. He's finally talking, and I don't want to discourage him.

"West was there when I escaped Hell. He was the first friendly I saw." Ryker offers a dry laugh. "Pretty sure he thought I was a mountain lion. Covered in dirt, blood, and shit. Running a fever of a hundred and two. Long, scraggly beard—in places." He rubs the scars on his jaw and cheek with his free hand. "Wearing a pair of gray pants...well, they were no longer gray. Or really even pants."

I stay silent, hoping he'll continue unprompted, but when he doesn't, I nudge my shoulder against his. "Sorry. We reconnected last year. Good guy. Solid."

"And Inara?"

"Sharpshooter. One of the best I've ever seen. We've worked together for three years. She's a translator when she's not doing K&R with us."

I sit up. "Does she speak Russian?"

"Yeah. Russian, Pashto, Arabic, French, Spanish, Italian, and one more. Chinese maybe."

"Can I send her some of the codes Zion left me?" For the first time in two days, I feel something akin to hope. "I kept trying Google Translate, but nothing I got back made any sense."

"I'll get you her email in the morning before we leave."

My fingers find their way to my wrist, but I left my bracelet by my bed. "Are you really that worried about taking me to Russia? Even with the arsenal out there?"

Ryker meets my gaze, and he doesn't have to answer me. The fear tightens tiny lines around his eyes and lips, and I blow out a breath. When his hand cups my cheek, then slides around to the back of my neck, I let him pull me down so I'm half on top of him.

"You're a civilian, Wren." His warm breath tickles my ear. "And you're...fuck. I haven't been ignoring you the past two days. I've watched you. How your mind works. You're brilliant. The way you tackle a problem...I want to know what's going on in that head of yours. All the time."

"All you have to do is ask."

I feel him nod against me, and then he eases me up slightly so he can slant his lips over mine. Before, his kiss was frantic, desperate. But this time, the tenderness in his touch makes my eyes burn—even though I can't remember how to cry. I don't want this to stop. I could kiss this man every day for the next month and it wouldn't be enough. I shouldn't need him. Shouldn't want him. There's a darkness inside him I fear will consume him one day. But I can't help myself.

He's broken in all the wrong ways. Perfect in all the right ones. And as he deepens the kiss and slides his hands down my back to cup my ass, I wriggle my hips, offering him more.

Too soon, he pulls away and tucks an errant curl behind my ear. "Stay with me, Wren. For just one night, I don't want to fall asleep alone."

I turn in his arms, letting him fit his big, solid body around mine, keeping me safe the only way he knows how.

13

Ryker

*E*ighteen hours after Wren fell asleep in my arms, we land at a defunct military airstrip outside of St. Petersburg. Ford arranged for a nondescript coupe waiting for us, and as soon as I usher Wren—her hair covered with a black scarf—into the car, she pulls her knees up to her chest and hugs herself tightly.

"Talk to me, sweetheart," I say as the engine sputters to life.

"I hate flying. And the hangover I get from doubling up on the anxiety meds. And my ears are still ringing. You fly like that all the time?"

"You get used to it." Stopping to check the GPS before I pull out onto the motorway, I slide my hand around the back of her neck and pull her closer. "Take a deep breath for me."

"I'm okay." She holds my gaze, but I can see her struggle not to go for one of her coping mechanisms like fiddling with her bracelet or tapping her fingers along the inside of her wrist. "Really."

"Sure. And I'm a short, underweight comedian."

Her laugh does something to my gut I'm not prepared for. I want to hear it again, but that joke's literally the only one I know. When she leans closer, I mirror her movements, and she touches her forehead to mine. "Don't let me distract you, Ry. I'm depending on you to keep us safe."

I nod and return my focus to the road. "Put on your sunglasses. In about twenty minutes, we'll be in range of the first traffic cameras." I tug a baseball cap down over my bald head, adjust my own shades, and tighten my grip on the steering wheel. We're about to head right into the lion's den, and I'm worried I forgot my whip.

By the time we get to the old house on the outskirts of town, Wren's fallen asleep. The street lights illuminate peeling paint, graffiti, and broken-down cars parked in several yards. Some things are universal, I guess.

"We're here," I say quietly as I pull up to the curb. She blinks and yawns, and I grip her wrist firmly. "You wait for me to come around. Understand? And once we get inside, you stay behind me until I've cleared the whole house."

She nods, her fingers dipping between her breasts for a quick moment until I take her hand. "Unless we're somewhere private, don't ever check to make sure the tracker's in place. Trust the tech. And trust me."

The little transmitter I asked Royce to send me is nestled inside her bra. Loc8tion, the mobile app he's been working on ever since a stroke left him unable to run his company, can track a person anywhere, and both Wren and I have the devices hidden in our clothes. The little GPS is small enough no one will find it if they pat her down—only if they make her remove her bra. And if someone does that, I'll kill them.

"Sorry," she whispers.

I want to reassure her, but it's good for her to be a little scared. On edge. She'll be more careful.

After I settle my pack on my shoulders, I skirt the car and open Wren's door, listening for anything out of place. A television drones on quietly from two houses away, and a dog barks on the next block, but no footsteps, no odd rustling in bushes, and no movement in the house I can see.

Wren's pack is smaller, but still easily thirty pounds, and I help her shrug into it before I ease the door shut and take her hand to lead her to the back of the house. My free hand rests on my pistol.

It's so fucking cold in the house, I can see my breath, but once we've cleared every one of the six rooms and the basement, I motion for Wren to take a seat on the ancient couch while I tape the draperies down so no light will escape the windows, then plug in the little oil heater.

"It'll be warm in an hour or so," I say as Wren takes out her laptop and starts getting us connected to the internet.

"I can deal." Despite her assurance, her teeth chatter as she works, and I pull out a couple of MREs, pour the water into the heating pouch, and wait for the beef stew to warm in my hands.

"Here. This'll help." Our fingers brush as she takes the packet, and I hold on a little longer than necessary. "I'll go out tomorrow and get some supplies. Scout around. But tonight, this is all we have."

"I need to get into the St. Petersburg Federal District offices. Here." Wren brings up a map on her laptop and points to one of the cluster of buildings I've studied for the past two days. "Give me fifteen minutes in their server room and I'll have access to the traffic camera network across the whole city. It'd be easier to go in at night." She holds my gaze, and I arch a brow.

"You want to do this now?"

"Well...yes." Digging a spork into the beef-flavored mush, she almost smiles. "You don't want me exposed. Right? So...let's get in and out while everyone else is sleeping."

I don't know if she's brilliant, brave, or reckless. But I can't argue with her logic. Heating up my own MRE, I sink down next to her. "All right, sweetheart. But once we're done, you're on lockdown. Understand?"

Multiple emotions flicker over her delicate features: anger, frustration, understanding, fear, and acceptance. Finally, she nods. "Understood. Just don't keep me in the dark, Ry. That's all I ask."

Cupping her cheek, I lean in and brush a gentle kiss to her lips, offering the only promise I can. "I won't."

14

Wren

$\mathcal{M}$y heart hammers in my chest hard enough I'm amazed Ryker doesn't hear it. At least my hands no longer shake, the anxiety pill working its way through my system. Even though I hack into government and private systems all the time, I rarely need to be on site to do so.

But I don't speak Russian. Inara, Ryker's teammate, is in my ear, and the glasses I wear transmit everything I see to her. Between the two of us, I hope this will only take a few minutes.

Ryker kneels by one of the building's side doors, concealed in shadows as he picks the lock. Pressed against the wall, I force slow, deep breaths and grip my small tablet in the pouch slung across my body.

In. Out. Back to the safehouse. And then I can sleep. Maybe with Ryker's arms around me again.

"Stay behind me," Ryker whispers as he opens the door. Gun in hand, he clears the hallway, then motions for me to follow.

Safety lights guide our path to the inner stairwell, then down two levels to the underground server room. An electronic keypad glows at the door, and I unzip my pouch while Ryker puts his back to the wall and sweeps his gaze up and down the long hallway. Tension keeps his shoulders tight and his lips pressed into a thin line.

Flipping through my stash of adapters, I find the right one, hook up the tablet, and launch my password cracking app. These little keypads are easy. The server I need to hack into? Not so much.

Sixty seconds pass, each one tenser than the last, and Ryker keeps flexing his fingers—one of his anxious tics I've discovered in the past few days. Finally, there's a quiet *beep*, the lock disengages, and I'm in.

After he plants a small camera on top of the door to keep watch on the hallway, Ryker follows me inside.

"Check the room for open terminals," I whisper. "On the off chance...it'll save me a ton of time."

Weaving among the server racks, we find nothing, so I choose a terminal at the back of the room where no one can see me from the door and pull out a keyboard on a swinging arm. "Okay. Are you ready, Inara?"

"I have a visual," she replies.

Plucking another adapter from my bag of tricks, I lean my tablet against the server monitor, plug it in, and let the two machines handshake. Lines of Cyrillic flash across the main screen, and Inara translates.

"You need an employee access code and PIN."

"Got it." This information takes longer, and with each minute, Ryker's tension ratchets up another notch. By the time I'm in, we've been in the building for ten minutes, and the hard stone sitting on my chest feels like it's about to suffocate me.

"Help me find the right directory." My code only works if I install it somewhere no one will find it. A utility folder is the best spot, but if I can't find one, I can try to hide it in the server's boot sequence.

We go back and forth with Inara providing a running commentary of folder names.

"How much longer?" Ryker growls as I seize on a good folder and launch my trojan.

Inara sighs. "Stand down, Ry. She's doing just fine."

"This program will allow me to access everything on the network from the safe house. But it takes a few minutes to install." I glare up at him. "And no amount of pacing is going to speed it up. Go wait by the door."

"Not letting you out of my sight."

"You're slowing me down. Go away." I try to ignore him and focus on my task, but I can hear him breathing just behind me, and I send an elbow gently into his side. "Go. Away."

"Ry. Listen to her. Go check the door camera." Inara sounds as frustrated as I am, and as the program runs and he stalks away, I send her a quick chat message.

Thank you. Is he always this overprotective?

A low, husky laugh accompanies the quiet sound of typing, and I have to stifle my snort when I see her reply.

He doesn't like anything he can't control.

While the trojan's final checks scroll across the screen, I run my fingers over the bracelet hidden under my black shirt. *I'm here, Z. And we're going to get Elena and Semyon out. I promise. If they're still alive, we'll find them.*

"How much longer?" Ryker asks over comms.

Annoyance prickles over the back of my neck. "Two minutes. Don't get your panties in a bunch."

"Not wearing any, sweetheart."

Inara clears her throat. "Um, you know I'm still here, right?"

"Fuck." Ryker lowers his voice, muttering, "I knew this was a bad idea."

"Focus, you two," Inara snaps. "I got out of a very warm bed to help you on this op, and it's fucking snowing here."

"Done." I disconnect my cables and shove everything back into my pack. "Coming to you, Ry."

As I reach his side, he wraps his arm around my waist for a moment, holding on like he thought I'd disappear. "Remember—"

"Stay behind you. Got it." Resting my fingers over his, I squeeze once. "Get us out of here safely, soldier."

So many emotions play over his rugged features: pride, relief, concern, caution... He's one of the most expressive men I've ever met, but he thinks he gives nothing away. He does, to those who understand how to read him. Or at least to me.

"Back the way we came," he mutters as he cracks the door. Grabbing the little camera, he creeps down the hall, gun at the ready. Compared to him, my footsteps sound like a herd of elephants, even though we're both wearing soft-soled boots. *Almost there. Almost safe.*

Ryker holds up his fist as he approaches the corner. I almost bump into him and have to grab the tablet pouch to stop it from banging into the wall. The cable ends clink together quietly, and Ryker flinches at the sound.

What's he waiting for?

Panic grips my throat as he whirls and shoves me back the way we came. Clipped footsteps—not rushed, but close— approach. Two men speaking in Russian sound a lot like bored security guards, but they won't be bored for long if we don't find somewhere to hide.

Door after door denies Ryker entry, and as we round the corner and I look back, the shadows of the guards loom steps away. Pushing me against the wall, Ryker meets my gaze, his multi-colored eyes desperate. "If we're compromised, you stay out of the way while I take care of the guards. And if I tell you to run, you don't look back."

I nod, clutching my tablet tightly against my chest. He holsters his gun, takes my hand, and races with me to the far end of the hall. Finding a bathroom, he pulls me inside, then lifts me so I'm standing on the toilet in the single stall. Holding his finger to his lips, he flicks the lock on the stall closed, then joins me. With his height, he has to crouch with his hands on his knees so no one sees his head over the top of the walls. If we're discovered...even if he manages to get us out of this mess, they'll know someone was in the server room. The door locks will log an entry, and if there are cameras anywhere...

"Monitoring all wireless signals in the area off your comms relay," Inara whispers. "Guards are checking in with control.

Wireless.

Sliding my tablet out of the pouch, I rest it on Ryker's back. The biometric scanner reads my fingerprint, and I open a shell program. My backdoor into this place gives me access to everything. Including wireless communications.

The bathroom door opens, and one of the guards calls to the other. In our ears, Inara translates.

"He...has to take a shit."

Spit-snacks. If I can't get these radios turned off, we're toast. I send the code to kill the wireless network when the guard is less than two steps away. Except...the word I think means wireless apparently means lights, as the bathroom goes dark. Quickly, I flip the tablet over, hiding the screen's glow against Ryker's back.

"Sergei?" A string of Russian words I don't understand follows, and the door slams open, then shut, before silence envelopes us.

"They're heading up to the lobby to check with the main guard. Lights are out all over the building," Inara says. "Get the fuck out of there now."

15

Ryker

The whole way back to the safe house, I try to find something to say to reassure her—or myself—we're safe. But the words won't come.

Too fucking close.

The guards should have been changing shifts when we were making our escape. Not patrolling the halls.

"Why the hell did you turn off the lights?" I ask after we're safely inside and she's huddled on the couch. "Of everything you could have—"

"I was *trying* to jam their wireless communications. Excuse me if reading Russian off a tiny screen resting *on your back* while trying not to have a panic attack wasn't *completely* accurate." She hugs herself tightly, shivering.

I should apologize for snapping. Or hold her. Or...anything but walk away. But we came so close to being discovered. Stalking into the kitchen, I rummage around and find a tea kettle. I need a drink. But until we're back in the States and the *bratva* isn't after Wren anymore, I won't let anything impair my focus.

The stove sputters to life, the gas burner crackling in oranges, yellows, and blues. For too long, I simply stare at the flame.

"Tell us what we need to know, Ryker. We do not want to harm you. Why were you in the mountains? What was your mission?"

"Fuck you."

"You leave us no choice. Burn him."

The fire licks up my left arm, a thin strip of flesh turning black as my captors hold the torch to my skin. I try not to scream, but when the asshole moves to my shoulder, I lose the battle.

"Ry?"

The kettle hits the floor, the still-cold water splashing over my boots. "Fuck!"

"Look at me." Wren grabs my arms as I start to shake. "Ryker! Stop. Listen to my voice."

I can't. I have to get out. The flames are coming closer. Somewhere nearby, Dax screams. I see the door. The bars. The rusted metal, stained with blood. My blood. I couldn't protect Dax. Couldn't stop those bastards from blinding him.

Honeysuckle surrounds me, and fingers flutter over my cheeks. Something warm curls around my waist. When her lips crash into mine, all my nightmares, my fears, my flashbacks fade away, and there's nothing but our kiss.

Wren. I'm with Wren.

The dank, cold caves dissolve into the monochrome gray of a Russian kitchen. And red curls. Creamy skin. She's wrapped around me, her hands stroking up and down my back, her tongue tangled in a lazy dance with mine, and my God, she's so fucking perfect.

I almost lost her. And now...I'll do anything to keep her right where she is. With me. But...not here. Not on a dusty kitchen floor with the stove blazing. Pulling away, I tuck a thick lock of auburn hair behind her ear and try to memorize the look in her eyes. Desire. Understanding. And...need.

"Hold onto me, sweetheart."

She's so light I barely notice her weight as I shift her in my arms, turn off the stove, and carry her into the living room. What am I doing? I don't...I can't...

"Ry. Stop thinking and kiss me again." Wren reaches for my belt, and I cover her hands with mine. Holding my breath, I will myself to wake up. This has to be a dream. There's no way this beautiful, intelligent, capable woman wants me.

And then she peels off her shirt.

"Wren..." Her skin almost glows in the light from the single lamp in the center of the room. A flush rises from her black silk bra, and my gaze travels lower, to the pants that mold to her ass. Why didn't I notice how tight they were before?

"Have you lost the capability to understand English?" Her hands stroke down her sides, fingers disappearing under her waistband, and I follow their trail. "I'm throwing myself at you, soldier. Catch me."

My shirt lands next to hers, and this time when she reaches for my belt, I run my fingers through her hair, trying to convince myself she's real. My dick strains against the thin, tactical material, and she skims her palm over me.

"So...were you serious earlier?" Her smile has the power to undo me, and copper flecks dance in her pale green eyes as she flicks open the button on my pants. "Are you really going commando?"

Swallowing the lump in my throat, I crush her to my chest. "I said no panties, sweetheart. Last time I checked, briefs didn't count."

"There you are." Wrapping her arms around my neck, she levers up on her toes so I can claim her mouth. She tastes like a summer day, and I might never get enough of her. "Let me see these briefs, soldier. And what's underneath."

Sinking to my knees, I bury my face against her mound, inhaling her sweet scent. "Not until I taste you."

"I...oh..." The tremble in Wren's voice urges me on, and I peel the leggings down her hips, finding the scrap of silk between her thighs soaked through. "Please..."

"Please what?" One finger dips under the edge of her panties, and her knees threaten to buckle. "Lie down, baby. And tell me what you like."

The sleeping bags rustle as she stretches out before me like a fucking banquet, and I cage her with my arms, holding myself over her as I wait for an answer.

"It's been a long time," she whispers. "But I'm not going to get what I want unless you're naked."

The laugh escaping my lips surprises me, but after I undo my zipper, I freeze. "Wren, the rest of me—"

She cups my arousal, her fingers stroking over the hard length through my briefs. "As far as I can tell, you still have the necessary equipment. Trust me, Ry. I don't know why you think I care about your scars. I care about *you*."

Shedding my pants, I watch her expression as she sees my legs. Parts of me look like a fucking jigsaw puzzle, but if she's shocked, she doesn't show it. "One day, you're going to tell me your whole story. But not tonight. Tonight, we're going to enjoy one another."

Enough of this slow dance. I need her like I need my next breath. I strip off my briefs, and her appreciative purr sends me to full mast in a heartbeat.

"Wow..." she says, her eyes widening as she reaches out to stroke me. I won't last if she keeps touching me, so I pin her hands over her head.

"Not yet." I barely manage to avoid ripping her panties as I yank them down her legs, and then her taste floods me.

"Oh God...Ry...yes!"

I have to hold her hips still. Her channel weeps for me, and I swirl my tongue over and around her clit. "Like this, sweetheart?"

"More..."

My cock throbs painfully trapped under my bulk, and I plunge two fingers into her channel as I continue to lave my tongue over her sensitive nub. Her whimpers rise at least an octave as her thighs tremble and she starts to tighten around me.

Scoring my teeth gently over her clit, I twist my fingers to find the little patch of nerves deep inside that will send her over the edge. With a strangled scream, she implodes, and I drink her in, savoring every sound. Every touch. Every second I have with her.

Sliding up her trembling body, I suck my fingers clean, then touch my lips to hers. "Kiss me, Wren."

With her arms around my neck, she pulls herself up so I can reach the clasp on her bra, and as she feathers kisses along my jaw, back to my ear, and down my neck, I toss the silk away, and palm her breasts. "You're fucking perfect," I whisper.

One nipple pebbles between my thumb and forefinger, the other between my teeth, and she gasps when I grind my hips against her mound.

"Inside me, Ry. Now."

Fumbling for my go bag, I search for a condom, unable to stop cursing until my fingers close around the foil packet. My crown's already dripping, and I won't last. It's been too long. My hands shake as I try to tear the wrapper, but Wren saves me, freeing the rubber and rolling it over my cock.

"You're...even more impressive than I imagined," she says.

"You...'imagined'? Are you trying to tell me you fantasized about me, little bird?"

Her cheeks redden as her hands stroke up my sides. "A little. Or maybe...a lot. Don't make me wait any longer, soldier."

"Hell no."

Nudging her entrance, I groan, fighting the desperate urge to bury myself deep in a single thrust. But I'll rip her in two, and I have to let her body adjust to me. "You're so fucking tight, baby."

I slide home by inches, and Wren's little whimpers and moans as I move only make me harder. And then...we're as close as two people can be. "What is this?" I ask, awe roughening my voice.

"Bliss." Her hips start to move under me, and it's all I can do not to slam into her over and over again. When she cups the back of my neck, I hold my breath, afraid somehow, I've hurt her, but the small smile that curves her lips banishes my fears. "I'm not going to break, Ry. And I need to feel you. All of you."

I've never wanted a gilded invitation. Until now. But the golden flecks in her eyes give me the permission I crave, and I claim her mouth as I thrust hard enough to make her gasp into our kiss. Her short nails rake across my back, and the tiny pinpricks of pain heighten every sensation.

"Fuck, Wren...I can't hold on..."

"Then don't," she manages, and when I swivel my hips enough to graze her clit, she calls my name, and I fly over the edge with her.

16

Ryker

*W*ren shifts against me, a soft sigh escaping her lips as she snuggles closer. She fell asleep as soon as I drew the sleeping bag over us and wrapped my arms around her.

But I lie awake trying to understand what the hell just happened. Besides the obvious—mind-blowing sex.

Since Colombia—since Coop's supposed "death"—I've drifted in a fog of uncertainty. In Hell, I trained my mind. Honed my memory into the sharpest blade. I escaped by memorizing everything. The sounds of the guards' footsteps. The scents that clung to them—different in the morning than at night.

Even when they kept me bound and blindfolded, I could tell you what time of day it was and where I was in the complex system of caves under the mountain. I counted steps. Turns. Learned the texture of the different walls. The way the sounds echoed.

So why didn't I see Coop's insanity? The signs were all there. Hell, looking back, I can see each one. The day he first lied to me.

The look in his eyes when he met West. I'd seen that look so many times in my captors. Pure, unadulterated hatred. But I dismissed it. Shoved it aside. And only after trying to stop West bleeding out in my arms did I start to put the pieces together.

Nothing makes sense. Except Wren. She sees me. The real me. The man under the scars. Under the pain. And when I slept curled around her the other night? The nightmares didn't find me. She soothes the constant whispers in my head. The ones telling me I'm not good enough. I didn't try hard enough. I failed Dax. Failed my men. West. Inara. Royce.

Threading my fingers through her hair, my heart squeezes in a way I've never felt before. Protecting her...it's all I have left. And if I fail, can I live with myself?

"I can hear you thinking," she murmurs against my chest. "Talk to me."

"You need sleep, sweetheart."

"So do you." Pushing up on an elbow, she peers at me through half-lidded eyes. The bruise on her cheek has faded to a sickly yellow, and I brush my knuckles along the edge of the discoloration. "We have a lot of work to do in the morning."

"I'll be fine. Going without sleep isn't a new thing for me."

"Ry." Her kiss quiets my protests, and she feathers gentle touches over the worst of the scarring on my chest. "You're like all of those notes Z left me in his book. A complete mystery—until you find the encryption key. I don't know why or how, but I have your key."

Shock steals any reply, and I can only blink down at her as she continues. "You didn't fail me tonight. You protected me. You got me somewhere safe, somewhere private you could take out the guards if you had to. And when the lights went out, you knew exactly where to go without being able to see a blasted thing."

"I...I remember things."

"You remember everything." Her lips twitch into a smile. "What was I wearing the day we met?"

"Green scoop-neck sweater, jeans with a rip mid-thigh, red Vans, a resin pendant in the shape of a teardrop, tiny silver hoops. Your smartwatch. Zion's bracelet." I don't tell her what I remember most of all is how she smelled. How her voice trembled—both in anger and fear. And how those two emotions sounded completely different.

"And what do I do when I'm nervous?"

"Run your fingers over your bracelet. You count the beads. Or if you're wearing your pendant, you trace the edges. Five times. Then you reverse directions."

A light laugh trips from her heart-shaped mouth. "Really? I didn't know I had a pattern." Her fingers dip between her breasts, searching for the pendant she left tucked in her pack before she relaxes into my embrace again. "You don't *do* uncertainty, Ry. You know why you're not sleeping. So...tell me. I'm not sleeping until you do."

The challenge in her gaze makes me want to bury myself deep inside her again, as does the way she's pressed against me. Her nipples tighten, and her sweet scent surrounds us. I want to live in this moment for the rest of my life. Because here, everything makes sense.

"I'm lost," I whisper. "And I can't see my way clear."

Her nod shouldn't shock me, but it does. Somehow, she understands—but how, when I don't? "Clear to what? The old you? The one who never asked for help? Who never let anyone in? Don't go back there. Ever. Stay here. Where you have people who care about you."

Sucking in a harsh breath, I try to free myself from the sleeping bag, but she tangles her legs with mine and holds on. Panic tightens a noose around my throat, and my words escape strangled and broken. "Wren, don't."

"You're safe," she says as she climbs on top of me, her hands on either side of my shoulders, and her mouth inches from mine.

"*We're* safe. And I'm not going anywhere. You won't lose me by letting me in."

"I don't know how." A strange, choked sound in my throat might be a sob, and I try to lock my emotions away, but Wren sees through my efforts and cups my cheek.

"By letting go."

Wrapping my arms around her, I bury my face in the soft silk of her hair and take a risk, letting a single ray of sunshine seep through the cracks in my black, cold heart. "I drive everyone away. I hate myself for it, but that doesn't stop me. I don't *want* anyone to get close. Because if I can't keep the darkness buried, it's going to swallow me whole. Me and anyone I care about."

I take a deep breath, unsure I can get the next words out, but I have to try.

"You're the first person in...forever...I want to see the real me. Please, Wren. Don't let me shut you out."

The determination in her eyes scares the shit out of me, but deep inside, a piece of my broken soul mends. And when she kisses me, an unfamiliar emotion settles over me.

Peace.

17

Wren

I wake up alone. I don't know why that surprises me, but it does. Cocooned in the sleeping bags, the scent of *us* surrounding me, my heart aches. I thought we'd turned some corner. But the space next to me is cold, and from down the hall, I hear Ryker pacing. And muttering to himself.

I could go to him. Make him talk to me like I made him kiss me last night, but selfishly, I want him to come to me. To show me he understands...something. Me. Us. What happened after I found him in the kitchen, trapped in his memories.

So I pull the sleeping bag up to my chest, tucking it under my arms to hold it in place, and reach for my laptop. With my back propped against the couch, I'm almost comfortable in this old, run down house with sputtering heat and dust everywhere.

An email from Inara waits for me, and as I scan through her possible translations, pieces start to fall into place. All of Zion's cryptic notes. Pulling up a map on my tablet, I scan the streets of St. Petersburg.

Wren, most of the letters and numbers you sent me don't add up to anything—in any language. But four sequences could be Russian. I cross-referenced the words with maps of the city.

On one of the pages, Zion highlighted "nevostochnyy" and "pod-voysk" and then had the letter X circled. What if he was indicating an intersection? Dal'nevostochnyy Prospekt and Ulitsa Podvoyskogo cross one another not far from the Neva River. Look at buildings around there. See if you can find anything suspicious.

If you give me access to the servers you hacked, I'll poke around in the morning and see if I can find anything interesting.

Take care of Ry. He's...difficult, I know. But there's a heart buried under all of those muscles and pain. Find it.

-Inara

Of course she'd end the message with a plea. I've never met the woman, but after our single brief conversation and last night's adventure, I feel like she's someone I...could be friends with. And it's obvious she cares about Ryker.

I glance down the hall. Now I *have* to go check on him. Well, as soon as I finish the code to search property records in a five square mile radius of that intersection.

"There you are," I mutter to the laptop when one of my searches spits out the addresses of two buildings owned by the same company. I recognize the name as one of the nonsense words Zion left in the margins on the page where Harry finds the Sorcerer's Stone.

Shoving to my feet, I snag Ryker's t-shirt from the pile of our discarded clothes and tug it over my head. It smells like him, and need twists my insides into a knot. If only anger wasn't simmering under my skin. He's been in the back room for an hour. I think he's working out, because I hear grunts and heavy breathing as I pad down the hall.

He's doing push-ups again. Holy roses. I could watch him for hours. The way the muscles of his back cord and flex as he presses his arms straight. And those arms. So strong, his tattoos almost come alive. As he moves, the skull tattooed on his back seems to watch me, the serpents winding through empty eye sockets slithering down his sides to wrap around his obliques.

"Ry?"

He jerks, pushes to his feet, and turns. The haunted emptiness is back in his prismatic eyes, and if I weren't so mad at him, I'd wrap my arms around him and demand he talk to me. But my anger flares, especially with his scent lingering on my skin, and his narrowed gaze at my attire.

"You're wearing my shirt."

"Your powers of observation are top notch, soldier. Next, you'll tell me I have red hair. Or that you're hiding out in here to avoid talking to me."

Regret twists his lips into a frown, and he rubs the back of his head. "I...needed to clear my head."

Fluttering my fingers over my bracelet, I swallow the lump in my throat. "Just what a woman wants to hear when she wakes up alone after a night of...whatever the horse-pucky we did."

"Horse-pucky?" With a shake of his head, Ryker snorts. "Where did that one come from?"

"If you're ever willing to have a real conversation with me, I'll tell you. Until then, I'm keeping my secrets." I hug myself tightly as I back out of the room. "I'm going to take a shower. I sent the addresses of a couple of buildings that might belong to Kolya Yegorovich to your phone. Thought you'd want to check them out while I get to work on the traffic cameras."

Stalking down the hall to the bathroom, I blow out a deep breath. "Damn you, Ryker McCabe. Why won't you just let me in?"

Ryker

Fuck. The sight of her in my shirt left me speechless, and now she's upset with me. I don't blame her. Leaving her sleeping this morning? I didn't have a choice. In a few hours, she broke through all of my defenses. And when I was buried deep inside of her, something in me cracked in two.

Outside the bathroom door, I pause, my hand on the knob. I should turn around. Go back into the empty bedroom and push myself through another hundred crunches. If I weren't worried about being seen, I'd go out for a five-mile run.

But...that would leave Wren alone. Unprotected. If this Yegorovich asshole weren't after her, I'd take her with me every-where. Then again, if she were safe, we wouldn't be here in the first place.

I need air. Wearing only a pair of loose shorts, I'm ill prepared for the elements, but I head for the back stoop. Times like these, I wish I still smoked, but I gave that shit up years ago. Fifteen months of my captors stubbing their cigarettes out on my chest, forearms, and inner thighs cured me of any cravings. The frigid spring air prickles along my skin, raising the fine hairs on the back of my neck. The sun filters through the trees, shadows dancing along the still-snowy landscape. Out here, I can breathe again.

And of course, all I can see when I close my eyes is Wren wearing my shirt. How the black cotton clung to her ass. The way her hips swiveled as she marched down the hall. The twin points of her nipples hardening as I stared her down.

Goddammit. I can't let her think I don't care.

Still, I take the time to check and double-check the locks before I head down the hall to the bathroom. The shower runs, and steam fills the room as I push my way through the door.

Training taught me to move silently. To enter rooms without

making a sound. To temper my footsteps. To glide, even when my muscles are screaming at me.

Fuck me. She's...*singing*. The sweet, light words of some musical I vaguely remember from my youth. Mesmerized, I watch as she moves behind the frosted glass door. When her fingers sink into her hair, the position highlighting her breasts and the curve of her ass, my cock stands at attention. Whatever I did, I have to fix it. Because if I don't get my hands on her again, right now, I'm going to explode. In more ways than one.

Shedding my shorts, I slide the door open. Her voice rises at the end of the song, and...shit. She doesn't know I'm here. But, I can't retreat now. I'm committed. Wrapping an arm around her waist, I hold on tight when she yelps. "Snack cakes!"

"I'd rather eat *you* than a Twinkie, little bird." Closing my teeth over the shell of her ear, I let my hand trail lower. Down the patch of trimmed reddish curls to her slick folds. When I slip a finger inside her, she shudders, her head falling back against my chest. "What do you want?"

"You..."

I kiss her shoulder, all the way up the curve of her neck, and score my teeth along the sensitive skin. "You taste like honey, sweetheart. Honey and..."

Hope.

Wren's fingers join mine, guiding me where she wants me. A breathy moan spills from her lips. "And what?"

"And..." I can't tell her the truth. That in a few short days, she's become my oxygen. So I spin her around and press her against the shower wall. Trapping her hands in one of mine, I pin them over her head, then capture one taut nipple between my teeth.

Her arousal mixes with the hot water, coating the fingers of my free hand as I play with her clit. My balls feel like they're about to implode, but she comes first. Always.

"Ry—" Her toes curl, her thighs tremble, and her eyelids flutter as I draw her closer to the edge. "Please..."

"Please what, sweetheart? Please make you come?" Peering down at her, I chuckle when all she can do is nod weakly and thrust her hips harder against my hand. "Kiss me, Wren."

As desperate as I am, she shocks me with the intensity of her mouth on mine. Her teeth capture my bottom lip, tugging sharply as I thrust three fingers deep inside her channel. My thumb presses to her sensitive nub, and she shatters against me, her legs finally giving out as I hold her through her release, whispering her name.

18

Ryker

I'm still hard as a rock when I wrap a towel around Wren and help her out of the ancient shower. "Are you hungry?"

She frowns, leaning against the sink as I wind another of the threadbare towels around my waist. I didn't think...this is the first time she's seen...this much of me...in daylight. I start to turn, but Wren grabs my wrist. "Stop."

My entire body stills, and I hold my breath as she cups my cheek. "Why is it so hard for you to talk to me?"

"I...can't." Despite the urge to look away, I hold her pale green gaze. I owe her that—and so much more.

"Not good enough, soldier." Her sweet scent invades my nose. "I fell asleep in your arms. And when I woke up, you were gone." The shadows of my nightmares haunt me, flickering in the corners of the room as she wraps her arms around my waist. "Trust me, Ry. Please."

With a sigh, I drop my chin to the top of her head. "I don't sleep much. Four hours is a lot for me."

"Next time, wake me." She peers up at me, one brow arched and challenge darkening her eyes. "Or better yet, stay with me. There are a lot of things we can do in a sleeping bag besides sleep."

Her breath tickles my chest, and if she doesn't step back soon, I'm going to lift her onto the sink and bury myself deep. "Wren... fuck. You don't know what you do to me."

"Oh, I think I have an idea." She cups my dick through the towel and a hum—almost a purr—rumbles in her throat.

Hauling her into my arms, I carry her back out into the living room, lay her out on the sleeping bag, and fish another condom from my go bag. "Tell me to stop."

"Why?"

This woman is perfect. Soft in all the right places, but with a steel spine and nerves harder than diamonds. She palms my hard length, running her finger over the head as she waits for me to tear the packet open. Damn. No one's ever...touched me the way she does. Like I'm not broken. Not a monster. Not...me.

Hooking her legs around my hips, she moans as I slide home. "Don't close your eyes, Ryker," she whispers. "Look at me when you come."

I can't. Can't let her see how much I need her. But...when she runs her hands over the scars on my back, pure acceptance curving her lips into a smile, I start to rock against her. "You're... so...tight and hot...little bird. Like you were...made...just for me."

"Harder." Flecks of gold brighten in her green eyes, and she swivels her hips in time with my thrusts. Balanced on my elbows, caging her small body, I let her see everything. All of me. All my pain. All my nightmares. All the raw need flowing through me every time I touch her. She doesn't understand—not caught in the heat of our coupling. But I do. And when my balls tighten, the pleasure shooting through me like a flaming sword, I let go as I shout her name.

I CLOSE my eyes and let my hands drift over my body. Burner phones—one in each of my jacket's side pockets. Wallet with fake ID and enough rupees to look natural. Moving slowly and methodically, I pat my lower back. A hidden pouch rests just under the waistband of my jeans with a couple thousand US dollars in case I need to pay someone off. A spare magazine in my hip pocket. Continuing my mental inventory, I verify the knife strapped to my ankle, the extra ear bud stowed in a slit in my sock, and the tracker tucked...where only Wren should find it.

When I finish and look back at her, she's fiddling with her bracelet, one of the sleeping bags wrapped around her.

"Promise me you'll stay inside," I say as I hoist my pack. "Get dressed. Make sure you have your tracker. But don't leave this house—"

"Unless you send me the 911 code or the perimeter alarms go off." Wren rises and pulls on a pair of black panties, and the contrast against her pale skin makes me ache for her again.

Turning around, I slide my pistol into its holster. "I'll be back before dark. You find any sign of Elena or Semyon, raise me on comms. You remember where the backup car is?"

Wren steps in front of me, thankfully mostly dressed. "Ryker," she says with an edge to her voice, "it's two blocks away. I have the key. I'll be *fine*."

Grabbing her around the waist, I kiss her hard enough to leave us both panting. "I'm...sorry. I don't know how to do this."

"Do what?" She blinks up at me, and God, I don't want to leave her.

It's one word, you stupid oaf. Tell her.

I touch her still damp locks, loving how she angles her head towards my hand. "Care."

"You'll learn." With a smile and a quick kiss to my cheek, she whispers, "Come back safe."

"I will, sweetheart. I want to know what other things you think we can do in a sleeping bag."

THE BATTERED old Ford Focus has seen better days, but I don't worry about blending in as I head into the heart of St. Petersburg. With my baseball cap, old denim jacket covered in patches, and gloves, I look like any other wannabe rocker bumming around the city. Well, except for my height. The oversized sunglasses cover the worst of the scars on my face, and I glance in the rear view with a sigh.

What does she see in me? I screw up every relationship I've ever had. My own team's proof enough of that. Yeah, Inara's helping us with this op, but she's distant. I know I hurt her when I left the warehouse. Hell, I wouldn't blame West if he quit after I bailed on his wedding.

But Wren...

"You'll learn."

She's a hell of a lot more optimistic than I am. But for the first time since I escaped Hell...I want to try.

I wish I could talk to her. Or...at least hear her voice, but we agreed to stay off comms unless absolutely necessary. I need to focus. Stay alert. No distractions. When I get back, though, I have to be...better. For her.

The morning rush hour is largely over, and I merge into traffic on the motorway, mentally inventorying the various weapons I have with me again, despite my pre-mission ritual back at the safe house. We all have our own little quirks. Inara uses head-stands to center herself. West has this long mantra he recites before every op. Me? I take inventory. Despite my memory—and my routines—I still worry every time I leave that I've forgotten something.

The addresses Wren sent me are less than ten miles from the little safe house, and I find a parking space across from a small town square with a fountain. Half a dozen kids—mid-twenties—gather, joking and roughhousing like only cocky boys can.

I can't hang out in the car too long. I need to blend in. Disappear. So I pretend to send a couple of texts from my phone as I snap photos and video of the area. Then, I unfold my large frame from the car and stick a pair of fake AirPods in my ears. With the occasional nod or shake of my head to non-existent music, I amble down the street, taking in everything.

The kids watch me. Well, two of them do. The others play it cool. I should have packed the telescoping mic.

At a small cafe on the corner, I stop, using the window's reflection to keep an eye on the kids. One of them is headed my way, so I duck inside. The place smells like boiled vegetables—cabbage mainly—and I try not to choke on the humid air.

Nodding to the older woman behind the counter, I point to a pile of pirozhkis in a glass case, hold up two fingers, and then gesture to the coffee pot as well. "*Kaffe und zwei bitte?*"

I don't speak Russian, but my German accent is passable, and my papers identify me as a German citizen.

"English okay?" With a scowl, the old woman slides two of the pastries onto a plate. "No German."

"Okay. How much?" I ask.

"Fifty. You want milk for coffee?" She stares past me, and when the door opens, her demeanor turns decidedly hostile. A string of Russian pours from her lips, and I turn, like any tourist would, to see one of the punks from the square.

He spits out a response that includes one of the few Russian words I do know—*cyka*. Bitch.

The woman points towards the door, and he flips her off

before leaving. "*Gopnik,*" she mutters before turning back to me. "You take sweet." Now, she's almost apologetic as she thrusts another plate at me with a powdered dough ball in the center.

"*Danke.*" This...is promising. Zion used the same word —*gopnik*—in one of his codes. Inara confirmed it's a general term for poor kids. The ones a cliché would call "from the other side of the tracks." This could be nothing. Just punks being...punks. But given my proximity to the buildings on Wren's list, I'm going to sit here and enjoy a cup of strong, hot coffee in this stuffy cafe, and see where it leads me.

19

Wren

Touching my swollen lips, I can still feel him. Taste him. And I want more. Ryker is one of the most infuriating men I've ever met. And I work for Dax Holloway. Pretty sure Dax has won the "Infuriating Man of the Year" award at least four years running. Not this year.

Turning my attention to the servers I hacked last night, I open a connection to the dark web and send Inara access credentials and an IP address. If I have to open Google Translate for every directory name I come across, this job will take a month.

Trapped in this house. With Ryker. For a month. An involuntary shudder runs through me—equal parts horror and desire. In a month, maybe I could convince him to open up to me. Or...he'd close himself off so completely, we'd end up never speaking again.

For the next few hours, I write code, using bits and pieces of some of my older programs to cobble together a hack that should get me into the traffic camera network without anyone noticing.

Inara helps, supplying a few translations here and there, but it's the middle of the night where she is right now, and eventually, I tell her to get some rest. She doesn't have any stake in this—other than being Ryker's...friend? Coworker? I have a feeling even she doesn't know.

She signs off the video chat with a yawn, then changes her mind and leans forward so her face is close to the camera as she narrows her tired eyes. "Are you okay?" she asks. "Ry isn't being a total dick, is he?"

"Maybe sixty percent dick," I say with a half-smile. "There's a good guy under there somewhere. He just doesn't want to admit it."

"Don't let him off easy." She runs a hand through her short-cropped hair. "I made that mistake a few months ago, and now... the wedge between us is industrial grade concrete instead of a pile of dirt. I'm not sure I'll ever be able to chip it all away."

"I won't let him get away with shutting me out. I may look..." I wave my hand, a little unsure what I want to say.

"Skittish?" She smiles. "You were so unsure of yourself when we first talked. Like you thought I was going to yell at you or something."

My cheeks flush, and I glance down at my bracelet, running my fingers over the beads. One. Two. Three. Four. Five. How did Ryker see the pattern when I never did?

"I have an anxiety disorder. If I don't take my meds regularly, it's...bad. I get tongue-tied, then I start to wonder why anyone would want to talk to me in the first place. And then I do my best impression of Road Runner." I don't tell a lot of people about my illness. I'm not close to anyone except a couple of my coworkers.

Inara nods. "My mother has anxiety. She was attacked when I was young, and after that night..." Her voice roughens, and she looks away, then murmurs to someone close by, "I'm all right." Turning her attention back to me, she sighs. "Ryker... when the two of you were trapped in the Federal Building...I've only heard him that panicked once in all the time I've known him."

"When?" And why is she telling me this?

"After West was shot. He was bleeding out, and we almost lost him. You've cracked through his outer shell, Wren. Keep going. You might be surprised what you find."

Ryker

Pulling a green army jacket from my pack, I change my appearance for the third time inside a McDonald's bathroom a mile from the cafe I spent the morning in.

I don't expect to find Elena or Semyon. Wren's facial recognition software will handle that for us—if they're even still alive. No. My entire purpose today? Reconnaissance. Learning patterns. When the kids come and go. Their communication methods. And scanning the buildings Wren identified for wireless signals, security cameras, and staff.

Thanks to a second-hand store I found when I left the little cafe, Wren and I have five or six different changes of clothes now.

With one final glance in the mirror, I tug the stained fedora a little lower and head for the car. I don't want to leave the vehicle in one spot for very long, and I can't risk being seen as two different people returning to the same piece of shit Ford.

One of the phones vibrates in my pocket. Wren. The message sends a little thrill racing up the back of my neck.

Got a partial match on Elena. Headed west from the intersection of Prospekt Bol'shevikob and Ulitsa Dybenko. Get a move on, soldier.

My lips curve as I imagine her with her hands on her hips, her head cocked to one side, and those gold flecks lending fire to her eyes. She has Royce's Loc8tion software loaded on her laptop, so she knows right where I am.

After I secure my pack in the trunk, I turn and start strolling east. This part of St. Petersburg is close to the river, so I make a show of taking a few photos of the boats and the bridges. Just another tourist out for a walk. But behind my sunglasses, my gaze never stops moving.

There. Three men flank her, all in suits. Ill-fitting ones that don't bother to hide the bulges of pistols at their hips. One of the assholes has his hand on her arm, and from the way she's holding herself, he's squeezing the muscle to the point of pain.

Her face is blank, dark sunglasses covering her eyes, and her blond hair shines, done in a fancy up-do with tendrils curling around sunken cheekbones. If she weighs a hundred pounds, I'll eat this hat.

Turning, I hold my phone up, faking a selfie with a big smile, but the camera records Elena as I shift forward and back, trying to get just the right shot. I mutter to myself, complaining about the angle and the sun and the glare off the water until they're only about ten feet away.

"Excuse me," I say to Elena in a thick, German accent. "Can you help me? A photo for my brother? He will not believe I am here."

One of her bodyguards—or captors, there's no way to tell for sure—growls, "No," and the entire group picks up their pace. The man closest to me had his hand under his jacket the second I started to speak, and the one holding Elena tightened his grip, drawing a gasp from her lips. Given how seamlessly they moved, they're pros.

I follow at a discreet distance, crossing the street and stopping at a news stand—cliché, but useful—when they reach a large, ornate building with white-washed masonry and bars on all the windows. Wren's research listed this place as a former hotel, now owned by a shipping company.

From my vantage point, I can't see inside the heavy metal door as they enter, but they practically have to drag Elena over the threshold, and as the door starts to close, she says something to the guards, a vicious expression on her face, and wrenches her arm free. The brute grabs her throat and squeezes, and she scratches at his hands as the heavy metal shuts with a loud *thunk*.

Fuck. If we have any hope of getting Elena out of there, we're going to need some help.

⊛

Wren

I can't sit still. Seeing Elena on a mall surveillance camera sent my heart rate shooting up and anxiety coiling in my chest like a snake ready to strike. Where are my pills? Ryker wouldn't let me unpack anything—in case we have to leave at a moment's notice —and I tear through my bag, shoving clothes and protein bars aside until I find the small bottle.

Five pills roll across the floor as I win the battle against the flipping child-proof cap, and I scramble for them, landing on my knees with a thud that sends a shock of pain lancing up my thighs.

Why hasn't Ryker texted me? I want to call him, but I know I can't. Distracting him at the wrong moment could get Elena killed. Or worse. Both of them.

Forcing slow, deep breaths in through my nose and out through my mouth, I pray the pill takes effect soon. My daily meds keep the generalized anxiety under control, but the panic attacks...they're a different animal. One I can keep in a cage as long as Ryker's with me.

Needing to do *something*, I go back to the translations Inara sent. Along with the street names that led me to Kolya's buildings, half a dozen other words stand out, and I do a search of Russian internet service providers.

"Holy mother of pearl!" A tiny company with a website that

looks like it belongs in the eighties matches one word—*ryba*—
and I scan my master list of everything I found in Zion's files. Yes.

Twenty minutes later, I'm in. Fifty-seven separate unread
emails wait for Zion, and my eyes start to burn as I realize he'll
never see them.

"Oh God." Elena didn't just send a video asking for Zion's
help. She copied some of Kolya's financial records. Z's spread-
sheets. He didn't just sell drugs for Kolya. He helped the man
with his bookkeeping. Elena even found bank statements. There's
enough here to keep an accountant busy for months. How the
heck did she get all this?

Most of her messages are in English, and as I scan through,
still too tense to process her ramblings, I open an email with a
photograph attached.

Four women huddle together in a room. Dressed in plain
black dresses, bruises dot their arms, legs, and faces. Their eyes
are wide, pupils dilated, and they look like they're scared to
death.

The entire message is only two sentences long.

*He says he is going to sell them. And if you do not come back, he
will sell me with them.*

20

Ryker

*W*hen I let myself in the back door of the safe house, my mood instantly lightens. Even though I know she'll want to talk—something I don't now how to do—the thought of seeing Wren...touching her...kissing her...it kept me going today.

"Wren?"

She doesn't answer, but I hear scrambling and a muffled curse —or what passes for a curse with her—from the living room. I find her trying to extricate herself from one of the sleeping bags, her cheeks pale and her eyes dull.

"Did you get Elena?" she whispers and then topples over.

Catching her in my arms, I haul her close, breathing in her sweet scent. We're both using cheap hotel soap, yet she still smells like honeysuckle. And her hair. Fuck. No one's hair should be this soft. "Whoa, sweetheart. What's wrong?"

"P-panic attack. Took a p-pill. Sometimes...I get...dizzy." She sags against me, resting her cheek against my chest. "Stop distracting me. Where's Elena?"

"In Kolya's fortress. With a shit ton of security." Easing her down to the couch, I don't expect her to shove at me, and my foot catches in the crumpled sleeping bag. I go down, hard, on my ass. "Fuck, Wren. What was that for?"

"For not...getting Elena!" Her breathing takes on a raspy edge, and she clutches at her sweatshirt like it's choking her. "She knows...too much. Kolya's...going to *kill her.*"

"What?" Shaking my head, I shove my questions to the back of my mind. Right now, I have to get Wren to calm down. Meds or no meds, she's on the verge of another panic attack, and I'm not going to get through to her unless she can breathe normally. "Never mind. Come down here." With my hands locked around her wrists, I tug her off the couch and into my lap. She resists for all of a second, then yields, collapsing almost bonelessly into my arms.

"She...took a picture...of the girls he's selling. And...there's so much...more..." A single, choking sob escapes her lips, and when I brush her hair away from her face, tears brim in her eyes. Tears. Despite being almost kidnapped, recounting her brother's death multiple times, and traveling halfway around the world to a country where she doesn't speak the language with a guy who looks like Quasimodo on steroids, she's shed exactly one tear before tonight. One. And now...she's barely holding it together.

"Shhh, Wren. Let it out, baby." Something twists inside me when she shatters, and as she cries into my jacket, I do the only thing I can. Protect her until the storm passes.

"Goddammit," she mumbles, and I draw back enough to meet her gaze.

"You just swore."

"I'm...I know *how* to swear." An indignant pout curves her lips, and she tries to extricate herself from my grip, but I'm not letting her go anywhere. "I don't cry. I haven't cried in...I just don't. I *hate* crying." Her cheeks flush a deep shade of splotchy red. "Please let me go."

"No. Talk to me."

Her snort riles my anger, and I stare up at the ceiling, counting to five so I don't lose my temper with her. "I know I suck at conversation, okay? When you spend fifteen months having the shit beat out of you every fucking day just so you'll *talk*, it... does something to you. But that doesn't mean I can't listen."

Her bloodshot eyes shine with fresh tears, and I risk loosening one arm so I can wick them away. "You're safe with me, Wren. Whatever Kolya's doing, we'll stop him. But we have to be smart about it. And me busting into his fortress with no idea what I'm going to find...that's not smart. We need help. And a plan."

"But—"

With a finger to her lips, I stop her protest. "Tell me what meds you need right now. Then after you take them, we're going to eat something and you can fill me in on what you found."

She doesn't move, and I arch a brow. "You're still panicky. I can feel your heartbeat, sweetheart. Your breathing's choppy and your pupils are half blown. Don't argue."

"Xanax. The blue ovals in my pill bottle. Just one." Her resistance gone, she leans back against the couch, sniffling quietly.

I go into the kitchen for a glass of water, and when I come back, she has her knees pulled up to her chest, staring at her darkened computer screen like it's going to bite her.

She doesn't argue when I hand her the pill and water and sits quietly while I mix up a couple of the better MREs—the ones West always snags for his fiancé because of their hard-as-a-brick brownies.

"Steak and potatoes," I say. "Tomorrow, I'll grab McD's."

Wren stabs a piece of meat with her spork and sniffs it. "I haven't had McDonald's since Z and I were kids."

"One of the most reliable places to eat when you're in the

middle of bumfuck nowhere and don't speak the language. A Big Mac is always a Big Mac." Her small smile rights my entire world, and I look away. What am I doing?

It's a relationship, stupid. Like normal people have.

Well, maybe not like normal people. Normal people don't hide out in Russian safe houses eating MREs with the mob after them and *enjoy* their nights.

"Tell me about him?" I ask.

Wren glances down at her wrist, and if she didn't have the spork in her hand, I know she'd be running her fingers over the beads. "He was a good kid. Quirky," she says. "He loved Harry Potter and soccer. When he was eight, he 'rescued' a bird that flew in our window. Tried to convince our mom it was a parakeet."

"What was it?"

"A pigeon. That chubby bird pooped all over the living room before Mom got home. Z had to wash the dishes by hand for a solid month before she forgave him. She took the racks out of the dishwasher and everything." Light dances in Wren's eyes, and she leans back against the couch, her shoulders finally dropping from up around her ears.

"My...brother hit a baseball through our neighbor's window when he was twelve. Pop made him clean Mrs. Sylverton's house top to bottom every week for a year." Shock at my own admission sends me digging in my MRE for the last drops of gravy, though the damn things only ever last me five minutes.

"You have a brother?"

"Had." Pushing to my feet, I head for the kitchen, dump the empty pouch, and dig another one out of my rolling duffel bag. Except, I'm not hungry anymore, so I brace my hands on the sink and stare out the back window into the darkness.

Until she finds me. I should have known. And dammit. She's still unsteady on her feet. "Come on. You're wiped." I sweep her up into my arms as she protests, but she rests her head on my shoulder.

"You're not getting out of this conversation," she says, and though she's obviously out of sorts from the meds, there's an edge to her voice warning me she won't let me off the hook, no matter how loopy she is.

"I'm not going anywhere, sweetheart. Except into the sleeping bag. With you. And without most of these clothes." Setting her down on the couch, I drop to a knee and pull off her boots. "My brother followed me into the army."

Slowly, savoring every inch, I run my hands up her legs to the waistband of her leggings. Touching her grounds me, and I can see Paul's face without the guilt and self-loathing that so often accompanies my memories. "His unit was on patrol outside Fallujah. Roadside bomb." Her pants land on top of her boots. "He died instantly."

"I'm sorry, Ry." Soft fingers skate over the back of my neck, and she pulls me close enough for me to feel her breath ghost across my cheek. "Were you close?"

"Yes and no. We were seven years apart. Didn't have a damn thing in common. But the year before I enlisted, we started to connect." With a shake of my head, I pull back the top sleeping bag, then wrap my hands around her waist and ease her down. "No moving," I say sternly as I rise and undo my belt. We don't speak until I lay each weapon, tool, and piece of gear in precise order down on the low coffee table.

"Are you always this...organized?" Wren asks.

"With my equipment? Yes." This isn't a conversation I want to have. All the possibilities running through my head every time I close my eyes. "You ready to tell me what had you so panicked earlier?"

She looks up at me with those pale green eyes, and the slightest shimmer warns me this isn't going to be an easy conversation. "Will you hold me?"

Shedding my pants and folding them neatly next to hers, I slip under the sleeping bag with her. "All night, sweetheart."

Wren

Despite how close we are—physically—Ryker still hides under the tight, black t-shirt. I shed my flannel as he arranged an arsenal on the coffee table, and I'm down to my panties and tank.

But he's here with me. His arms around me. And I feel safe for the first time today. "I found a private email server Zion set up for Elena." Every time I close my eyes, I see the photo of those girls. Huddled together. Terrified. Abused.

"She found enough dirt on Kolya to put him away for life—if we were in the United States. Financial records. Payments from his organization to government officials. And...so much more." Turning to grab my tablet, I press my thumb to the biometric scanner and type in my ten-digit password. "I made back-ups of everything. All encrypted." The last email from Elena fills the screen, and Ryker swears under his breath. "When Kolya gets tired of one of his...girlfriends, he ships them off to God-knows-where. Sells them."

Anger rolls off Ryker in waves, and he forces out a breath, purposefully loosening his grip on the tablet. "I can't get in the building without help. Every inch of the exterior is covered by cameras. Two blocks away, a group of boys—probably about Zion's age—hang out at a public fountain. They rotate on and off throughout the day. Three or four at any one time head out, come back two hours later and disappear inside. Thirty minutes later, they're back at it again."

"Selling drugs." A cold weight settles in my chest, and I close my eyes, trying to slow my heart rate, even as the second Xanax threatens to knock me out completely. "Zion never talked a lot about what happened over here. Only that he worked for someone—helping with the guy's accounting in exchange for drugs. He sold drugs too. Like those boys you saw today."

"Kolya Yegorovich is a fucking asshole." Ryker's arms tighten around me, and I give in to the pull towards oblivion.

"I know." My words slur a little now, and I sigh over the lump in my throat. After a minute, I shake my head, remembering the other email that sent my panic rising. "There's more."

I bring up another video—one I only found when I went looking through the deleted messages. On the screen, Elena huddles in a tiny, but pristine bathroom. Blood stains the side of her face, and she can only open one eye.

"Zion, Misha is dead. Kolya...he knows I convinced Misha to help you escape. And he was so angry with me. Even more than before. You have to get me out of here. He swears he will sell me if I go against him again. If he finds these messages... I do not want to end up like Sveta and Ilsa. Please. Hurry."

"When did she send this?" Ryker asks.

"A week before Zion disappeared. Two days after the video I showed you in my apartment. Misha went from trusted employee to dead in forty-eight hours." I swallow hard, then pull up another message. "This is Z's reply."

I'll fix this, baby. I promise. I just need a little more information. Then...I can go to my sister. She's brilliant. And she works with the baddest guys on the planet. By next week, I'll tell her everything. Love, Z.

"Fuck." Ryker pushes to his knees, sets the tablet on the couch, and punches the cushions with enough force the old sofa creaks. "He intercepted this somehow, didn't he? Kolya?"

"I...I think so. And...maybe that's why he came after me?"

Ryker's brows draw together, and though I'm a little dizzy now, and my vision's gone fuzzy from the meds, I can still see his mind working. His multi-hued eyes shift and darken when he thinks, and I'm mesmerized by his intensity.

"Wren?"

"Oh...sorry. I'm..."

"Half-comatose." Easing me onto my back, he plays with a lock of my hair. "Sleep, sweetheart. We can finish this discussion in the morning."

There's something else I have to tell him. Something important. But I'm so tired. And I hate how the Xanax steals my focus. But his lips are on mine, and he tastes so good, feels so good, I don't care. Until I close my eyes.

"She's...his favorite," I mumble against his chest. "Elena. She's...Kolya's favorite of all his...girls. And she...knows too much."

Ryker's voice rumbles under my ear. "He'll kill her long before he'll sell her."

"Uh huh. We...have to...help her."

Whatever he says in reply fades until all I can hear is a deep, comforting baritone, and I let myself slip under.

21

Ryker

I *need help. How fast can you get to St. Petersburg?*
The text message waits on the screen as my finger hovers over the send button. Against me, Wren sleeps soundly, and I press a kiss to the top of her head. My instinct is to get up and force myself through a punishing exercise set, but she needs me.

Jabbing send before I can change my mind, I throw my phone on the couch cushions. I hate asking anyone for anything. Let alone...this. I still think rescuing Elena and Semyon is a suicide mission, but we can't leave her to Kolya and his goons. I keep replaying her last glance out the door in my head. Fear. Stark, naked, fear churning in her eyes. I know that feeling. Better than most people alive. I won't leave anyone behind if there's another option.

My phone vibrates, and the text message settles my nerves—at least a little.

Eighteen hours. How deep is the shit you're in?

With a grimace, I thumb out a reply.

It's the fucking Grand Canyon.

♥

HONEYSUCKLE FLOATS IN THE AIR, and something soft tickles my cheek. Jerking awake, I try to make sense of my surroundings. A pale glow from a laptop. The rustle of a sleeping bag. And Wren. She sighs, almost a hum, in her sleep and shifts closer to me. I bury my face in her curls to center myself.

I haven't woken up screaming once since I brought her to my bed back in Boston. Something about her soothes what's broken inside me, but this can't last. Soon, she'll figure out I'm too fucked-up to be worth her time. Once we rescue Elena and Semyon, I'll have to go back to Seattle, and her life is across the country. Mine isn't. There's nothing for me there anymore. Not after losing my brother, my parents, and any hope of a normal life.

"Stay," she murmurs when I roll onto my back and slide my palm under my head. Sleep isn't going to come for me anytime soon.

"Not going anywhere, sweetheart."

Though her eyes don't open, she drapes her arm over my chest and says, "Promise?"

That one word led us here. Halfway around the world. Too close to a veritable army with guns, drugs, and a penchant for murder and human trafficking. My every instinct screams at me to rub her back and coax her to sleep without answering, but instead, I brush a kiss to her lips. "Promise."

♥

"WE DON'T HAVE ANY HONEY," I say as I set a cup of instant coffee in front of her.

Wrapped up in the sleeping bag with her laptop balanced on her thighs, Wren smiles up at me. "I'm amazed we have coffee."

Taking a seat next to her with my own mug, I take a sip of the bitter brew. "This isn't coffee. It's caffeinated swill."

She snorts and covers her mouth, coughing as she tries not to let said swill shoot out her nose.

"That's not funny." I don't understand why she's laughing.

"It is the way you said it. Like you expected instant to taste like anything but flavored water. You've gone soft, soldier."

"Soft?"

"Yes. Soft. Don't you spend days in foreign countries all the time? You can't tell me you have access to the good stuff there."

"Actually...I do. West is responsible for the coffee. Frogman doesn't go anywhere without his hand-roasted Guatemalan reserve."

"Sounds like a smart guy. But...Frogman?" Wren presses her index finger to her laptop's biometric sensor and then types in a ten-digit passcode while I wonder how I can feel so...comfortable around her now. Is this what normal people do? Have coffee together in the mornings and talk about their coworkers?

"Ry?" She touches my arm, her fingers warm from the mug. "Where'd you go?"

"Nowhere." Does she remember what she asked me last night? And my answer? "Sorry. Frogman is what guys like me—Special Forces—call a SEAL."

"What does West call you?" she asks with a smile.

"Asshole, probably. Show me what else you found last night."

Wren takes a deep breath, then blows the air out slowly. "Zion spent two years here. He kept a diary—kind of. I found it thanks to Inara's translations. Every few days, he'd write me a letter. But he never sent them." She shakes her head. "He knew I'd come for him.

"For a few months, he thought everything was great. He had a steady supply of heroin, but he wasn't using so much he couldn't function. Kolya likes to keep his runners sober at least half the time. He uses the drugs as...a carrot, I guess. Motivation. Sell enough and you get a present. A bonus. A few days off to shoot up and do nothing."

A chill raises the hairs on the back of my neck. After long enough without any basic need—and to an addict, heroin is a basic need—you'll do anything for it.

"By the time two years had passed, Z and his best friend Semyon were shooting up every day. They started stealing from Kolya. Keeping just a little bit of the take. It was easy for Z. He handled some of Kolya's books. But then Kolya found out and he had two of his generals beat the crap out of them."

"I'm surprised he didn't just kill them."

"Semyon is Elena's brother. I think—well, Z thought—Elena begged Kolya to keep them both alive."

"Kolya's never going to let Elena walk out of there. If she's *that* special to him, he's going to kill her before he lets her go. But he might sell Semyon to teach her a lesson first."

Wren shows me a few of the diary entries, and it's obvious Zion was in a bad way. And completely in love with Elena.

By the time she's done, the entire bleak picture spreads out like a frayed, old canvas. A megalomaniac with an empire built on fear and the desperate need for what he provides. A scared twenty-something girl hoping this American kid with connections can free her from an abusive boyfriend-slash-owner. Her drug-addict brother who may or may not still be alive.

"And she doesn't know where her brother is?"

"Nope." Wren pulls up the last message the girl sent Zion just a week ago.

I am scared, Z. Kolya will not let me see my brother. He brings in girls every few days. At the last auction, he sold five. He tells me every day if I do not behave, he will sell me too. Where are you? I have not heard from you in so long. Please do not leave me here.

Bringing up a spreadsheet, Wren shakes her head. "He's not

making enough money off the drugs anymore. I ran the numbers. He's losing hundreds of thousands of rubles every month." Wren shows me her calculations, and I ease the computer off her lap to scan through the various files.

"The human trafficking won't be enough either. Not with this bottom line. He'll be out of business—or dead—in six months." Wren stares at me like I've grown a second head. "I went to college, sweetheart. Got a minor in math."

"I'm sorry...I didn't mean—" Her cheeks flush with color, and she stares down at her hands, twisting in her lap as she plays with her bracelet.

Silencing her with a kiss, I savor the way she leans into me. How she stills, as if nothing can touch her when I'm around. And she's right. I'll protect her until my last breath.

22

Wren

*R*yker starts slowly and methodically assembling the gear he'll need for the day, and I sit with my arms wrapped around my knees. "Take me with you."

"No." He doesn't spare me a glance as he picks up a second magazine and tucks it into a strap on his shoulder harness. "You're safer here."

"Physically, maybe. But I hate not knowing what's going on. Please. I can't take another day like yesterday. You might as well lock me in a closet for all the good I'll be here alone." Just the thought of needing another Xanax has my stomach twisting into a knot.

He stops, so still I'm not sure he's breathing. The look in his eyes...for a split second, he's not here, but then he shakes his head and sighs. "I have to plant at least eight cameras around Kolya's fortress today, Wren. He has lookouts everywhere. I can't watch out for them and for you."

My lips twist into a frown. "You don't have to 'watch out for me.' Set me up in a cafe and I can monitor the whole square." Turning my tablet around, I show him the view I have from the three traffic cameras in range of the former hotel. "And as you bring the cameras online, I'll have an even better view."

"Too dangerous."

"Is it? What's worse? Me having coffee in a cafe with you on comms? Or me here, hopped up on Xanax? I hate taking them. They make me loopy. You saw me last night. What good would I have been if you'd been followed back here? None." I stand, going chest-to-chest with him, but even throwing my shoulders as far back as I can and rising up onto my toes, the top of my head only reaches his chin.

I've got him, though. Even as messed up as I was last night, I understood how worried he was about me. About us. "I have anxiety, Ry. The meds I take every day help keep it manageable. But the panic attacks...they make me feel like I'm going to die. I can't breathe. I can't think. Let me help you. It'll help me too."

Dropping his head so our foreheads touch, he wraps his arms around me. "You need to do everything I tell you. No questions. No arguments. No hesitation."

"I will." Relief flows through me, loosening the knot working its way up to my heart. "I'll stay put. I just want to be close."

"If I tell you to run, you run." He draws back and meets my gaze. "I don't care what's happening to me or anyone else. You run and you don't stop until you get to the backup car. Then you drive yourself to the airport and get on a fucking plane to any friendly country you can find. You understand?"

"Yes. Western Europe, the US, Canada, or Japan."

With a nod, he releases me and then reaches for my pack. "All right. Show me what you need to bring."

AN HOUR LATER, we walk into a little cafe half a mile from Kolya's fortress. A black scarf hides my hair, and Ryker's wearing coveralls, hoping he can pass as a sanitation worker. On the way here, he must have asked me twenty times if I had my tracker and my earbud.

"Stay here until I come back. If you have to leave for any reason, go to the restaurant I showed you. Order a meal. Read a book. Act—"

I rest my hand on his forearm and squeeze the tight, corded muscle. "Normal. I know, Ry. I'll be fine. I'll connect to the cameras and watch your back."

"Keep off comms as much as you can." The strain in his whispered words and the furrow in his brow make my heart hurt a little. As hard as staying back at the safe house would have been for me, this is just as hard for him.

"I will." Cupping his neck, I pull him down for a slow, deep kiss. Luckily, we're tucked back in the corner of the cafe. "Thank you."

"For what?" His gaze takes a quick trip around the small space before returning to mine.

"For everything. For believing me." The lump in my throat threatens to cut off my words, so I force a smile. "Be careful."

With a nod, he's gone.

Despite my complete ignorance of the Russian language, I manage to stumble through ordering a small lunch plate with strong coffee and pull out my tablet. The cellular data card gives me quick, encrypted internet access, and before my food arrives, I've brought up all three traffic cameras with views towards Kolya's headquarters.

The kids he told me about—all Zion's age or a little younger —gather around the fountain, laughing and roughhousing like kids do. They seem...happy. At least for the moment, and I hope Zion's life here wasn't all bad.

Bringing up another of his diary entries, I search his words for the barest hint of hope.

Sis, I wish I could talk to you. Semyon and I went out for dumplings last night. You'd love how they make them here. I tried to get Elena to go with us, but the boss wouldn't let her come. She's the reason I can't just leave. I think I might love her. Maybe one day you'll meet her. I just need to figure out a way to get my passport back and get out of the country. Semyon said he'd help. I don't know why I keep writing to you. I don't want you to ever read these letters. But sometimes...they help keep me focused when I just want to escape from everything. Love you.

From all accounts, Semyon was Z's best friend here. I bring up a photo of the young man I found when I poked around St. Petersburg's prison records. He has that vacant, "I don't care about anything" stare of an addict, bad teeth, and a smattering of pimples across his forehead. But otherwise, he's a good-looking kid. Blond hair, blue eyes, full lips. Arrested for property damage —at a restaurant Kolya owns. Probably how he got trapped in this life in the first place.

Shifting my focus to the cameras, I search for Ryker. Anxiety twists my stomach until I find him. With a large rubber bin slung over his shoulder, he trudges along the edges of Kolya's hotel-turned-stronghold, using a long pole with pincers to pick up trash in the gutters.

He slows, checks all around him, and then drops to his knees next to a tall set of windows covered with bars. I zoom in, mesmerized as he places something small and black on the side of one of the bars. A moment later, his voice rumbles in my ear. "Mic one. Set."

I switch to the list of locations he sketched out early this morning and mark off the first one. Only ten more to go.

THREE HOURS LATER, I start to worry the cafe owner will think I'm trying to take advantage of her warm, quiet shop, so I order two pastries and a soda. I don't need any more caffeine—my anxiety is already through the roof, but I don't know where else go to, and Ryker only has two mics and one camera left.

"Something's happening," he mutters in my ear. "North of the square. Get eyes over there."

Cracker Jacks. My fingers tremble as I bring up both traffic cameras and the surveillance cams he planted earlier and try to find the disturbance. When I do, I gasp before clapping my hand over my mouth.

"Wren. Talk to me," he snaps.

"Two big guys are beating the crap out of a kid. I can't tell if they're his men or not. Or one of his kids. They're dragging him into an alley and...frankincense. I can't see them anymore."

"Going to check it out. Be ready to move if I tell you."

My heart thuds so loudly I think he can probably hear it over comms. But I force myself to move slowly, calmly, as I pull out a handful of rubles for my bill. Tucking the book I've been pretending to read all afternoon back in my bag, I scan through all of the camera images. Nothing. I can't find Ryker or the goons.

When his voice returns to my ear, it carries a hint of panic. "Something's wrong. Get the fuck out of there. Rendezvous point three. Five minutes."

With a little squeak, I shove the tablet into my bag, throw the rubles on the table, and try not to run for the front door. My first breath of fresh air helps center me, and I remember to check for anything or anyone out of place before I set off for the bar Ryker showed me this morning.

A handful of people are out and about. A businessman talking on his cell phone, a mother with a small child holding her hand, and an older couple—maybe fifties, heading for the cafe. No one *looks* like a threat, but would I even know?

Two blocks later, I'm almost in control of my emotions until a young man rushes past me, his shoulder slamming into mine. I stumble and snap, "Hey. Watch where you're going."

When the kid stops, turns, and meets my gaze, time stands still.

"Semyon?"

The boy from the mug shot curses under his breath as he races down the street and then darts into an alley on the next block.

"Ryker? I just saw Semyon." I follow, clutching my bag tightly against my stomach as I start to jog. "I'm turning down *Ulitsa Tel'-mana* to follow him."

"No!" Ryker growls over comms. "Get to the rendezvous point, Wren. Now!"

I should listen. But the look in Semyon's eyes—it was like he recognized me. And if I leave him now, I might never find him again. At the mouth of the alley, I stop, warning bells going off in my head. Except...Semyon is at the other end, banging on one of the building doors. "He's right here. I can see him..."

"Wren!" Ryker's voice sounds both in my ear and from a few blocks away. I glance back at him, seeing the pure terror on his face as he sprints towards me. A shout rings out from the alley, and I turn, seeing Semyon struggling with a big burly man.

"Let me go," he shouts and tries to kick at his attacker. I don't think. I have to get to him. To save him. For Z.

Ryker begs me to stop, but I can't, and as I race down the alley, Semyon manages to wrench his arms free and escape out onto the street. I try to stop my forward momentum, but I skid, my heart rate skyrocketing and my feet tangling with one another. Unable to find my footing, I crash to the ground, scraping my palms. As Ryker curses and shouts, rough hands grab me.

"Ry!" I flail my legs, but the man holding me slams me into the wall, and the side of my head explodes in pain. Fear wraps icy fingers around my heart as his scent invades my nose. Sweat and onions. I can't...I can't move. Can't think. I have to get away. But he's too strong. Too big. Pressed against me. "Ryker," I choke out, and a shot explodes close to my right arm, sending bits of concrete flying up to hit my arms.

"Let her go, fucker!" Ryker shouts, and I find enough focus to squirm and land a solid kick to my attacker's shin.

"Stupid *cyka*," the man grunts and whirls around. Something hard smacks into my cheek. As my world goes dark, I hear Ryker scream my name.

23

Ryker

*T*wo shots is all I can risk. I could hit Wren. But they're not enough. Small bits of concrete explode from the side of the building as a dark-haired man with tattoos running up and down his arms tosses Wren over his shoulder and disappears inside the building. The other asshole—this one blond—sends a return shot my way before following his partner.

"Wren! Wren, sweetheart, talk to me!" I shout over comms. She can't answer me. I saw the blond one punch her hard enough to knock her into next week, but I have to try. She'll be lucky if she doesn't have a broken jaw. What am I thinking? She'll be lucky if she lives.

I reach the door, but it's locked, and my pounding does nothing but bruise my fist. "Let her go, you dumb fucks! I'll hunt you down and rip you apart!"

Footsteps slap on the concrete at the other end of the alley, and I spin, raising my gun. "Freeze!"

A young kid—no more than twenty-five—stops, stares at me

for two seconds, and then darts around the corner. My shot misses him by inches, and indecision paralyzes me. Pick the lock or go after the kid?

Muffled voices echo over comms. Not Wren, but the men who have her. I can't make out what they're saying, but I think I hear a door slam. The sound frees me from the terror gripping me, and I abandon any thought of picking the lock. Stepping back, I fire two quick shots at the deadbolt.

The door swings open, and I slip inside and press my back to the wall, listening. Laughter, I think, and another door.

Fuck. Get your bearings, soldier. She needs you.

I take a deep breath. Scent the air. Sweat. Gunpowder. And honeysuckle. This is some sort of warehouse, I think. Stacks of boxes halfway to the ceiling hide the other end of the room from me, and light glows from somewhere behind them.

I know in my heart, she's gone. This was a targeted, planned attack. Somehow, they knew she was here. Knew just how to get to her. But I can't give up. Not this time. I've failed everyone I've ever cared for. I can't fail Wren. Can't lose her. Not now. She's...everything.

Creeping silently around one stack of wooden crates, I find an open door leading to a hallway. With a quick check to verify no one lies in wait, I follow Wren's scent. Until something glinting on the floor stops me.

Her bracelet. The purple and green beads are smooth between my fingers, and I say a silent prayer of thanks they didn't break when they fell off her wrist. Except...she needs her bracelet. Without it, her anxiety...her panic attacks...

Keep going.

I can't let myself dwell on what might happen to her. Because I know what *will* happen to her if I can't save her. Bursting through another door out into the sunlight, I'm seconds too late. The dark-haired goon grins through the side window of a shiny new car as the vehicle pulls away from the curb, tires squealing, and Wren's gone.

I DON'T REMEMBER how I get to the safe house. I only have vague memories of running back to the car. I know Kolya has her. But I can't get into his fortress without a hell of a lot more fire power—and help.

Wren's laptop sits on the couch. Nestled amid the sleeping bags. Dropping my pack, I sink to my knees. Her scent is everywhere in this house. But nowhere more than right here. In the makeshift bed where I found peace for the first time in...forever.

My heart pounds in my ears. Rhythmic thumping I can't stop. I failed her. This morning, she kissed me right here. I ran my hands over her small breasts, down her stomach, to the patch of reddish curls over her mound. The pressure inside my head builds, more thumping threatening to drive me insane. I can't get myself under control.

Wren kept me calm. Centered. Focused. And now...

My phone buzzes in my pocket.

Open the damn door.

The pounding. It's not in my head. Inara.

With Wren's bracelet still clutched in my hand, I fumble for the lock.

"About time." Inara pushes past me with a rucksack half her size on her back, and I start to close the door, but a hand shoots out and slams into the wood.

"Is that any way to thank me for postponing my fucking wedding?" West raises a brow, and I stagger back, shocked. "Jesus, Ry. Did you seriously expect me to stay back in Seattle?"

"Where's Wren?" Inara asks as she drops her pack and West shuts the door behind him.

I look from one to the other, suddenly unable to speak. One.

Two. Three. Four. Five. I trace patterns over the beads in my hand.

Inara grabs my arms and tries to shake me. But she's half my size. "Ry?"

"They took her." Saying the words suddenly makes the horror real, and then I'm on the floor. I don't remember sitting. Or falling. My ass hurts. All I can smell is honeysuckle.

Cool fingers touch my cheek, and for a second, I think...she's here. I dreamed the whole thing. But then the scent of lilies and vanilla drives the honeysuckle away, and Inara's face swims in and out of focus. "Ry. Talk to me. Where's Wren? Where did they take her?"

"He's too far gone. If she's wearing her tracker, Royce's program can find her." West pulls out his laptop, and even though I should get up, should help him, should do *something*, all I can do is stare at the beads in my hand and think about what Kolya is doing to my sweet Wren, right now.

24

Wren

a hard slap sends pain exploding in my cheek. "Wake up, *cyka*."

Dizzy, I struggle to focus. I'm in a chair—plush, leather—and I try to bring my hand up to soothe the pain, but it won't move. Oh God. I'm tied up. Ankles secured to the legs of the chair, wrists bound behind me. And the sickening scent of too much aftershave in my nose.

I whimper as another hit sends my head rocking. "Stop. Please." I can barely manage a whisper through the throbbing in my cheek and the nausea churning in my stomach. Ryker. Where's Ryker? He was close. I heard him. And then...nothing.

Someone grabs my hair and forces my head back. "You will look at me when I am talking to you."

Kolya Yegorovich. Oh shit. I'm dead. He's going to kill me. Panic coils around my heart, and I start to hyperventilate. "P-please..." I beg through rasping, wheezing breaths. "Need... my...meds..."

With a snarl, he punches me in the stomach, and the shock makes me retch as his fist drives the air from my lungs. I hiccup, but after the room stops spinning, I can breathe again. Who knew a punch could stop a panic attack? The absurdity of what just happened makes me want to laugh—or perhaps that's the terror talking.

"You and your brother have caused me much trouble. I disposed of him too quickly. You...you will beg me to break you." His hand tightens around my throat, and I try to pull away, but the back of the chair stops me. As my body runs out of air, tears stream down my cheeks.

Darkness tinges my vision, and I see Ryker's face, hear the panic as he screamed my name over the roar of my heartbeat in my ears. Ryker will come. Won't he? He'll save me like he saved me in Boston.

Except he doesn't. My arms and legs spasm in their bonds, and pressure builds behind my eyes until I'm sure I'm going to pass out. But then Kolya lets me go, and I suck in huge lungfuls of air until I can see again.

Kolya paces back and forth in front of me, and two large men —blondie and the handsy guy who grabbed me and felt me up at the same time—stand between him and the only door I see in the room. Arms crossed. Guns in shoulder harnesses. Tattoos cover their arms, even up to their necks.

"I thought taking care of you back in the States would be simple. But the stupid fucks I hired could not manage such a simple task. Imagine my surprise when I saw all of those pitiful emails Elena sent your brother had been read. How much did you tell that brute with you?"

Horror clenches in my gut. He knows about Ryker. Does he know about the cameras? The mics? I swallow hard and force myself to meet Kolya's steely-blue gaze. "Go to hell."

His deep laugh makes my skin crawl. "You are in no position

to demand anything, *cyka*." A slap to my other cheek makes my ears ring. "What information did your piece of shit brother steal from me? Did you know he tried to blackmail me? Me!" Grabbing my upper arms, he squeezes hard enough to bring tears to my eyes. "He thought he could get me to let Elena go. Her *gopnik* brother too."

"You...don't need them," I say as another tear rolls down my cheek. "You have...an empire. Zion just...wanted to be...free. Let us all...go and you'll never...see me again."

"Stupid bitch," he mutters as he shoves the chair so hard, it topples onto its side, with me still tied to it. My head hits the rich wood floor, and I see stars.

"Pick her up," Kolya barks to one of his men, and the blond giant lumbers over and winds his beefy hand in my hair, using my curls to lift me—and the chair. I whimper at the pain, and my throat tightens up again. Please...just let me pass out. I think I'm still wearing my tracker—I'm fully dressed, though my earbud is gone. If Ryker's alive, he'll know where I am. Maybe...he'll be able to save me.

With his back to me, Kolya digs through something on his desk. My bag. Dammit. My tablet's in there. Except, it's encrypted. As long as I don't give him the password, he won't know what I know. Won't know about the cameras. The tracker. All of the financial data Elena and Zion stole.

"Give me access," he orders as he thrusts the tablet in front of my face.

"No."

"You think you are so brave?" Leaning closer, he stares me down, and his breath threatens to suffocate me. He smells like onions and sour milk, and I fight not to lose my lunch.

"Not brave," I whisper. "But not stupid either. The minute I tell you, I'm dead. You might as well just kill me now. Because I'm never going to give you what you want."

Kolya's lips curve into a sneer. Perfect white teeth fill his wide mouth, so perfect they have to be fake. Oh God. I hope I haven't just made a terrible mistake. "Never? If you are at all like your brother, little Red, you will beg to tell me very soon." He turns to Blondie. "Take her to the bath. I will be along shortly with proper...motivation."

Motivation? Oh God. He's going to rape me. Or try to drown me. What else would he do in a bathroom? The big guy pulls a jackknife from his pocket and flips it open, waving it menacingly at me as he comes closer. His partner moves behind me, and in seconds, they've cut me free, but I'm too stiff, sore, and dazed to run for the door before Blondie grabs my legs and the Groper yanks my arms over my head and pins my wrists together. They carry me almost like a hammock, swinging me between them, letting my back hit the floor every couple of feet. I struggle, but it's no use. They're too strong. With every step, my panic rises, until I'm half-sobbing, half-screaming as I thrash and buck.

Down a short hallway, then around a corner and into a lavish bedroom. I wheeze as the panic attack hits its apex and try to throw my weight from side to side, anything to get them off balance, maybe force one of them to drop me. Screaming like a banshee, I give up on all of the polite and cute curses Mama taught me. "Let me go, fuckers!"

And the Groper does. My head slams into hard, black tile, and the entire world tilts, darkens, and quiets as I fight not to lose consciousness. "There," the Groper says in a thick Russian accent. "I let go."

Blondie kneels down next to me and fiddles with something close to the floor. When a cold, solid weight settles around my ankle, I try to push myself up. A chain runs from the thick, metal cuff to a pipe under a gleaming black sink. Shit, shit, shit.

Heavy footsteps approach, and my heart leaps into my throat. Kolya looms in the doorway, that same, sneering grin plastered on his face. He has a small bag in his hand, and I can't look away it as it swings from his short stubby fingers.

"Take her clothes," he orders.

"No!" I flail my arms, trying to scramble back, but the Groper grabs my hands and uses his knees to pin them to the floor.

"If you do not want to end up bleeding to death, little Red, I suggest you hold still."

Blondie's knife waves in front of me, and I tremble as he slices through the button on my pants, then drags the blade down one leg. I'm cold. So cold. I can't look away as he cuts through the other leg, then yanks the black material out from under me. My boots are next. Then socks.

"Stop, please," I whisper when Blondie uses the flat of the blade to trace up my outer thigh. His sick laughter is too much, and now I'm sobbing uncontrollably. My blue shirt is next, the knife making quick work of the thin, insulating material. I start to shiver, my teeth chattering, and then the tip of the knife presses between my breasts.

"No, no, no," I moan, but Blondie laughs as he jerks the blade through the black lace, and the bra falls away, sending my tracker tumbling onto the tile. "*Der'mo*," he says, turning the small receiver over in his hand. "What is this, boss?"

Kolya snatches the device away and narrows his eyes at me. "Answer him, *cyka*."

"Fuck you."

With a snarl, the drug lord kicks me in the side, and I whimper as I struggle to breathe. Everything hurts. So much I hardly notice when my panties are cut off and yanked away. Naked, terrified, and with three huge men leering at me, I realize Kolya's right. I'm ready to beg him to kill me.

Ryker. Please. I'm so scared. Where are you?

Crouching a few feet away, Kolya opens the bag. "Sit her up and keep her still."

I can't stand their hands on me, and I'm shaking all over—from fear, panic, cold, and then...from sheer terror as the Groper holds my arms and Blondie sits on my legs so he can palm my breast with lust in his eyes.

"This is how I train all of my new girls," Kolya says as he dangles a rubber tube from his fat fingers. "You will do anything for me soon." He wraps the rubber around my upper arm, tying it tightly, and the reality of what he's about to do slams into me, stealing my breath.

He lights a thick, squat candle, and sulfur burns my nose. I whimper when he withdraws a vial of brown powder and pours some into a spoon. As the heroin starts to bubble, I beg, "Please. Just kill me. I can't...I can't do this..."

"You would be surprised how easy it is, *cyka*. Your brother was hooked with his first taste. After a few days...you will do anything I ask. Willingly."

"I won't. I can't." My voice turns into a squeak, then I'm crying so hard, the world takes on a watery glow and my head throbs.

"Tsk, tsk, tsk," he says with a sneer. "You will do whatever I say, little Red. Or maybe I cut you before I take the pain away."

Blondie takes the knife and traces a line up my stomach, and blood wells as he gives the blade a flick along the side of my breast.

I'm gasping for breath as the heroin liquifies, and when Kolya drops a cotton ball into the spoon and then sucks the drug into the needle, I start to wheeze and my entire body strains. "No, no, no," I beg, but it does me no good.

The needle breaches my skin with a little pop, and I scream, thrashing until the needle slips free, but that only makes Kolya angrier. "Hold her still," he growls again, and the Groper tightens his grip on my forearms. The second time, Kolya holds my elbow himself as he pierces my vein. With a chuckle, he pulls the plunger out slightly, and blood mixes with the heroin, sending a burning pressure consuming my upper arm.

He pauses, raising a bushy blond brow. "Is this your first time, little Red?"

"Please...stop..." I whisper.

"Enjoy the ride," he says, and my body freezes in a silent scream as he depresses the plunger.

25

Ryker

"*D*rink this." West sets a cup of coffee on the table in front of me. "And then get your ass up and help us."

The scent of his favorite brew is almost comforting, except... Wren's gone, and Kolya's either raped her, killed her, or tortured her by now. Will she tell him where we are? Can she? She fell asleep on the way here, and she might not remember the route from the safe house to town today. I don't think she'll break—for a while. But she's not trained. She doesn't know what an interrogation can do to a person.

Screams—mine, Dax's, my other men's—echo in my memories. I smell burning skin, my captors' sweat, fear.

If he sells her...I'll rip each one of his fingers from his hand and feed them to him before I cut his dick off. And then I'll find her and kill every single man who's touched her.

"Ry?" Inara kneels next to me. "We're flying blind here. Wren's laptop is password protected. Her tracker's dead, but its last location was inside that big building by the square. But we can't tell if she's was wearing it at the time or if it was sitting in some drawer somewhere. It died an hour or so ago, but before that, it showed small movements inside the fortress. I'm heading out on reconnaissance. But you *have* to help West."

Don't leave. I don't know how to fix this.

I can't say the words, but as she meets my gaze, I think she understands. With a quick squeeze of my arm, she offers me the only comfort she can, and I nod my thanks. As she hefts her pack and heads for the door, I find my voice. "Be careful."

"I'm sticking to the rooftops. They'll never see me. You two stay on comms. Both of you."

I don't move for almost ten minutes, the mug of coffee cupped in my hands, Wren's scent surrounding me. Will honeysuckle soon be nothing more than a memory?

Shoving my ear bud into my ear, I shake my head.

Focus. She's out there. She needs you.

Looking up, I find West arranging his gear. "You shouldn't have come, Sampson."

"You're right. Cam and I are supposed to get married in two days. *Were* supposed to get married. We have tickets to Costa Rica in a week. A private resort. Non-refundable." He glares at me, his intense blue eyes unforgiving. "Instead, I'm in an empty house in Russia, three miles from one of the most dangerous drug lords in the Eastern Block, staring at a man who looks like he's lost everything." West ambles over to me and holds out his hand. "You going to sit there wrapped in that sleeping bag all night? Or are you going to help me get your girl back?"

"My...girl?" I stare up at him, the coffee in my hand long forgotten.

A dry laugh—almost a snort—escapes his lips, and he shakes his head. "You're so far gone it'd be funny if she weren't in danger, Mr. I'm-Never-Falling-In-Love."

"I don't..." The truth crashes down on me. I don't want to be without her. Not now, not ever. She calms my demons. She understands me. Doesn't let me get away with any bullshit. Is this...love?

"Stop fighting it, Ry. I swear, both you and Inara. Stubborn as fuck." He stares down at his extended hand, brows raised. "On your feet."

"What does it feel like?" I clap my hand against West's and let him pull me up. "Finding...that person."

"Like you're home." He sighs, the barest hint of a smile tugging at his lips. "Like...you don't *have* to tell her your deepest, darkest secrets, but you want to. And when you do...she understands. Doesn't judge."

"I had a brother."

"What?" West frowns, running a hand through his dark hair. "You've never talked about him."

"Not good memories. He...died. I told Wren." I pull her bracelet over my fist, and the beads warm against my skin. "Didn't mean to. Didn't mean to tell her a lot of things."

"Do you love her?" He studies me. Watches me for any sign I'm lying to him—and myself. SEALs are some of the most goddamned observant men in the world.

"Y-yes. Fuck. Yes."

"So...let's get her back." West passes me Wren's laptop, and I stare at the biometric sensor. "You know what to do. Supplies are in my kit."

As West spreads a map of the city out on the dining room table, I open his rucksack and dig out the black leather infil kit. With silicone spray, ultra-fine charcoal powder, and a rubbery finger-condom, I lift Wren's print from the sensor, apply it to my thumb, and pray.

Enter passcode:

Closing my eyes, I think back to the first time I saw her fingers flying over the keys. The ten digits roll out of my memory easily, and I'm in. "Got it."

One-by-one, the cameras come online. Kolya hasn't found any

of them. Not yet. She hasn't told him everything. The streetlights illuminate a couple of kids lounging on the front steps of his building, but no one else is out. It's well after nine, and this part of St. Petersburg rolls up its sidewalks after eight. At least on a Sunday.

"In position, Whiskey," Inara whispers over comms, using West's code name. We never use real names on a mission—just in case someone's listening. Inara is India, I'm Romeo, and West is Whiskey. New guy—if we ever go on another mission again—will be Golf. "I can see into the top floor of that monstrosity. Four rooms, I think. One's an office. Blinds open. Desk, chair. Dark colors. Another might be a bedroom. Kind of looks like the video with the girl."

"Any signs of life?" West asks.

"No. Switching to thermals."

I hold my breath. If Wren's there…

"One heat signature. Indistinct. Like someone curled in a ball. Could be a fucking dog for all I can tell. In a room off the bedroom. Floor level." After a pause, she mutters, "Most everyone's on the first floor. Got…fuck…at least fifteen. Maybe twenty."

"Wren?"

"How the hell would I know? These are heat signatures. All the shades are drawn down there. I'm going to try to get closer and use the parabolic mic. Going dark."

I cycle through the cameras, looking for anything out of place. The kids head inside, passing through the front door after a security check from a big, burly guy with a semi-automatic slung over his shoulder. That's new. They're expecting trouble.

They're expecting *me*.

"Bring it, you fucking bastard," I say under my breath. "You're mine."

West chuckles. "That's more like it." His grim smile matches his tone, and he waves me over. "Cam found the blueprints for the building."

"What're we looking at?" I carry Wren's laptop over to the table with me, keeping one eye on the cameras while West opens the black and white schematics for Kolya's fortress.

"Former hotel. Ten rooms on each of the two middle floors. Dining room and kitchen on the first floor, ballroom, a couple of storage closets. Fourth floor has three penthouse-style suites with full bathrooms. Electrical and storage in the basement. Server room, too, I think. Six exterior doors, and one ingress point on the roof." West twists the 3D model on screen. "If she's in there—"

"Three hostiles are climbing the stairs with the girl—Elena. Caught a glimpse of them as they hit the second floor. Kolya and two guys. One blond, one dark."

"Where's the unknown signature?" West asks. "What side of the building?"

"North east corner."

"That's a bathroom," West confirms. "Switch to thermals and give me a visual."

She does, and West answers the incoming video call. The indistinct heat signature starts to move, and as its shape changes, I suck in a breath. Definitely a person. Small. Moving so slowly it's almost painful to watch.

Oh God. Is that Wren? If so...what have they done to her?

Wren

I'm lying in something sticky. And...disgusting. The sour smell of bile burns my nose. Oh my God. Vomit. I try to push myself up, but my limbs don't want to respond.

Everything's fuzzy. An undercurrent of fear runs through me, sending my heart thudding in my chest and my stomach clenching. The needle. The terror as my arm went numb. The sudden,

violent retching. My head slamming into the sink. And then...
peace. No pain. No fear. No...anything.

But now, my entire body screams in agony. My head. My
arms. My ribs. And I'm cold. So cold. Naked, bruised, bloody,
and covered in my own sick, I bury my face in my hands
and sob.

Ryker, please find me. I can't...I can't do this. I'm so scared.

The whole time...however long it's been...I knew I was in
trouble. Knew I was hurt. But...I didn't care. Nothing mattered.
And now, my emotions are overwhelming me. Stronger than I
can handle. I reach for my bracelet, but it's gone, and only rough,
reddened abrasions from the ropes decorate my wrists. My arms
and legs feel...heavy. Something stings all along my neck. Forcing
my gaze down, I see deep, red scratches all the way to my breasts,
and a keening cry catches in my throat.

*"All of your problems...they just go away. You itch. Everywhere.
And nothing matters but that next hit. You'll do anything so you don't
have to hurt again."*

Part of Zion's recovery involved telling me how heroin made
him feel. I don't want another hit. Or...do I? Drawing my legs in
closer, the cuff around my ankle pulls tight, and the reality of my
situation crashes down on me.

I'm naked. Locked to a water pipe in Kolya Yegorovich's bathroom. Beaten and bruised. And he's drugging me. My fear is an
oily, bitter taste in my mouth and the pain grips every muscle in
my body, but...my anxiety's almost non-existent.

I try again to sit up, and this time, I manage. The room spins
around me, and drying vomit clings to my hair. Water. I need
water. Using the sink, I pull myself up, almost fall over again, and
force my knees to lock.

It takes me three tries to turn on the faucet, but once cold
water flows freely, I stick my whole head under the stream. The
chill helps me focus, and after most of the vomit's out of my hair,
I turn my head and suck down as much water as I can without

making myself sick before turning the faucet off and sinking back down to the floor.

The door opens, and a blurry figure approaches. Small. Not Kolya. Still, I whimper.

"Wren?"

"Who...are you?" I try to focus, but I'm too scared. And I can't concentrate long enough to make sense of what I'm seeing. Blond hair. Bruises. Arms so thin they don't look real. Her voice, though...I know her voice.

"I am Elena." Cool fingers touch my cheek, and I wince as pain spirals down my jaw. "Zion...?"

I shake my head, immediately regretting the motion as I topple over, rapping my temple against the pipe. "Please...help me," I whisper.

"Give me the password to your computer," she says as she helps me sit up and takes my hands. "I can talk to Kolya. Maybe... he will listen. Let you out of here."

I blink hard and meet her gaze. Blue eyes, terrified, shadowed. "I can't. He'll...kill me..."

Heavy footsteps approach, and I shrink back against the wall, trying to make myself as small as possible as Elena darts a glance over her shoulder.

"Did you enjoy your first trip, little Red?" Kolya looms in the doorway, grinning at me. "You were a joy to watch. You moaned. Such a pretty sound."

"Let me go...please," I whimper, my words slurred. "I'm no danger to you. I just want to go home."

His snort sends a jolt of panic through me, but the aftereffects of the heroin temper the emotion quickly. "You are much too valuable for that. And pretty. Zion never told me how beautiful you were. I think I will keep you."

Keep me? Oh God.

"You can't—"

"I can. Leave us, Elena. Into the bedroom. Strip." Kolya shoves her out of the room, and she stumbles, a soft sob escaping her swollen lips. As he kneels next to me, he pulls a fresh needle from his jacket pocket, handing it to the goon behind him. "Prepare the next dose, Victor."

Blondie crouches a few feet away and lights the candle. I can't look away from the flame as he starts heating the heroin. I'm scared, my entire body shaking, but...then...an eerie calm settles over me. I won't care about anything once the drug hits my bloodstream. I understand now. How Zion could want this more than anything.

"Please don't." My voice is barely audible, and my fingers flex, almost aching for the release he's promising, even as my heart jackhammers half out of my chest and a dull roar fills my ears.

Kolya grabs my arm and yanks—hard. I topple over, right into him, and he takes the opportunity to cup my breast and pinch my nipple. "I can do whatever I want with you, sweet Red. And right now, I want to hear you moan again."

With deft hands, the Groper tightens the rubber tube around my arm. I start to struggle, but then his massive hand wraps around my throat, squeezing just enough to make breathing difficult as he growls, "Be still."

I'm numb...I let my body go slack. What good would fighting do me? Blondie—Victor—and the Groper are at least twice my size, and I'm still locked to the pipe. Kolya could carve me up into tiny pieces and I couldn't do anything to stop him.

"Do you want this, my little red-headed pet?"

Something deep inside my rational brain tells me to say yes. Even though I know I don't. *Trick him. Find a way to survive this long enough for Ryker to rescue you.*

Except...as he waves the needle in front of my face, I think... maybe I *do* want it. What's the alternative? Passing out from a panic attack? Screaming until I don't have a voice left from the pain, the sheer terror of being in the presence of pure evil?

"N-no...I...mean...I...please..." Tears burn my eyes, then spill onto my cheeks. Kolya laughs as he whisks one away with a bent finger.

"So pretty when you cry." Kolya shoves the needle into my arm, and my skin burns, the pain sending sparks racing up to my shoulder until a warm, heavy peace settles over me and there's nothing. No fear. No pain. Nothing. And I float away.

26

Ryker

*W*atching Kolya and his goons—or at least their thermal images—gang up on what has to be Wren sends anger prickling over my skin. After they leave, she—I can't believe it's not her—doesn't move. Prone, almost curled into a ball. Two of the men head back down the stairs, and the third— Kolya I assume—grabs Elena and drags her to the far corner of the bedroom, laughing. A hard knot twists in my gut as her cries and the unmistakable sounds of rough sex, of rape, come over comms.

"Get me a better visual or a way to hear what's going on inside that bathroom," I bark at Inara, but I know it's no use. There's a door, so even if Inara could find another rooftop, the best she can do is change the angle on the thermal imaging. The parabolic mic only works if there's a window to aim at, and even then, it's limited.

West tightens his hand on my arm. "Romeo, breathe. If we're going in there, we're doing it with a solid plan. India, get me footage of all sides. Heat signatures and night-vision, then find somewhere to hunker down."

I know he's right. Hell, this is what I pay him for. Infil and exfil. The man can run a dozen different scenarios in his head at once. But I can't just let her think I'm not coming for her.

Bracing my hands on the table, I stare daggers at the laptop, willing it to show me something—anything—useful. Like Kolya jumping out the window to his death or Wren running from the building, whole and unharmed.

"Whiskey."

The former SEAL holds up his hand and turns off his transmitter. "I know. But we're three against...twenty? Those are shit odds under the best of circumstances, and right now, you're not firing on all cylinders, Ry. Sit down, shut up, and let me think."

I slink back to the couch and run my fingers over those damn beads.

When I was in Hell, I spent my days—when I could focus—memorizing everything. Sights. Sounds. Smells. But so often, the pain chased clarity away, and I tapped patterns on the floor, the wall, the inside of my wrist...whatever I could reach based on how they restrained me that day. I revert to my old habits now.

Tap. Tap-tap. Tap-tap-tap. Tap-Tap. Tap. Against Wren's beads.

Please, sweetheart. Hold on for me. I'm coming for you.

The cameras cycle as I stare unblinking at the screen on the table a few feet away. A lone figure darts across one of the shots, and his blond hair and build look hauntingly familiar. "India. Where are you right now?"

"Rooftop of some dirty restaurant that smells like beets."

"South end. Get a visual on the kid hustling towards you. If you get a close-up, send it." Leaping up, I race over to the laptop and motion West to join me.

"What? I'm a little busy here."

Inara zooms in, and I suck in a sharp breath. "That's him. That's the kid I saw when they took Wren. Elena's brother."

West clenches his fists over the map, crinkling the paper. "India. You have non-lethals?"

"This isn't my first rodeo, Whiskey," she whispers. "You want him?"

"Hell no. But we need him. If you have a shot, take it. But for fuck's sake, be careful."

"Roger that." She clicks off comms, and her body cam shows her creeping along the top of the building, following the kid. He's moving quickly, but once he turns the corner alongside the back of the building, he stops and sort of collapses against the wall. A fumbling hand digs into his coat pocket and he comes away with a pack of cigarettes. The subtle red glow illuminates his face, and Inara stops moving. I can picture her. Getting into position. Flat on her belly. The long-range rifle wedged against her shoulder. She's one of the best snipers in the world with more confirmed kills than anyone in the past decade. And the first woman certified. Since then, three others have come up through the ranks, but Inara's still the best.

Semyon glances up and down the alleyway, smoking like his life depends on it. The butt glows brighter as he inhales, and then he jerks, staring down at his chest. Another jerk, and his hand lifts to his neck, but as if in slow motion, his entire body crumples to the ground, the cigarette landing a few inches from his lips.

"Got him. Will confirm after retrieval," Inara says, and then she starts to run. West and I don't speak until we see the boy's body land in the trunk of a beat-up car. "This better be worth it." She's out of breath. Though she's strong, and Semyon's rail thin, she's carrying a hell of a lot of gear. "Turning off the camera. I'll be back in fifteen minutes."

"Roger that," West says. "You're sure this kid knows something?"

"He lured Wren down that alley." I crack my knuckles, itching to beat the truth out of the boy. "He knows a hell of a lot more than something."

West sighs. "I hope you're right. Because this is going to be Colombia all over again. Way too many hostiles, only one safe ingress and egress point, and we have no clue what condition Wren's in."

"Don't," I snap. Grabbing him by the arms, I barely stop myself from shaking him. "She's going to be okay."

"Ry." His gaze locks onto mine, and I know what he's thinking. Kolya's the worst of the worst. Drug lord, pimp, murderer, and more. The likelihood of Wren living through his wrath is...almost non-existent.

"She has information he wants. He needs. He won't kill her until he knows he's safe. I have to believe that. If I don't...I might as well just go in there guns blazing and take out as many of those fuckers as I can before they kill me."

"No." Shaking me off, West takes a step back. "If we get confirmation she's dead—" he holds up his hands when I growl and raise my fists, "—fucking listen to me, McCabe. If she dies—we'll blow that entire building. Together. And then we'll all go home. As long as we think there's a chance she's alive, no one's giving up on her."

For a long moment, neither of us move. Finally, I lower my hands. "I have to get her back."

"I know. And we're with you. Whatever it takes." He turns back to his maps and laptop, and I scoop up the sleeping bags and carry them into one of the back bedrooms. Wren is coming back to me. And when she does, I'll take care of her. In private. Where she can feel safe. Nothing will ever hurt her again, and I have to tell her. She's it for me.

27

Ryker

By the time Inara arrives, I have all of Wren's things set up in the bedroom. I found a few candles in the kitchen and unrolled the extra sleeping bag we brought and never used. It's not much, but it's all I can do.

West mutters from the front room every few minutes, and once or twice, I hear him on the phone to Graham back at our base in Seattle. I'm glad they didn't bring him. The kid's brand new, and this isn't a mission for amateurs. Though, a couple of extra guns wouldn't be a bad idea.

"A little help?" Inara calls.

I race out and lift the still-unconscious kid off her shoulders. Tossing him onto the couch, I grab a set of zip ties and secure his hands behind him, then bind his ankles together.

Propped up against the cushions, he looks so young. Twenty-three maybe? "Wake him up," I say, and Inara pops the top on a vial of smelling salts.

Semyon snorts and coughs and tries to squirm away from the

stench, but West slaps his hands down on the kid's shoulders from behind. "Don't move if you know what's good for you."

A string of Russian escapes the kid's lips, and I glance at Inara. She shakes her head as if she can't believe he's that stupid. "Half of your text messages are in English, kid. Don't pull that shit with us." Waving his phone in the air, she smiles. Not the friendly, I'm happy to see you grin she can sometimes affect, but a lethal, try anything and you're dead smile.

"Who are you?" Semyon asks.

"Try again." I lean forward, putting my face right in front of his. "You recognize me, asswipe. I know you do. And you know where Wren is."

He starts to tremble and writhe against the zip ties. "He will kill me if I talk to you."

"I'll kill you if you don't." Whatever he sees in my eyes and hears in my calm, flat tone convinces him I'm telling the truth, and he deflates.

"She's with Kolya."

Even though I knew it, hearing the words still shakes me to my core. "Is she alive?"

"Da. Yes. He wants her for himself. He says…if I help him…he will let Elena go. The redhead…Wren…will be his new *shlyukha*."

Inara grabs my arm and holds on tight before she translates. "Whore."

I want to snap this kid's neck—after I break every bone in his body, but he's my only link to Wren. I meet Inara's gaze. "I'm in control."

"You better be," she mouths, her back to Semyon.

Returning my focus to the kid, I cross my arms over my chest. "Here's what's going to happen now, Semyon. That is your name, right?"

He nods.

"You're going to help us get Wren back. And in return, we're going to get you and your sister out of the country where Kolya can never touch you again. Deal?"

Wide, blue eyes stare back at me, and he shakes his head vigorously. "You will fail. And Elena will die. We all will."

"I don't fail, kid." Jerking my thumb at my chest, I arch a brow. "Special Forces. The guy behind you is a SEAL, and she's the Rangers' deadliest sniper in the past fifteen years. We're your best shot at living through the next few days. But we need intel."

Semyon presses his lips together, determined not to speak. West grabs a handful of his hair and yanks his head back. "Listen, you little shit, all three of us are trained in enhanced interrogation. And we hate pulling those skills out of the deep, dark box they live in. Because it's messy. You're going to piss yourself. Bleed all over this couch. Probably shit yourself too. And you're definitely going to cry. In the end, you'll tell us whatever we want to know while begging us to kill you."

The kid looks from me to Inara. She shrugs and pulls a knife from a sheath strapped to her thigh. The serrated edge gleams in the light, and I shove down a laugh as she uses the tip to clean under one of her fingernails. There's a reason every movie on the planet uses that ploy. It works. At least on civilians.

"Okay, okay," Semyon squeaks. "You get Elena out? If I help you?"

Crouching down so we're at the same level, I hold his gaze. "We came here for you and Elena. We're not leaving without the two of you. But right now, Wren comes first."

He nods, relief spreading over his young face. "What do you need to know?"

Wren

Light pours through the frosted window, almost warm on my bare leg. I threw up again. A little. The bitter taste on my tongue makes me gag, and I try to stagger to my feet to reach the sink, but I crash to my knees, slip in the mess, and can't manage to force myself upright again.

"Ryker," I whisper to no one. "Where are you?"

How long does heroin last? It was dark when they locked me in here. And now it's not. I feel...hollow. Nothing but a shell of me left. I can't muster more than an ounce of energy to care, even though the fear starts to worm its way back into my mind, icy and cold.

"Wren?" Elena knocks at the door, then slips inside the bathroom. She has a washcloth in her hands, and as I try to shrink away from her, she turns on the water in the sink. "I clean you up."

"Help me." I can't manage more than a whisper, but I curl my fingers around her ankle. "Get me...out of here."

"He will kill me. Or make me wish I die." She shows no emotion, so resigned to her fate as she drags the warm cloth over my cheeks, rinses it out, and then cleans the dried vomit off my chest. The scratches burn, and I curl myself into a ball when she starts wiping up the floor. "He will not stop. You must give him what he want."

"I can't."

How long until I won't have a choice? Until I'll do anything Kolya asks?

"Zion...loved you."

Elena's tears spill over, dripping onto the floor, and she chokes back a sob. "I know. He was...my angel. Kolya tell me. What he do to Zion. Is my fault."

I reach for her hand, wincing as one of my many bruises

aches. Panic wraps its bony, icy fingers around my heart as a shadow falls over us, and Elena scurries away from me.

"I clean, baby. No more smell."

Kolya grabs her hair and pulls her head back as he gropes her through her thin, red dress. "Very good, kitten. Go to your room and I will bring you a reward."

Her nipples tighten under the silk, and the look in her eyes, I shudder as I recognize the raw need, the desperation. I'll be her soon, and I curl away, desperate to forget, to avoid more pain. Ryker's face flashes behind my swollen lids, and I try to hold on to him, to the memory of his voice, his touch. But when Kolya runs his rough hand down my arm and digs his fingers into the bruises, I cry out, and Ryker's gone.

"Tell me your password, sweet Red. I can take the pain away." His voice is almost kind now, and I want to give in. To let him do whatever he wants. "You will be happy here with me."

With him. Not with Ryker. I want to be happy with Ryker.

I can't let him get my password. No matter what he does to me. And I know he'll break me down. How much longer until I can't resist? Until I crave the nothingness heroin provides with every breath? I force myself to look up at him. "Make it stop," I whimper. "Please."

"Her tablet, Victor." Kolya sits me up against the wall, and I bring my knees up to try to shield my body from his lecherous gaze. When he has the tablet in his hand, he brushes my cheek with the backs of his knuckles. "Do this for me, sweet one and I will make sure you have your reward. No more pain. I promise."

My hand shakes as I press my thumb to the biometric sensor. The tablet beeps in error, and I try again, steadying the thin screen with my other hand. Fear tightens in my gut. I don't have a choice.

"Elena!" I whimper as I look over Victor's shoulder. The men both turn, and I yank the tablet out of Kolya's hands and slam it into the sink with all of my remaining strength. Glass shatters, and the tablet snaps in two. Blood wells from a cut on my left hand, and Kolya roars out an oath.

"You stupid bitch!" He grabs me by the hair, pulls me to my knees, and then punches me in the stomach. I retch, but there's nothing left for me to throw up. Gasping for breath, I'm helpless as he throws me against the wall.

"You think you can beat me, *cyka*? Soon, you will beg me to take the pain away. And I will refuse until you are screaming." With a vicious kick to my upper thigh, Kolya snarls at Blondie, "Bring her medicine."

"No more," I beg. "Please."

Panic squeezes my chest so tightly I can't breathe, and I claw at my neck, opening up the barely healing scratches. Blondie lights the candle, and Kolya slams my head back against the wall, leaving me too dazed to move as he ties the rubber around my arm.

I'm going to die. My heart will keep beating, but Wren will die. And maybe...maybe that will be for the best.

28

Wren

$\mathcal{F}$ ive times. Five times Kolya's come and drugged me. I think. Everything's blurring together now. I smell like bile and sweat and blood, and my stomach is twisting itself into a pretzel. And God. I'm so hungry. Except...when I'm not. Which is most of the time.

It's dark again outside the frosted glass window. Has it been one day? Two? How can I not know? Ryker hasn't come for me. If he's dead...Kolya would have told me. He wants me to suffer. To beg him for another dose of relief. But...why hasn't he tried to rescue me?

I stifle a sob as I remember Ryker's kiss. How he smelled. His touch. I...was so stupid. If I'd listened to him...maybe I'd be in his arms now. The walls shift and almost pulse as I force myself to my knees, my anxiety returning with a vengeance as my heart rate skyrockets.

My arms and legs feel like they weigh a ton, and my head pounds, the room spinning around me as I try to pull myself up.

I think...if Kolya plans to dose me again, he's late. I don't have a watch, and there's no clock in this bathroom. But though I'm weak, disoriented, and woozy, my thoughts are clearer now than they've been since he first drugged me.

Everything hurts. My ribs. My arms. My head. The last time he came...he was so angry with me he didn't even speak. Just wailed on me with his fists until my lip split and blood filled my mouth, half choking me. I begged then. Begged him to stop. To take the pain away.

I begged for him to drug me. The realization sends more tears streaming down my cheeks, and I wonder if I'll ever be able to stop crying.

Z explained to me once...what it felt like. Why he couldn't stop getting high.

"It's like you don't care about anything, Wren. All your problems... they just go away. I...hated myself. Hated my life. And heroin...took all my pain away."

Not just the pain. The terror. The sickening anticipation of what's coming next. I...remember...a little. As soon as the heroin hits my vein, I'm not afraid anymore. I don't hurt. Or...I don't care if I do...I'm not sure. It's like...I'm at peace.

I understand Z better now. His addiction. Because I want that peace. I *need* it. There's no anxiety. No panic. But...there's also no me.

The mirror shows the horrors of what he's done. Sunken, blackened eyes. Blood staining my lip and chin. Deep scratches down my neck and breasts. There's still vomit in my hair. I splash a little water on my face, cup my shaking hands under the flow and try to drink, but I can't hold more than a few drops at a time.

I'm so scared. Panic tightens a knot in my chest and I sink back down to the floor, my head between my knees. When I fall over, my fingers brush my ankles, tangling in the chain keeping me locked to the sink.

The sensation distracts me enough to draw in a shaky breath.

It's...almost thin. Forcing my head up, I rub my eyes to try to clear my vision. In college, I had a couple of epic hangovers, and this... this is ten times worse.

"Focus," I whisper to myself as I blink hard and stare at the chain. The cuff is thick. Maybe two inches tall and heavy. But the chain...I...I could break it. I think. If I get free...can I escape before he kills me?

Wedging my other foot against the pipe, I grab the cuff and pull as hard as I can. Not enough leverage. Maybe if I scoot over towards the toilet. I try again, and I think I feel a little give. Sweat dampens my brow, and my head pounds hard enough I fear it'll split in two, but with one final tug, the chain snaps, and I tumble back, my head slamming into the porcelain bowl.

I lie there panting, willing my ankle to stop sending sparks of pain racing up my calf. I don't know how long it takes me to move. Five minutes maybe—though my sense of time is so warped, it could be an hour.

Ten inches of chain hang from the cuff, and I wrap it around my ankle, tucking the end between the cuff and my skin. On my hands and knees, I crawl towards the door, but stop with my hand on the knob. I need a weapon. Even as weak as I am...something.

But this bathroom is as empty as I am. Tears choke me as I look wildly around the room until I remember...the toilet tank has a metal float arm inside. It's not much, but it's something.

My stomach pitches as I lift the lid, but Kolya seems to be obsessed with cleanliness. This bathroom is spotless. Elena cleaned up all of my messes, and I swipe at my cheeks as I remember the last time I saw her. Strung out, Kolya's handprint across her cheek.

Focus. Weapon. Escape

The metal arm snaps off easily, and I take a few unsteady steps towards the door.

A wave of dizziness threatens to send me back down to my

knees, but I force a deep breath, lean against the wall, and press my cheek to the cool wood door. *You can do this, Wren. Get out.*

Cringing as I crack the door, I expect Kolya to be standing on the other side, laughing with a syringe in his hand. But the bedroom is empty. The lavish, four-poster bed takes up much of the space, and my bare feet land on thick, plush carpet.

I'm halfway across the room when I hear his voice. "Wait downstairs," he says. "I am tired of her resistance. She needs additional...motivation. And the first time I take her...should be private."

Oh God. He's going to rape me. I barely have time to slide my pitiful weapon under the pillows before he slams the door, his lips curled into a snarl.

"Clever girl," he says as he stalks towards me.

"Please..." I throw up my hands. "I...I need...more." I have to try to convince him I'm not a threat. "Don't...leave me...like this..." Forcing myself to take a step towards him, I plead, "I need you to...take the pain away."

His eyes narrow, blond, bushy brows drawing together as he dangles a syringe from his fingers. "You want this, sweet Red? Medicine to make everything fun again?"

"Yes. Please." I'm so scared, my whole body is shaking, and if I can't get out of this room in the next few minutes, I'll pass out, and he'll do...God knows what to me.

The syringe lands on the bed. "Not yet." Kolya lunges for me, and I'm too slow, too weak to get away. His fingers tighten on my arm, hard enough to leave yet another bruise, and he spins me around and bends me over the bed. I yelp and thrash, but he pins my arms at the small of my back. "I am not going to kill you, sweet Red. I am going to keep you. And I want you to understand what that means."

"No!" I scream. "Don't!" He's hard already, grinding against me through his pants. "Get off of me!"

Kolya laughs, pulls a thin rope from the nightstand, and has it looped around my wrists in a few seconds. Helpless, terrified, I kick him, and I must find his dick, because he goes down with a groan. I have to get free. I aim another kick in the same general area, and this time, I hit his balls.

Working my wrists, I rub them raw in seconds, but he never knotted the rope, and it starts to loosen. My right hand pops free, and I lunge for my hidden weapon. Swinging wildly, I connect with the side of his head.

"*Cyka!* Kolya growls as blood wells at his temple. My pitiful strike did nothing but daze him and piss him off, and I try again, grunting as I bring the metal down on the top of his skull. But the impact sends the piece of metal clattering to the floor, and I scramble back, almost falling on my ass. The needle glints in the lights. Can I dose him before he overpowers me?

I pause for a single second, the lure of not caring when he rapes me stronger than I expect, but then I hear Ryker's voice in my head. *"I care, Wren. I care."*

If he's alive, I have to get out of here and get back to him. Because...I care too. More than I knew. Snatching the needle from the bed, I lunge at Kolya. He tries to knock my arm away, but my knee lands on his already abused dick, and his reflexes kick in, his hands trying to protect his family jewels. My heartbeat roars in my ears, and my fingers tremble, but I make a fist and punch him in the eye. Pain sings up my arm. I grab a metal lamp from the nightstand and swing it towards his forehead. But it's too heavy, and it glances off his temple. Still...it's enough to make him slump to the floor.

Forcing a deep breath, I angle his head and aim for the pulsing vein on the side of his neck. *Please. Please work.* As soon as the needle pierces his skin, I depress the plunger.

Koyla lunges for me, and I go down hard as he jerks my ankle. But his grip loosens a few seconds later, and he groans, then curls into a ball. His limbs move slowly, like he doesn't quite know how arms and legs work, and as I watch, his entire body goes slack.

"Hey, asshole." I should run. He doesn't answer, and I wave my hand in front of his face. His eyes barely track my movements. I stumble towards the bedroom door, then realize I'm naked. A wave of nausea has me retching, but there's nothing left in my stomach to throw up. Still, my eyes water, and I can't move until the sensation passes. *Get your marbles together, Wren. Find your stuff and get the hell out of here.*

There. In the corner by the bathroom. My bag. I destroyed my tablet, but dammit...I don't want him to have anything of mine. My shredded clothes are gone, and I try to remove his shirt— needing *something* to cover my body, but I can't manage the tiny mother-of-pearl buttons. The ankle chain digs deeper into my skin as I creep towards the door. Listening carefully, I hear laughter, but it's far away, like maybe downstairs, and when I peer out into the hall, I'm alone.

With one last glance back at Kolya, who's staring at the ceiling with a blissed out look on his face, I creep towards the stairs. But voices head my way, and I stifle my gasp as I dart into another room and try to quietly shut the door.

Kolya's office. The chair he tied me to still sits in the middle of the room, righted now. On the desk, his computer is on...and Cracker Jacks...unlocked. I crouch down, ready to dive under the desk if the door opens. But when nothing happens after a few minutes, I stare at his computer screen.

Elena copied a lot of his financial records. But not everything. The men outside the door are joking and laughing, and I'm trapped. Digging into my bag, I pull out a USB stick and slide it into his computer. My breath catches in my chest as the progress bar fills the screen. All of those idiotic espionage shows where a rogue hacker transfers the contents of someone's hard drive in five minutes, whispering, "come on, come on, come on," at the screen? Total horsepucky. But my little drive installs a trojan so I can access his computer from the safe house. If I ever get back there.

Fifty percent, sixty, seventy... I glance at the door, praying the men don't come in here. Or go check on Kolya. At one hundred percent, I yank the stick out of the drive and tuck it into my bag. I need the encryption key on it to open the portal.

I stand up too quickly, and the room spins around me. A moan escapes my lips before I can control myself, and the voices stop. Looking around wildly, I stumble over to French doors that lead out onto a balcony. I can't fight. I have to get out of here now.

My first try, my hand is so sweaty and shaky it slips off the handle. Rubbing my palm on my bare thigh, I try again, and an icy wind chills me to the bone. The door snicks shut, and I creep towards the far end of the balcony.

The freezing concrete makes the soles of my feet tingle. I suck in a breath, my lungs rattling. Crashing to my hands and knees, I sway, falling against the metal railing.

In the dim light seeping through the drapes, I catch sight of the multiple, red, swollen puncture marks from Kolya's injections.

Move, Wren.

My fingers curl around the top of the railing, and I pull myself up, staring down at the frosty ground four stories below. I can't... I'm trapped. My chest tightens, and I wheeze, fighting for breath as I search for any possible escape.

An awning one floor down. But it's so far away. I'll have to jump from this balcony to the next. And the next. Then let myself fall. I can't do this. I'll die.

Except...I'll die here if I don't try.

Throwing my leg over the freezing metal, I struggle to focus. *Fight through it. You can panic when you're free.*

I catch my foot when I try to jump to the next balcony, and

flop over the other railing, the impact driving the air from my lungs.

My head hits the concrete as I crash to the ground. "Get up, Wren. Keep moving."

Dizzy, shivering, and desperate, I scramble over the next railing and leap, barely managing to stay on my feet. Oh Cracker Jacks. This balcony is at the end of the upstairs hallway. And the drapes are open. Shadows move in my periphery, and as I reach the corner closest to the awning, muffled shouts send terror coursing through me. Blondie and the Groper burst through the doors, guns drawn.

I don't think—can't, anyway—and let myself tumble down onto the awning. I roll, unable to stop myself, until I fall off the edge with a scream.

As I hit the concrete on the second floor, my knee explodes in pain. A shot pierces the still, quiet night and my left arm starts to burn. Screaming, I throw my hands over my head, curling into a ball.

Another shot splinters the concrete a few inches away. Everything hurts. I can barely breathe, and when I try to push myself up, my arm collapses under me. *Move. Move. Move or die.*

"Wren!"

Ryker's panicked shout is so close. I'm hallucinating.

"Wren. Get up! Now!"

Oh my God. He's really here. The look in his eyes—terror, pain, desperation. He'll save me. If I can get to him.

The next shot comes from below, followed by three more, and my heart leaps into my throat. Glass shatters, raining down on me as another sound, more solid, lower, echoes from across the street.

"Wren! Please! Jump, baby. Jump and run."

Bullets fly overhead, and I squeeze my eyes shut. I can do this.

White hot pain pulses through my arm, but I grab onto the

railing and haul myself to my feet. The ground is so far away. But there's Ryker. Firing more shots over my head.

Fear glues my bare feet to the concrete until the Groper lands on the other end of the balcony. "You will be sorry, *cyka*."

Another dull thud, and red blooms on his white shirt. He clutches his chest, sinking to his knees, and I throw myself over the edge, praying Ryker will catch me.

29

Ryker

*W*ren falls, and I'm a second too late. Her legs crumple under her, a gasp escaping her lips, followed by a moan, and then her eyes flutter closed. Firing another five shots towards Kolya's men, I kneel at her side. "She's down. Not moving. Cover me."

"Roger. Four hostiles north corner," Inara says calmly. A shot flies across the square. "Three."

Blood stains the frosty grass under her naked body, and she's covered in bruises. Sliding my arms under her, I cradle her to my chest. "Fall back!" I shout.

"Hostiles neutralized. Falling back." Inara clicks off comms, and I run for the next street over.

"Stay with me, sweetheart," I whisper. "You're going to be okay."

Will she? There isn't an inch of her unmarked, and she's so cold, her skin is almost blue.

As I skid around a corner, the car—with West at the wheel—

screeches to a stop right in front of me, and I yank open the door and fall into the backseat. "Go, go, go."

"Elena?" West asks.

"No sign of her. Got a hundred yards away and saw Wren climbing across the fucking balconies." Brushing her hair away from her face, I watch her breathing. Shallow, but as I bite down on the tip of my glove to pull it off so I can check her pulse, her eyelids flutter.

"Wren? Can you hear me?"

A little whimper escapes her chapped and split lips, and my instinct is to tighten my grip, but I don't know if she broke anything in the fall. "I've got you, baby. You're safe now. But you have to tell me what hurts."

"Ry?" The single word is so faint I only hear her because I'm watching her lips so carefully.

"Right here."

She turns her head into my chest and starts to cry, and I give up being careful, crushing her against me and rubbing her back as West takes a corner on two wheels, slams on the brakes, and leans over to open Inara's door.

"Holy shit. Your girl's insane," Inara says as she tosses her gear bag next to us and turns in the seat. "And braver than half the guys in my last unit."

"She doesn't like being called a girl." The retort comes out sharper than I intended, and I curse under my breath. "Sorry. Turn up the heat in here. She's an icicle." Wren's tears soak into my shirt, and her entire body shakes in my arms.

"She's naked." Inara shrugs out of her jacket and hands it to me. "Put this on her." I don't want to let Wren go long enough to get her arms through the sleeves, so I just drape the black material around her upper body.

The clink of metal draws my gaze to her legs. "Fuck. Get me a pair of bolt cutters." The thick metal cuff on her ankle is bloody, several inches of chain dangling from a ring on one side.

Her hair's matted and dirty, and there are deep fingertip bruises around her neck. I can't tell what else is wrong in this position, but as long as she's breathing, the rest...we'll deal with together.

Inara leans into the back seat and rummages around in her bag, coming away with a pair of heavy-duty shears. "I'll take care of it." A couple of cuts and a curse later—mine as Inara nicks Wren's pale skin—the metal falls to the floor.

Halfway to the safe house, Wren's sobs fade away, and her body goes slack. Asleep or unconscious, I don't know, but I can feel her heartbeat, and it's steady. My mind won't stop racing. Thinking about all of the horrors Kolya could have put her through.

West meets my gaze in the rear view mirror. "Semyon's going to be pissed."

"Keep him the fuck away from Wren. We're not abandoning the mission. Yet. Not until she can tell me what happened to her. But we're sure as shit not going back there unless we *know* we can destroy him."

"I killed six." Inara pulls off her black cap and runs a hand through her short-cropped hair. "If Semyon's numbers were right, we're still looking at fifteen of Kolya's loyal muscle men, plus his team of runners. Though hell, some of those kids might easily be turned to our side."

West and Inara run a short post-op analysis as we weave through the darkened city streets, but I don't pay attention. West and I were on opposite sides of the building when I saw a door open out onto a fourth floor balcony and Wren stumbled outside. I didn't think. Told West the op was FUBAR and headed straight for Wren.

After West pulls the car around the back of the safe house, Inara opens my door. "Take care of her. We'll get the gear."

I pause for a beat, holding Inara's gaze. I don't have the words. I never do—except with Wren. But Inara added six to her tally sheet tonight. Every one takes a toll on her. And she did it for me. For Wren.

"Go," she says quietly as she lays her hand on my arm and squeezes. "We're square."

We're not. I'll owe her for the rest of my life for this. But I nod and carry Wren straight into the bathroom. She's still freezing. Once I have warm water running into the tub, I sit with her in my lap and take off my boots. "Sweetheart, can you hear me?"

Wren flinches, and her entire body stiffens. "No, not again... no more...I can't..."

"Wren. Wake up. You're safe. It's Ry. Open your eyes and look at me."

Cupping her cheek, I run my thumb gently over her lips. When she forces her eyes open, they're so bloodshot, I can barely see any white in them, and her pupils struggle to focus. "Ry? Oh God. Ry. You're...real." Fresh tears tumble over her cheeks, and I brush them away.

"I want to get you into the tub, baby. You're freezing."

"Don't let go."

It's not easy stripping out of my pants, socks, and shirt while holding on to an injured woman, but I manage. And then I shift her and get my first good look at her body. *I'm going to kill him. Slowly. Painfully. And I'm going to make sure he knows every scream, every cut, every broken bone is payback for what he did to her.*

Her arms bear multiple distinct finger bruises, and blood runs down her left bicep, to her elbow, and half down to her wrist. Long scratches mar her neck and breasts. Ligature marks on her wrists. A fucking boot print on her side, right under her ribs. Deep purple and black spread across her hip. I'm too terrified to look lower. What if he raped her?

I rest a tentative hand on her thigh, and when she doesn't flinch, I release the breath I'm holding. "Is this okay?"

She must understand my hesitation, because she blinks hard and reaches for my cheek. Her hand shakes as her fingers skim my jaw, and she whispers, "He didn't. He tried, but I stopped him."

Thank fuck. I shove my briefs down my legs, kick out of them, and sink down with her into the tub.

"Hurts," she whimpers. "Too hot."

"It's only because you're so cold, baby. Give it a minute or two. I promise it'll feel better soon."

Ten minutes later, she's stopped shivering, and I pull the plug. The water's red from the blood still trickling from her arm, but the wound isn't serious. "Can you stand?"

She looks up at me, pain, fear, and shame welling in her eyes. "N-no. I don't think...I'm so tired. Everything hurts. Make it stop..." Panic swallows her words, and she struggles to pull away.

"What? What do you want? Anything, Wren. Name it."

"He...Kolya...told me...oh God. He was right. I can't... breathe..." Her voice rises in pitch, and she starts to wheeze, her fingers curling around my bicep.

"Listen to me, baby. You're safe. He's never going to hurt you again. Do you understand me?"

"He...every time...it was worse...I tried to fight...but...I don't want to hurt anymore."

What the fuck? Calm her down. Now.

"Wren. Repeat these numbers. Twelve, two, ninety-seven, sixty-one, five." I don't know if she's coherent enough to hear me, but I have to get her panic under control before I can find out what's wrong.

She loses focus after the third number. "Ry..."

I do the only thing I can. I kiss her. Cupping the back of her head, I brush my lips to hers, then trace the seam with my tongue. My dick rises to attention, jutting firmly against her ass, and she parts for me, letting me in for several seconds before she pulls away with tears brimming in her eyes.

"I need...to tell you...show...you..." Her head bobs a little as she tries to extricate her left arm from between us, and I gently take her wrist and help her. Ice creeps through my veins, despite the steam filling the bath. Half a dozen needle marks dot the inside of her elbow.

"Heroin." The pieces start to fall into place, and it's almost like I can hear them click together. The scratches on her chest and breasts. The dazed look in her eyes. The scent of bile in her hair. Kolya drugged her. "How many times?"

"Dunno. Nothing hurt then. And everything hurts now."

"Wren, listen to me. When was your last dose?" I cup her cheek, rubbing my thumb in small circles over a patch of unbruised skin.

"Wore off. I could think again. Had to...get out."

"A few hours then. Five, six at least. I promise, baby. You'll feel better after I get you clean and we sleep a while."

Her eyes unfocus, and though she's staring right at me, I don't think she sees me. "You...?"

"I *promise*, Wren. I know what that word means to you. And I promise. I'll take care of you. He won't hurt you again. We'll get through this. Whatever you need, I'll be here."

The words catch in my throat. The three words I knew I had to say to her the moment I saw her fall off that balcony. But my promise must be enough, because she rests her head on my shoulder and whispers, "I believe you."

30

Ryker

"Arms around my neck, sweetheart. Can you hold on long enough for me to wash your hair?"

"I...think so. I'm so tired, Ry."

Stepping under the spray, I help her tip her head back, then start to massage shampoo into her hair. "I know. We'll sleep in a few minutes. Tell me what hurts."

"Everything," she murmurs against my chest. "How long did... he have me?"

"Thirty-three hours." I could tell her the minutes. Tell her how I kept checking my watch. Pacing. How West threatened to tie me up next to Semyon if I didn't stop hovering over his shoulder.

"I kept hoping...you'd come for me."

The sudden tightness in my chest steals my breath. If she'd shot me, I'd be in less pain. "I'm so sorry, baby. I..."

"S'okay. I know...Kolya had too many men."

As the blood and dirt wash down the drain, Wren falls silent, and I don't know if she'll ever truly come back to me. Not after what that bastard put her through. Thirty-three hours. *Thirty-three hours.* Even if she spent much of it high, her body shows the horrors he visited upon her, and I'd bet my life he didn't hurt her until the drugs wore off.

I keep my touch light as I skim my hands over her mound, her hip, her ass. She doesn't react—to anything—and I whisper her name. "Wren?"

"Uh huh."

Thank God she's still with me. "Let's get you into bed, okay?"

"Uh huh."

Maneuvering a limp woman into a sweatshirt and fleece pants isn't easy. Not with her injuries. But I bandage her arm and ankle, and then sit her up against my chest and press one of her daily anxiety pills to her lips. "Open, baby."

"No. No drugs." Her whimper holds so much fear, but she needs this. Needs to feel...normal again.

"It's just your anxiety medication, Wren. The one you take every night. Trust me. You need this."

She's too out of it to protest more, and after a sip of water, I lay her down, and she's asleep almost immediately.

I won't leave her side, despite the curses and sounds of scuffling coming from the main room. Semyon's understandably worried about his sister, but Wren was always my priority. And as far as we know, Elena wasn't in mortal danger tonight. Wren was.

I watch Wren until I can't stay awake any longer. Then I wrap my arms around her and bury my nose in her damp curls. "I'm so sorry," I whisper. "I'll never fail you again."

"Ry?" Her weak voice permeates my dreams, and I'm instantly awake.

"What is it? What do you need?"

"I don't feel well. I think...I'm going to be sick."

I scoop her up in my arms and carry her into the bathroom. She retches, but nothing comes up. "I don't...know what's...wrong."

"When was the last time you ate?" I brush her hair back from her face, and I see the answer before she says a word. "Fuck, baby. I'll get you something. What do you want?"

"Don't leave me." Wren clutches my arms, and the fear in her voice shatters something inside me.

"I won't. West and Inara are here. You want McDonald's? I'll send one of them."

She collapses against me, winding her arms around my waist. "I want to forget."

"I know. But let's start with some food, okay?" Everything she's feeling...I understand. I had the same thoughts when I escaped Hell. She'll never forget. Not really. And a rational Wren wouldn't want to. This Wren...she's terrified. In pain. And too raw to understand what she's feeling.

I carry her back to our makeshift bed and text West.

McDonald's. Big Macs and Fries. Cokes. She hasn't eaten in more than 36 hours. Please.

A few seconds later, I hear the front door open and shut. "Talk to me, Wren."

"It won't change anything." She tries to turn over, but something hurts, and she hisses out a breath. "Shit."

"Shit? No Cracker Jacks? Fudgsicles? Shoot the Moon?" I ghost my knuckle along her cheek, just below one of the darker bruises. "I was working on my own variations for you. Like...'go to Hollywood' or 'shut the fudge shop.'"

One corner of her mouth twitches in what might be a hint of a smile. "I...don't mind if you swear...like a normal person."

"Oh, I'll always swear, sweetheart. You don't have to worry about that. You spend as long as I did in the army, you can't help it." I ease her against me, mindful of her various bruises. "But before I enlisted, I was a kindergarten teacher."

"What?" For the first time since she escaped, her voice holds an emotion other than fear. "You're just trying to distract me."

"Is it working?" I duck my head and press a kiss to her temple. "I'll never lie to you, Wren. I taught little rug rats for three years before 9/11. Loved every single minute of it."

"Why didn't you go back?" Her words slur a bit, but she relaxes into my embrace and trails her fingers over one of the thicker scars on my chest.

Now that I have her back in my arms, I refuse to hide behind the walls I've built and reinforced for years. She's too important. She's mine, and I want to be hers. But there's a fuck ton of shit she needs to know about me first. Still, I don't know how to admit my truth.

"When I went home...for the first time after Hell...no one recognized me." All of a sudden, I'm back in Quincy, knocking on my aunt's door. "Mom and Pop were gone already. So was my brother. But my Aunt Lindsay was still alive. Her son—my cousin—has two little girls. Well, they're teenagers now. Nicole was seven. She answered the door. Then...screamed and ran for her grandma."

Wren's fingers tangle with mine, and I try not to grip her hand too hard. Her knuckles are bruised and raw.

"Brittany—she was two years older—told me I was a monster. And my aunt...she asked me to leave because I was scaring the kids."

"Oh God. Ryker. She's your family."

"Not anymore. I walked away, got in the car, and drove straight to the airport. Caught the next flight to Seattle." I bend my arm under my head and stare up at the ceiling. "Figured if my own family couldn't stand to look at me, a classroom full of kids wouldn't want to either."

A knock at the door makes Wren jump.

"Food," Inara calls. "Can I come in?"

I want to say no—I'm only wearing a pair of basketball shorts, and Inara's never seen the worst of my scars. But as I glance around, I realize all my clean clothes are in the living room. And Wren needs to eat. "Yeah."

My wounded little bird curls against me when the door opens, regarding Inara with a wary, nervous gaze. But the scent of french fries and greasy burgers makes her stomach growl.

"Wren?" Kneeling next to us, Inara holds out her hand. I don't expect Wren to move...not as weak and scared as she's been, but she pushes herself up to her knees with some effort and hugs Inara.

"Thank you," she says quietly.

Inara gently pats Wren's back and whispers something in her ear before the two women part. "You have Big Macs, Chicken McNuggets, fries, Cokes, and three kids meals in there."

"Holy shit. You do realize Wren's all of a hundred pounds soaking wet, don't you?" I peer into the bag and suddenly realize how hungry I am.

"I do. And you haven't eaten since she was taken either, asshole." With a jab to my shoulder and a quick glance at my scarred chest, Inara pushes to her feet. "Besides, what better way to throw any potential tail off my scent than to order three kids meals."

"She has a point," Wren says as she pulls out a hamburger and peels off the wrapper.

Inara pauses at the threshold and turns back to us. "We're monitoring the cameras. So far, there's no indication they know where we are. You're safe, Wren. And we'll make sure you stay that way. West is working on a new plan to save Elena right now, and as soon as you're okay to travel, we'll get her and get the fuck out of Russia."

After Inara closes the door, Wren turns to me, a bit of ketchup smearing the corner of her mouth. "West is here? He's...the other member of your team, right?"

"The damn fool postponed his own fucking wedding." I tear into a Big Mac, pausing only to swipe the little red smear from Wren's cheek. Not eating for twenty-four hours was stupid. If my reaction time had been any slower, I could have gotten her killed. "I didn't ask him to come."

One hamburger gone and another half-eaten, Wren stops and reaches for my hand. All I see every time I look at her is the bruises. The pain behind her eyes. But she links our fingers and holds on tight. "They're your family, Ry. They've always *been* your family. You just didn't see it."

"They work for me," I say after a swig of Coke.

"Bullpucky." She tries a smile, and though it's lopsided and doesn't light up her eyes like it did before she was taken, I think something's settled inside her. "They care about you. And you care about them. Why is that so hard for you to admit?"

Because I hurt everyone I care about.

"Ry?" Wren sets the half-eaten carton of fries back in the bag and scoots closer to me, a grimace of pain twisting her lips until she blows out a breath. "I...I care about you."

I should tell her. Everything. Say those three words I've never said to anyone. But...if I do, I'll fail her. Like I failed Dax. And West. And Inara. Like I failed my brother. And most of all, like I failed myself.

The light in her eyes fades, and she picks up her soda and takes a long drink. "I'm going to sleep a while now. You won't leave?"

"No, baby. I won't leave." As she slides under the sleeping bag, I want to run as far and as fast as I can. But a promise is a promise, and despite my fear, I love this woman. And I'll try as hard as I can to never let her down.

Wren

Ryker groans quietly and drapes his arm around me. I wish I could sleep, but I'm about to crawl out of my skin. Every time I close my eyes, I hear Koyla threatening me. Or feel the needle piercing my vein. I can't settle.

After what I now know was more than twenty-four hours chained to a sink in a tiny bathroom, I feel like the walls are closing in on me. But...at the same time, everything's just...too much. Every sensation is magnified a thousand times. I can't get comfortable. Falling off the balcony bruised my tailbone, jammed my shoulder, and twisted my knee. I don't even know if I can walk. Ryker carried me to this little oasis he created. Three sleeping bags, candles all around the room—thankfully unlit as I don't know if I'd be able to handle them right now—a bottle of water and food within reach, and him.

Every time I came back to my senses after the drugs, I half-expected him to be there. Rescuing me. Protecting me. I know why he couldn't. Too many guns. Too many men. But the disappointment...it's one of the only feelings I can remember besides fear. And...the relief, every time Kolya depressed that plunger. A moment of complete and utter terror, and then...nothing.

I wish I could feel nothing again.

Unable to lie still another second, I try to slide out from under Ryker's arm, and beads click together. Oh my God. He found my bracelet. The lump in my throat threatens to choke me as I ease the band off his wrist and onto mine, praying he won't wake up. He'll want to talk, and I...just can't.

Across the room, a single window is covered with a thick blanket. Ryker's doing. Privacy. Making sure no one knows this house is occupied—or how many people are here. I need to see out. Need to see something besides four walls crushing me.

Not trusting my legs, I use my hands to scoot myself across the floor on my less-bruised hip. My eyes burn at how broken I feel—how broken I *am*—but I won't let myself cry any more. I can't. After I pull out the tacks holding the bottom of the blanket in place, I peel back a corner and stare out at the deserted street.

Without lamplight, I can see the stars, and I run my fingers over the beads around my wrist. One. Two. Three. Four. Five. Z used to do the same thing. He said it calmed him when he wanted to use.

Z...I'm so sorry. I never understood you. Not truly. Not until now.

If I had...would things be different? Would I be back in Boston with him? Safe? Cocooned in my own little bubble with Pixel on my lap watching *Firefly* for the fiftieth time?

My lower lip wobbles as I try to shove my emotions back down where they can't hurt me. If I'd known what Z was going through, would I have met Ryker? He's the one good spot in my life. The one thing I know I need. Want.

Staring at his face, relaxed in sleep like it never is when he's awake, I wish I'd listened to him. I never should have gone after Semyon. Maybe then...we'd still have a chance. Because now...I don't even know if *I* have a chance. Or if I want one.

31

Ryker

The chill at my side wakes me from a deep sleep, and I sit up, looking around wildly until I see her curled by the window, a flap of the blanket pulled back so she can stare into the street.

"Get away from the window," I snap and claw my way out of the sleeping bag. I'm at her side in three steps, pulling her into my arms. "What the hell were you doing?"

In the dim light from the single bulb, her eyes shine, wide and terrified, the pale green almost gray. "It's...too much," she whispers.

"What's too much?" I smooth a hand over her hair, and she leans into my touch one moment, then tries to scoot away the next. "Talk to me, Wren."

"Everything. All of it." Her breath catches in her throat as she extricates herself from my arms and leans back against the wall. Fingering her bracelet—the one suddenly no longer around my wrist—she counts silently, fighting against her anxiety and panic.

I scramble for her pill case, find a Xanax, and press it into her palm.

"Take this, sweetheart. Then come back to bed and tell me what's wrong."

Instead of swallowing the pill, she holds it up to the light, turning it over and over between her fingers. "It's worse now. Knowing there's an alternative."

She's speaking in half sentences and generalizations, and I can't put the pieces together. But I feel like I'm losing her. "What's worse? What alternative? Baby, you have to tell me what's going on in that head of yours. You're scaring me."

Her entire body shudders as she forces a breath, and the pill falls to the floor. Scooping it up, I try to hand it back to her, but she shakes her head gingerly. "Z had anxiety and panic attacks his whole life. Mine...didn't get bad until college. I thought...I thought I had them under control." Gesturing to the pill in my hand, she offers me a weak smile. "Even though Xanax never took all the pain away, never left me feeling...totally calm. But Zion... he found the secret."

Wren stares up at me, uncertainty welling in her eyes. "What do I do now that I know the secret too? I can't forget it." Her voice lowers, fading away to almost nothing. "I was terrified. Kolya locked me to a pipe in his bathroom. And he made me watch. He had his men hold me down while he cooked the heroin and told me how I'd do anything once he had me hooked. I'd tell him anything he wanted to know."

"You're—" She holds up her hand and shakes her head before I can tell her she's okay, that she only had a taste, and she's strong enough to know drugs aren't the answer.

Swallowing hard, she presses her lips together, and I spot the tremble. The struggle for control. I can't move. Every piece of me aches to hold her, but whatever this is...she has to get through it.

"I've never been so scared. Until he drugged me. And then...I felt nothing. No fear. No pain. It was like...I was at peace for the first time in my entire life. Nothing mattered. *Nothing.* And every time he came for me...he'd let the effects wear off just enough so I'd be afraid. And he'd beat me and threaten and taunt, until I'd start to shake or cry or cower, and then he'd dose me, and it felt... so good. Like all my problems went away."

"But it wasn't *real*, sweetheart."

A tear balances along her lower lid. "I know. But you don't understand... When I escaped...he was late, I think. I felt...more clear-headed. And I realized the chain he used was so thin, I could probably break it. So I did. But before I got out of his bedroom, he came in with another dose, and a threat. He was going to rape me. Make me his. And I was going to feel every-thing because he wasn't going to give me the drug until he was done."

Rage sparks across my skin, the heat of it setting me ablaze as I ball my hands into fists and try not to scare Wren any more than she already is. I want to destroy Kolya. Piece by piece, and I want to make sure he's conscious for every fucking second.

Wren stifles a sob. "I fought him off, kicked him in the balls a couple of times." A little snort, almost a laugh, mixes with her next sniffle. "And then I saw the needle. And, Ry...I *thought about it.* Did I want to use it on him and try to escape? Or use it on myself so I wouldn't care when he raped me?"

Somewhere under my anger, understanding dawns. Why she's so scared. Why she can't fully trust that I'll protect her.

"It's so much worse now," she says softly. "Knowing I could make all my fear and pain go away, if I were willing to pay the price."

For a few seconds, I don't move. Wren runs her fingers over her bracelet, and I let her finish her ritual before I offer her my hand. "Can I hold you, Wren? I...need you to know about Hell."

Wren

I don't know if I can settle against him, but he needs me. It's in the timber of his voice, the sadness in his eyes, the arch of his brow. So I nod, and he helps me shift onto my side, the sleeping bags cocooning us. He's chilled, and for as long as I've known him, he's always been warm.

"Intel is everything in war. We had this new guy working the radios. And he screwed up. Forgot to encrypt the signal. So the enemy knew exactly where my team was going to be. But they didn't know why we were there."

The rumble of his voice soothes me, and the hard knot in my chest lessens slightly.

"We were pinned down on the side of a mountain. No way up or down. I lost three men in the fire fight. The rest of us...we ran out of ammo. Couldn't raise ComSat on the radio to have them send backup. So...we surrendered." Ryker takes a deep breath. "Five of us. Hab, Ripper, Gose, Dax, and me. We knew they'd make our lives hell. Knew we'd be separated. Tortured. But...we didn't have any idea how bad it'd be.

"They knew who we were. Capturing a Special Forces team? Taking their commander alive? Shit. They were celebrities. Hab died pretty quick. Lucky bastard."

Lucky? I peer up at Ryker, but he's not here with me anymore. He stares at the ceiling, his arm around my back, but his mind— and heart—back in Afghanistan.

"For a couple of months, we were paraded in front of every Taliban bigwig, beaten to shit, starved. And then...they sent us to Hell."

"Where were you before?" I ask to bring him back to me.

"Somewhere near the Uzbeki border. In a wood and cement block building where we could sometimes see the sun." Longing tinges his voice, and he sighs. "That place was a fucking paradise compared to Hell. The insurgents dug out a massive cave system under a mountain. Built a dozen cells. A couple of deep holes they'd throw us down and cover with plywood. If you went into the hole, you stayed there until you were so disoriented, you didn't remember your name."

"Ryker," I whisper, but he doesn't hear me.

"It's easy to turn a person into an animal. Easier than most people expect."

Running my fingers over one of the jagged scars across his chest, I try to comfort him, but he covers my hand with his and holds me still. For an hour, he talks. The stories they all stuck to —as long as they could. Ripper's disappearance. How for months, they'd torture Ryker in front of Dax, trying to break both of them. I can sense this strong, capable man struggling not to fall apart in front of me. His voice roughens, and he's so tense, I fear he'll shatter into a million pieces.

"As bad as it was," he whispers, "there are worse things than a life of torture."

"My God. What could be worse?"

He flinches, like he forgot I was there, and buries his nose in my curls, inhaling deeply. "You always smell like honeysuckle," he muses.

"Ry?"

With a sharp shake of his head, he gazes down at me. "Getting out. Trying to...fit back in with society. Reclaiming a normal life."

"You wouldn't go back there...?"

"Fuck no. But at first? I couldn't sleep. Anywhere. Everything smelled too clean. I spent fifteen months surrounded by the scent of shit, fear, sweat, and blood. Catching a few minutes of sleep at a time on rocky, uneven ground, usually tied up. Even the hospital floor was too soft for me." Ryker shifts his legs under our sleeping bag and almost chuckles. "I hadn't seen a blanket—or even a shirt—in six months. The nurses weren't thrilled to come into the hospital room and find me naked on the floor. I scared them."

"I'm sure you didn't—"

"I wasn't a man then, sweetheart." He plays with a lock of my hair, his voice going raspy again. "The quiet killed me. Screams, begging, the shouts of our guards? That's how I could tell my men were still alive. My first year out? I had to find a horror movie on TV just so I could catch a couple of hours."

Silence fills the room, and I want to ask Ryker how he found his way back. I feel so lost. Except...he had fifteen months of torture a million times worse than I could have imagined. And I was Kolya's plaything for a day.

"You want to know how you forget the secret? How you don't turn to something that makes the whole world fall away? How you know even if you're tempted, you're strong enough to resist?"

"Yes," I whisper.

"You find something real. Something to hold on to." Cupping the back of my head, he threads his fingers through my hair and kisses me. My entire body reacts to his possessive claim, the rumble in his throat, the hardness of his cock pressing against my thigh. By the time he pulls away, I'm wet and all I want in this moment is more. More kissing. More touching. More...Ryker.

But he rises up on an elbow and holds my gaze. "This is real. *You're* real. *We're* real. I won't lie to you and tell you it'll be easy. But I will promise you one thing."

"What?" I'm not proud of the need in my voice or how my fingers are digging into his side.

"You'll never be alone. I love you, Wren."

I draw in a sharp breath, and he cuts off my reply with a chaste kiss. "Don't say anything, baby. Please. Just...let me hold you tonight and trust me to keep your demons away—like you've banished so many of mine."

32

Wren

I didn't expect to sleep, but when I open my eyes, light seeps from behind the tacked down drapes. Ryker is curled around me, our fingers intertwined.

"I love you, Wren."

I wanted to tell him how I feel. But...like so many times since we met, he protected me. I think...I do love him. I know I want him. Need him. But he was right to stop me. If I say the words—when I say the words—I want to feel like...me. Not the old me. I'll never be the woman who left Boston with him again. But...a version of me who knows the temptation of heroin and doesn't want it to be the answer.

I'm not there yet. As I stretch my legs under the soft sleeping bags, pain lances through my hips, and the bullet wound to my arm burns. I'm terrified Kolya will find us—me—again, and I'll be back in that bathroom, trying desperately not to beg for the blessed release of oblivion.

Ryker's real. And he loves me. And for today...that's enough.

Maybe more than enough. Staring down at my coping mechanism—the green and purple beads I never wanted to be without—I ease my bracelet back over his hand, then run my fingers along the beads. Right now, I need to see the crystals around his wrist. Know he has a piece of me. Even if I don't know who *I* am anymore.

"Zion would have loved you," I whisper.

The scent of coffee—real coffee—wafts under the door, and I hear voices. Slowly easing out from under Ryker's arm, I use the wall to brace myself as I stagger to my feet. My left knee throbs with each step, but I stay upright as I make my way to the door.

With one last glance at a sleeping Ryker, I slip into the hallway.

In the living room, a dark-haired man with piercing blue eyes stares at a computer screen, a mug of steaming coffee in his hand. "I don't know," he says. "He brought in another six overnight."

"Well, shit." Inara comes around the corner and stops short when she sees me. "Wren."

"I couldn't sleep. And I smelled coffee." I take another three steps towards the kitchen—awkwardly—before Inara rushes over to me and wraps her arm around my waist.

"You look like you're about to topple over. Sit down. I'll get your coffee." She helps me to the couch, and the man skirts the makeshift command center set up along the far wall. Maps cover the tall table, along with three laptops, a handful of legal pads, and several small, rectangular devices I don't recognize.

"West. Sampson," he says as he holds out his hand. "You look...better."

My cheeks heat as I realize he probably saw me naked the night before. Inara jabs him in the ribs as she heads for the kitchen and mutters, "Idiot."

"It's okay." I offer him my hand, then realize how bruised my knuckles are when he closes his fingers around mine. "Except... maybe no more shaking."

"Let me see." He drops to one knee, then examines the swelling. "Make a fist." I do, and he watches my face the whole time. "Okay, now try to hyper-extend your fingers." Again, he pays attention to my expression, and when I only wince a little, he nods. "Not broken. I have some arnica in my kit. It'll help."

"Thanks." Cradling my hand in my lap, I stare at the various pictures strung up around the living room. All different views of Kolya's fortress. Some have red dots on them that look almost like...people. Clear, block handwriting covers others, words like "dining room" and "sleeping quarters" and "Wren?" strategically placed around those red forms.

"You...knew where I was?" I ask when West sinks down next to me with a tube in his hand and Inara returns from the kitchen with two steaming mugs.

"Not for sure. But Ry thought from the way the heat signature moved," Inara says, "you were on the top floor. In a bathroom."

Nodding, I try not to flinch when West takes my hand and starts massaging a cool gel into my knuckles. "I was. Kolya, uh, chained me to a pipe under the sink." My voice cracks, and Inara passes me the coffee.

She pats my knee—the bad one—and a little of the dark brew spills over the rim of the mug as I stifle my whimper. "Shit. Will that stuff work on a twisted knee?"

"You should have Ry take a look. But yeah. It'll help." West caps the tube and sets it next to me. "Take it. I have an extra." He's up and back at the table before I can even sip my coffee, and I realize I must look like death warmed over. Even Inara watches me with a wary eye.

"What...what are you planning?" I tug the sleeve of my sweat-shirt, suddenly worried they can see the needle marks, but the cuff is only slightly above my wrist.

The two share a glance, and Inara inclines her head towards the hall. Towards Ryker.

"Tell me." Forcing strength I don't feel into my tone, I hold

225

her gaze. "I'm not fragile. I want to help. That's my computer over there after all. I'm the reason you're here...risking your lives. And I...messed up." My cheeks heat, and I stare down into my mug. "If I'd listened to Ryker...maybe we'd all be home by now."

"Stupid *cyka!*" The angry shout sends my heartbeat pounding in my ears, and I drop the mug, scrambling away from the sound as footsteps thunder towards me. Hands close around my throat, and I try to scream, but I can't. I can't move. Can't think.

Until a roar comes from behind me and the pressure at my neck falls away. "Get the fuck off of her!"

I only see a shadow as my attacker flies into the wall, and then I'm in Ryker's arms, his scent surrounding me, and the hard muscles of his chest under my cheek. "Are you okay?"

"I...think so," I croak, the combination of the brief strangulation and my own panic combining to leave my voice unsteady and rough.

Across the room, West kneels down in front of the man and growls, "You try anything like that again, we'll leave you for Kolya with a pretty pink bow in your hair and a full recording of every fucking thing you told us. Understand?"

"*Da. Da!* I am sorry! Please do not hurt me!"

West pulls a zip tie from his back pocket and binds the guy's hands together behind his back.

"Wait," I manage as I try to extricate myself from Ryker's iron grip. "What's going on? Ry? Who is that?"

"A fucking coward," he mutters, but loosens his hold enough so I can turn in his arms as West hauls the man to his feet.

Blond hair. Pale blue eyes. The last remnants of adolescent acne still sprinkling across his cheeks. "Oh my God. Semyon. You found him?"

"A few hours after you were taken," Inara replies. "Little shit handed you over to Kolya because he thought the world's most *honest man ever* would just let him and Elena go."

Betrayal stings my eyes. Not for me, but for my brother. "Z

loved you," I whisper. "He tried to get you out. He *died* for you and Elena."

"Zion was *tupoy*. He fucked Elena. You want to know why he came back to the United States, *cyka*? Because Kolya found out." Semyon's voice trembles, and he juts his chin into the air and looks away, blinking his shimmering eyes rapidly. "No one see her for months after that. She was beautiful. Not now."

I rest my cheek against Ryker's chest, unable to argue with the boy's anger. But since we're not all on a plane heading back to the states, I know she'll be free. Ryker and his team won't let her stay Kolya's prisoner. "I'm sorry," I say quietly, risking a quick peek at Semyon. "I can't undo what happened. But we're here...for her. And for you."

Semyon spits in my direction and utters a string of words in Russian I assume is mostly profanity from the look on Inara's face.

"Get him the fuck out of here," Ryker says sharply. "He doesn't come anywhere near Wren—or me—unless he wants to be sent back to Kolya in pieces."

"Ry..." I try to link our fingers, but he won't open his fist. I'd go after Semyon as West shoves him down the hall, but I'd probably topple over, and Ryker's tense enough already. "I think someone needs to tell me what happened after you found Semyon."

33

Ryker

*W*aking up without Wren at my side scared the shit out of me. To see her with that asshole's hands around her throat and terror in her eyes...I might never let her out of my sight again.

After West secures Semyon in the basement, he and Inara disappear into the kitchen, and the scents of eggs and bacon waft in. Wren sits stiffly at my side, cradling her right hand in her lap.

"Are you okay?" I reach for her fingers, and the purple and green beads around my wrist catch the light. "Sweetheart? This is yours..."

She stops me before I can give it back to her. "Not yet. I don't... I need you to keep it for me. For a little bit."

"I don't understand." Turning to face her, I notice the bruises on her hand. "Fuck, Wren. Did you...punch the bastard?"

A hint of a smile tugs at the corners of her lips. "Hurt like hell. But...it dazed him enough for me to get away."

Gently folding her hand into a fist, I adjust her grip. "Next time, keep your fingers flat to the first knuckle, and your thumb curled between the second knuckles of your index and middle finger. Like this."

Wren's gaze shifts between my eyes and her hand. "Okay."

"Then, when you throw the punch, tilt your wrist down just slightly. You want to keep your first two knuckles in line with your forearm."

Scooting back on the couch, I hold up my palm. "Try it."

"It'll hurt."

"Not if you do it right. Not even with those bruises. Go slow. Don't put any force behind it. Just try the motion." I don't know why it's suddenly so important to me that she learn how to punch. I'll protect her with my life. But whether out of fear or just because I don't want to ask why she needs me to keep her bracelet, I have to do this.

Extending her arm, she touches my palm. "Good. A little more of an angle." Again, and this time, she's dead on. "Harder."

Though the uncertainty on her face makes my heart hurt, she punches my hand with enough force to sting a little. "Ow," she whispers, but her smile belies her words. "When...this is all over, will you teach me how to fight?"

"You'd be better off learning from West." I push to my feet, an intense need to pace, to move, to burn off all this nervous energy consuming me. When this is all over...we live on two different sides of the country. And I'm so fucking in love with her I don't know how I'll survive if she doesn't want me.

Luckily, Inara and West save me from this conversation by setting plates of food on the small dining room table.

"Breakfast," Inara calls before disappearing back into the kitchen.

Wren limps awkwardly until I offer her my arm. When we're alone again, I'm taking better stock of her injuries. All I cared about last night was getting her into bed with me. I didn't even think she might have needed food.

You're shit at caring for people. Why would she ever want you?

But she seems to sense my thoughts—damn woman can tell what I'm thinking even when I can't. As I help her into a chair, she squeezes my hand and offers me another weak smile.

"Hey! Are you assholes going to let me starve?" Semyon calls from the basement.

"Yes," Inara and I answer in unison.

West shakes his head. "We need him. For now." Raising his voice, he calls, "You eat when we say you eat. Now shut up and let the grown-ups talk."

Another string of Russian cursing ensues, and Inara stalks over and slams the basement door. As she returns to the table, she meets Wren's horrified gaze. "His hands and ankles are bound, but not uncomfortably. He's sitting on a soft mattress, and there's a little heater a few feet away. He's *fine*. Lucky, even. Kolya probably would have killed him by now."

Wren's breath catches in her throat, but she nods and picks up a piece of bacon. In the light, the ligature marks around her wrist stand out dramatically against her pale skin. "How did you find him?"

I tell her the basics—Inara going to surveil the area, breaking into her laptop to access the cameras, seeing Semyon running from Kolya's fortress a little after one in the morning.

"And my password?" Wren asks, a forkful of eggs halfway to her lips.

Downing a large gulp of coffee to give myself time to formulate my next words, I look to Inara for help. She's the only one who knows my secret, and even she doesn't understand everything I can do. But she just arches a brow.

"Ry has a memory like no one I've ever seen," West says.

"My password is ten digits long." Wren turns slightly in her seat, pinning me with her stare. Her eyes are mostly clear today, though bruises mar her delicate features, and every time I notice another scratch, another subtle swelling, I want to cause Kolya ten times the pain he caused her.

"One of the last books I read before I was captured...it taught me how to associate patterns and words and letters with memories. You ever heard of Sherlock Holmes and his mind palace?"

Wren nods.

"Kind of similar. If I have a couple of minutes to think about something I want to remember and pick a pattern...I can remember it for years. It's how I escaped Hell."

"I don't understand." Wren slips her small hand in mine. "How did a good memory help you get out of that place?"

"You never told me that story either, Ry." Cupping his mug of coffee, West sits back in his chair. "We can't do anything until sundown. Now's as good a time as any."

"Not here. After Wren eats." Glancing at the door hiding Semyon, I jerk my head towards the living room. In truth, I don't give a shit if he hears me. But Wren looks like she's about to collapse, and I need a hell of a lot more of her touching me than just her fingers if I'm going to recount one of the worst experiences of my life.

But staring into the faces of my team, knowing there are only four people in the world I trust and three of them are in this room, I have to tell them. Because I think Wren's right.

This is my family. And families don't keep secrets.

WITH WREN TUCKED against my side, I stare at the ceiling. Easier than trying to make eye contact. Despite how much I told her about Hell last night, there are some memories too awful to willingly dredge up. Except...I have to.

"Down there...we didn't have any sense of direction. They'd designed Hell to be a maze. When I got out, I realized they'd painted dots and lines on the walls for identification. But every time they moved us, we were blindfolded. They'd take me from one cell, bring me to an interrogation room, beat the crap out of me, and then throw me in another cell. Or one of the holes." The stench of fear and sweat and onions fills my nose, and I bury my face in Wren's hair for a moment, try to remind myself I'm not back there.

"No pattern?" West asks.

"Whatever cell was the dirtiest at the time. The bloodiest. Or the emptiest." Screams. Fear. Darkness. Wren rubs my leg, and I meet her gaze in silent thanks. "Even without any sort of routine, there are tricks you can use to help you remember long lists of things. I'm very good at them."

"Like a mnemonic for memorizing the names of the planets?" Wren asks.

I stifle a chuckle. "Not exactly. Think about your neighborhood. Everything you see on your way to work. There's a way to train your mind so that you associate a different number or fact with each lamp post. Each car parked on your street. It's hard to explain, but I can teach you...if you want."

God, I want her to say yes. Because maybe...that means she'll stay with me. But West leans forward expectantly, and I force out a deep breath. "I knew every guard by sound and smell. I could tell if it was morning or night based on their scent. And when they brought us down into the caves the first time, I memorized every turn. Every step. How the ground felt under my feet. How sounds echoed off the walls. I had a mental map of the way out the minute they threw me in that hole. Every time they moved me. A couple of times, I was unconscious. As soon as I'd wake up, though, I could figure out where I was by the smells, the sounds, and the feel of the rocks or walls around me."

I swallow hard and stifle my shudder as I turn to Wren. "How long have you known Dax?"

Her brow furrows a little. "Almost four years."

"Ever wonder why he's so damn good at getting around?"

She huffs. "All the time. He's scary. I swear he doesn't need that cane."

"We spent maybe half our time in Hell unable to see. There were times they'd leave us tied up and blindfolded for days. If we could see, we'd be in near darkness or with bright lights shining directly in our faces."

"You never saw a damn thing outside of the cells?" West asks, shock infusing his tone.

I shake my head. "Not until the day I escaped."

With a long, low whistle, West leans back, lacing his fingers behind his neck. "Fuck, Ry. The guys in my unit...we had recon and logistics exercises every week. And we were never anywhere near that good. Those damn caves were like an Escher drawing. When you led us back there...I kept expecting you to pull a map out of your kit."

"Sorry. I probably owe you a hundred bucks."

"Try two." Running a hand through his hair, West snorts. "Why didn't you ever tell anyone?"

"Didn't think anyone would believe me." I shrug. "And after Dax...I didn't ever want to think about those fifteen months again." Silence fills the room, West and Inara looking a bit dazed.

"So my password..." Wren's gaze holds a mix of awe and humor as she intertwines our fingers.

"Piece of cake, sweetheart. Had it memorized before we left Boston."

34

Wren

A thud from the basement sends West and Inara to check on Semyon. Ryker's so tense, I'm worried he's going to implode. He hasn't let go of my hand, and my fingers throb from his tight grip, but last night's words ring in my ears.

"You find something real. Something to hold on to."

Ryker is real. Real and flawed and perfect. And he loves me. Meeting his gaze, I cup his cheek with my free hand. "Are you okay?"

West's footsteps interrupt any reply as he stalks into the kitchen muttering, "Fucker expects to eat. Should I tell him the Geneva convention doesn't apply here?"

"We need him." Inara brushes her hands off on her black pants as she returns to the living room to study one of the laptops on West's table. "He's the only one who knows the hotel layout. And we can use him. I hope. The old plan probably would have worked."

I touch Ryker's arm. "Was…there actually a plan?"

His eye roll speaks volumes. Yes, there was a plan. No, he didn't like it. But he couldn't figure out a better option.

"We took everything into account." Ryker snorts softly. "Except you, baby."

As his words sink in, I start to tremble. "You couldn't rescue Elena because I escaped. What if Kolya kills her before we—you —can get her out?"

"Stop." Ryker's growl reassures and frightens at the same time. "You will not blame yourself, Wren. There was no way in *hell* I was going to lose you. The second I saw you, we dumped the plan."

Elena's desperate blue eyes are all I can see. "Can you just... use the same plan?"

With a shake of his head, Ryker sighs. "Between Semyon's information and the blueprints Cam found online, West had the whole thing mapped out for us. We were going to breach the hotel through the roof. West approached from the north, and I came from the south. Inara was five hundred yards away on the old clock tower."

Ryker pauses for a sip of coffee, and his eyes darken. "That roof hatch leads to an attic crawl space. It's hard to tell on the blueprints, but I think it opens up to that bathroom you were in. You were my first priority. If you hadn't jumped off the balcony, I would have been there less than ten minutes later."

"Oh." I stifle my shudder. "You would have been too late." I can't force my voice above a whisper, and Inara leans forward as Ryker cups my chin and urges my head up to meet his gaze. "Kolya was done waiting. He was going to rape me—without drugging me—so I'd be so desperate to...forget...I'd do anything he wanted...just so he'd take the pain away."

"Drugging you?" Inara stiffens as West silently returns to the room. "Wren? What did he do to you?"

Ryker saves me from the admission. "Heroin."

I don't know how to say the words. How to confess how much I still want to forget.

"Shit." Setting his coffee mug down with enough force to slosh the dark liquid over the rim, West braces his hands on the table. "And Elena? Did you see her at all?"

I nod. "Twice. I think. He made her clean me up. So much of what happened is fuzzy. Like…I was watching a movie out of focus. A movie I didn't care about at all." My head starts to throb, and I pinch the bridge of my nose. "I begged her to help me, but she said she couldn't." The lump in my throat threatens to choke off my next words. "And then he shoved her into his bedroom and told her to strip. After that…there was another needle and I don't…I can't…"

"Shhh. It's okay, baby," Ryker says as he threads his fingers through my hair. The warmth of his touch calms me, and I sink into his embrace. "He won't kill her. But now they know Inara's hidey-hole. My approach vector. And if they were observant… they noticed my rappelling gear."

"So…what do we do now?" I look from Inara to Ryker, shame at getting myself captured flooding through me. Despite the bruising at my elbow, I hook my arm around Ry's, needing to feel him, to feel pain, just to keep myself grounded.

"We wait for West to figure something else out," Inara says with a wry smile. "He's the brains of this whole operation. I'm the bullets." She angles her head at Ryker. "He's the brawn. Well, and the bank."

"Semyon couldn't tell us anything about the top floor." West gestures to the blueprints spread out on the table. "Our thermal cameras have been recording the whole time, and Kolya's holed up in this back room—here."

Ryker helps me up and keeps his arm around my waist. A part of me rails against his overprotectiveness, but I'm starting to feel woozy, so I let him hold me as I stifle a yawn. We slept less than five hours after last night's confessions. I'm exhausted, everything hurts, and my mind wants to wander. To dark places where nothing can hurt me. Except, Ryker won't be there. And maybe that's enough to keep me here. In this painful, overwhelming, frightening reality.

Ryker presses a gentle kiss to the top of my head. "You look like you're about to fall over."

"I am. But I want to help." I look up at him, and he seems to understand my need to be useful. "I'll lie down in a few minutes."

Studying the plans, I point to the main suite. "This is Kolya's bedroom. And the bathroom where he chained me up." A hard swallow and Ryker's warmth at my back helps center me. "The room across the hall is his office. Oh!" I can't believe I forgot. "Ry...I think...I had a USB drive in my bag. Did I still...have my bag when I jumped?"

My brows furrow, and the motion makes my head ache even more, as does trying to fight my way through my fuzzy memories. "I had to hide. Two of his goons came up the stairs. And...his computer was unlocked."

"You okay for a minute, sweetheart?" Ryker asks. "I'll get it for you."

"I can manage to stand up on my own." I offer him a small smile, and as he strides into our little bedroom oasis, Inara scoots closer, a not-too-subtle indication of how bad I must look. "This is another suite. Like his. I...I think it's Elena's. Or at least...where she stays sometimes. I didn't see her, but the door was open when they took me from the office into Kolya's suite. It was...purple and pink. Like the video."

"So he's locked in with Elena." West shakes his head as Ryker returns to my side. "There goes any hope of getting her out without confronting him—and half his army."

"Maybe...if we have something he wants," I say, "he'll give her up willingly."

Ryker snorts, and I arch a brow. "Don't look at me like that, soldier. You don't know what's on this thumb drive."

In truth, I don't know if I have anything. Not really. But even in my drug-addled state last night, I had the presence of mind to leave myself a backdoor. "Slide my laptop over here," I say. The adrenaline fuels me, helps ease some of my aches and pains. Or maybe the coffee is finally kicking in.

"Wren..." With a gentle hand to my lower back, Ryker tries to draw me away from the table. "You need to rest."

West clears his throat. "Ry. We're on borrowed time here. Inara swapped out the cars, but how long do you think it'll be before Kolya figures out where we are? We either need to draw him out or call for backup. Do *you* have a dozen men—" with a quick glance at Inara, he continues, "—and women you can mobilize by tonight?"

"If I *had,* do you think I'd have called you?"

The two men stand chest-to-chest. Sort of. Ryker towers over West, at least five more inches of bulk and brawn, his muscles stiff and hands balled into fists at his sides.

"And that's why this is never going to work long term, man. Not unless you start trusting us." With a shake of his head, West stalks away. He pauses at the door to the kitchen. "We're your fucking family, Ry. Have been ever since we pulled your ass out of that hole five clicks from Hell. It's about damn time you realized it."

The back door slams, and I flinch.

"Well, now you've done it," Inara says. "You better go after him."

Pain swims in Ryker's eyes, and I slide my hand up his arm, over thick ropes of scar tissue and solid muscle. He's so angry he's practically vibrating. "I'm not leaving Wren."

"Oh for duck's sake. Give us a minute?" I ask Inara. She quietly slips from the room, and I wind my arms around Ryker's waist. "Why is it so hard for you to admit you care about them?"

For too long, Ryker stares over my head towards the kitchen. When he finally does speak, his voice is rough and raw. "What we do, Wren...every single time we go out, we might not come back."

In some of my lucid moments in that bathroom, I wondered. If I loved him. Now, I know. I can't say the words yet, but I can give him this. Give him the family he's denied himself for years.

"It's easier not to care. Or...not to let on that you care. Because if you care...you might lose them? Is that it?" His body stills, and I'm not sure he's even breathing. "I saw how you looked at Dax. The pain. The guilt. He's family too, isn't he?"

A single nod, and he's a statue again.

"And me?" Now I'm the one holding my breath.

"Baby, you're my everything." Ryker's voice breaks on the final word, and he wraps his arms around me, shudders wracking his bulk as he struggles to draw in ragged breaths. "I can't lose you."

"You won't. But you won't lose them either. Not if you let them in."

Jerking back, he scrubs his hands over his face. "I let Dax in. Hab. Ripper. Gose. Naz. And look at what happened to them."

I reach out and press my palm to his heart. "They're all still with you, Ry. Here. Can't you feel them? You carry them with you every day. Just like I carry Zion. I know it's a cliché. And not a very good one. But...even with all the pain and tears Zion caused me when he was using...I still loved him. And now? Everything I...I just went through? Am still going through? The few years I had with Zion are worth all that." I sniffle and brush away a hint of dampness under my swollen left eye. "Now go find West and make this right. I'll be here when you come back."

Ryker leans down and touches his forehead to mine. "Do you promise?"

"I promise."

35

Ryker

*T*he sun slashes across the stoop where West sits with his arms crossed over his bent knees. "I never should have come back," he says bitterly. "All my years in the SEALs and I was never as close to death as I was in Colombia. And now...my fucking wedding is—was—supposed to be tomorrow."

"I was wrong." Forcing my feet to move, I plod down the stairs until I'm standing in front of him, my hands shoved into my pockets. "And I'm an asshole."

West narrows his eyes. "Say that again? I think my hearing's going."

"You heard me."

"And you think this makes us solid again?" He jerks up and turns to head back inside, but I grab his arm.

"Wait. Hear me out and then...after we get out of this fucking country, you never have to see me again." I don't know how to make him stop and listen, to make him understand when I can't figure this shit out for myself. "Please."

"You're never going to change, are you, Ry?" Shaking off my grip, West puts several feet between us as he stalks into the small backyard. "Who the hell said I never wanted to see you again?"

"You did. 'And that's why this is never going to work long term, man. Not unless you start...' Shit." My ass hits the stairs, and I drop my head into my hands.

"Finally figured it out?" With controlled, precise movements, West scoops up a handful of stones from the neglected land-scaping and aims at a dead tree in the corner of the yard. *Plunk.* "I know you lost your team, Ry." *Plunk.* The second rock lands a mere inch from the first. "But so did a lot of us. I had to watch my men die too." *Plunk.*

"You didn't leave a man behind." My words don't rise much above a whisper, and as a fourth stone lands—all in a tight, circular grouping—West blows out a long, slow breath.

"Neither did you." When he turns to me, frustration gathers between his dark brows. "If you hadn't escaped when you did, you and Dax would have both died."

"You don't know that," I snap, jumping to my feet and advancing on West. "I cost Dax his fucking eyes. And worse. I left him there. Alone." I shove the former SEAL, but he anticipates my rage and spins away.

"You want a fight? Or you want to fix things?" His fist plows into my jaw, and before I can recover, he sweeps my legs out from under me. "Stay down."

Sucking in a sharp breath, I fight the instinct to get to my feet and tackle him. I've only seen hints of this side of West. The savage, tightly restrained anger we're taught to use to our advantage—if the situation's desperate enough.

"I called Dax before I got on the transpo in Seattle. If you think he blames you for his sight, you're a fucking idiot."

"But—"

"Oh, he's pissed at you. No question. But not for any of the reasons you think." Crouching down next to me, West jabs his finger against my chest. "You could have fixed things with him a hundred times in the past six years. Just by picking up the phone. The two of you went through something no one else in the world can understand. You didn't take his vision, Ry. You took his closest friend. And isolated yourself in the process. If you don't stop that shit, pretty soon you won't have anyone left."

Standing, West holds out his hand, and I let him pull me to my feet.

"When Coop took Royce, you didn't think twice about going after him. About breaking more than a dozen laws to get Royce back and keep me and Inara safe. Is it so hard to believe we'd do the same thing for you?"

His fingers tighten around mine as he pins me with a hard stare, and I try not to look away. "Yes."

"Why?"

The question throws me, and for the life of me, I don't have an answer.

"Because you're so caught up in your misplaced guilt over what happened in Hell, you can't see straight. I didn't invite you to my wedding out of obligation. You're the reason I'm alive. The reason Cam and I have a future—if we ever get out of this godforsaken country. I invited you because you're practically my brother."

The truth of his words is written all over his face. Have I really been that much of an idiot? Missed out on six years of my life— six years where I could have had friends? Family?

I pull West in for a quick, one-armed hug. I don't like being touched—except by Wren—but it feels like the right thing to do. "I didn't know what was wrong with my life," I say, the words thick and awkward, "until I met her. And now...fuck. I'm sorry. Tell me how to fix things."

After two thumps to my back, West releases me. "Come to the

wedding. Bring your girl. And maybe...next time someone asks you how you are, think about giving them an answer longer than a single word."

"I'll...try."

Nodding, West holds the door open for me. "That's a start."

36

Ryker

*W*ren looks so tiny and frail hunched over her computer. Bruises cover the left side of her face from her eye to her jaw, and every time I see the finger marks around her neck, I want to punch Kolya so hard, his teeth come out his ass.

But her green eyes are bright, and she grabs Inara's arm as I follow West into the living room.

"Look at this. Fifty million rubles to another *bratva*?" Wren shakes her head, then winces.

Inara's lips curve into a smile, but there's no mirth in her eyes. Only cold, calculating intensity. "He'll be lucky to live another month. West, get over here. If we play this right, we can take him down for good—and keep our hands relatively clean."

I peer over Wren's shoulder, wrapping one arm around her waist. "How'd you find this?"

She smiles, a little lopsided with her swollen lower lip, and leans her head against my chest. "When I was hiding in his office,

I installed a backdoor into his computer. I have access to his entire hard drive. Including his email."

"Stupid idiot's barely covering his tracks," Inara says as she jabs her finger at the screen. "Any halfway competent law enforcement agency that cared could put him away for the rest of his life."

"I can work with this." West nods at Wren. "You're good. Could probably give Cam a run for her money."

"Cam?" Wren's brows furrow. "Wait. You live in Seattle. Cam... from Emerald City Security?"

The former SEAL beams. "Yeah. That's my girl. She remembers you. Was pretty disappointed when you turned down her old boss's job offer."

Wren looks dazed, and I can't help filling in the last little detail. "And that old boss?" I crack a smile, though the sensation feels foreign. "That's who gave Inara that pendant there."

Understanding dawns in Wren's eyes as Inara's fingers brush the pink stone I don't think she's taken off since Royce clasped the chain around her neck. Some emotion I can't read flits over Wren's face. "Wow. I...wait. *Old* boss?"

"Cam runs Emerald City now," Inara explains. "Royce—" her voice wavers for a beat, "—had a stroke last year. He's good now, but he signed the company over to Cam and spends his time writing apps. That tracker Ry gave you? The Loc8tion software on your laptop? Those are his."

"Oh..." Wren sways against me, and I tighten my arm around her.

West and Inara share a look—those two are so in tune, it's ridiculous—and Inara angles her head towards the back bedroom. "You should get some rest. Let us see what we can do with this new intel. No matter what, we're staying put until dark, so you've got some time."

Nodding, Wren grabs a piece of paper and pen. "This is the key you'll need to decrypt my notes. Everything I have from Elena and Zion." After she scribbles down a series of eighteen letters and numbers, her writing shaky, she turns into me, and I scoop her up into my arms. She's asleep before we even make it into the bedroom.

COOL FINGERS BRUSH MY JAW. "RY?"

Instantly awake, I inhale sweet honeysuckle and find her green eyes almost ablaze with streaks of copper. Wren presses her lips to mine, and her little moan sends the blood rushing to my cock. I want to claim her, to feel her come apart in my arms, to taste her release as it floods my tongue, but she's so battered and broken.

"Please," she whispers. "I need you. You won't hurt me."

"How do you do that?" I thread my fingers through her hair, tightening just enough to hold her head still so she can't look away. "Know what I'm thinking?"

Her smile is my sunshine, my oxygen, and I'd do anything to see her smile at me every day for the rest of my life. "Your eyes. You think you're so mysterious. Or...maybe...stoic. But I've never met anyone who says so much with just their eyes." At my frown, she draws her thumb across my lips. "When I met you, your eyes were...blank. Hard. Cold. I don't know when they changed. After I was attacked, maybe?"

Avoiding her bruises, I feather kisses along her jaw. "I've trained for years to hide my emotions from the enemy. It's how I survived Hell. But...it also cost me. I don't want to be that person anymore. You make me...a better man."

Wren shifts her hips to press against my hard length. "You did that all on your own. Now are you going to undress me? Or do I have to do everything around here?"

The challenge in her eyes snaps my control, and I roll her onto her back, straddling her and curling my fingers around the edge of her fleece pants. But then in the dim light seeping around the curtains, I see her bruises. "Promise me, Wren. If I hurt you, tell me."

"I need you to hurt me," she whispers. "Pain is real. You're real. *We're* real."

Every protective instinct I have screams at me to stand down. To gather her in my arms and insist she sleep more. Or simply hold her and talk to her. But her short nails dig into my shoulders, desperate, and I yank the waistband over her hips.

Copper curls glisten with her arousal, and the scent of her fills the room. I try for gentle as I ease the sweatshirt over her head, and then she's bared to me. In the light of day, her injuries look so much worse, and she cringes as she watches my gaze travel the length of her body, settling on the angry, red needle marks at her elbow.

"Ry...I'm...sorry." Tears well in her eyes, one slipping down her temple, close to her ear. I wick the salty drop away with my kiss, then claim her mouth, my tongue meeting hers in a slow, languid dance I don't want to ever end. But I have to reassure her, to tell her how beautiful she is. Or...show her.

Stretching out next to her, I trail the backs of my fingers along her cheekbone. "You're perfect, sweetheart. Don't ever think otherwise."

"I let him—"

"You didn't *let* him do anything." I take her hand, kissing the bruises on her fingers. "You fought back." My lips trail down to her wrist, to the reddened burns from whatever he used to tie her up, then along the back of her forearm, where a bruise darkens her pale skin. Another defensive wound. Blocked punch, if I had to guess. "You protected yourself. You're so fucking strong, Wren. When I saw you on that balcony..."

"I was a mess. I still am—"

"You were beautiful." A smile tugs at my lips, and for once, I don't fight it. "I stopped dead in my tracks. Couldn't even speak for a few seconds. I've never been so scared. Not even in Hell. But then...you jumped onto that awning without a moment's hesitation. You're so fucking strong, baby. You don't see it. But I do."

Reaching her elbow, I press a tender kiss to the needle marks, and under my touch, her body starts to relax. I wish I had the words to tell her how much she's changed my life. The pieces of my heart she's mended by simply being her. By seeing me. The man behind the scars.

Her nipple pebbles as I score my teeth over the tender nub. "More, Ry. Please..."

"Oh, I'm just getting started." Pinching the other taut bud between my fingers, I kiss down the line of her stomach, all the way to her copper curls. "You taste like rain," I murmur against her clit, and when my tongue traces lazy circles between her folds, she fists the sleeping bag and keens softly.

"Oh God. I need...I need..." Her heels dig against the floor, and she jerks and thrusts against my mouth. Wrapping one hand around her hip, I freeze as she whimpers in pain. But in the next breath, she begs, "Harder."

I can't get enough of her—the quiet gasps, the way she arches her back, the flood of arousal coating my tongue. Slipping two fingers deep inside her channel, I twist my hand, finding her G-spot as I suck on her clit.

"Ryker!" She slaps her hand over her mouth as she shatters, her entire body bucking helplessly, the waves of pleasure overtaking her.

My little bird gasps and shudders as she comes down from her release, and I hold her as gently as I can, taking in every curve, every freckle, and every bruise. I don't need any fancy memory techniques for Wren. I'll never forget a single detail. I can't. They're all written directly on my heart.

"Off," she whispers as she tugs at the hem of my shirt. "I need to feel you. And see you."

She's seen me naked half a dozen times now, and I still pause.

But though she hasn't said the words, the love in her eyes spurs me on, and I reach behind me, grasping the collar and sliding the shirt over my head. Her palms skim my pecs, fingers tracing over my scars.

"You're real, Ry. Every mark...every burn...is a part of you." Wren offers me a small smile as she pulls off my briefs and strokes my cock. I'm so hard, her gentle touch threatens to undo me, and a bead of precum coats my crown, slips against her fingers.

When she wriggles down my body and swirls her tongue around my shaft, I groan. "Fuck, Wren. I won't last if you keep doing that." Her lips envelop me, and my balls ache with desperate need. "Baby, I don't want you on your knees. I need to see your face. Look into your eyes."

A quiet *pop* as she draws her lips over my crown accompanies the crinkle of the condom wrapper, and then the tight heat of her channel grips me as I slide home. A feeling I don't understand spreads from the center of my chest, warm and soft and...right. Bracing myself over her, I thrust deep, and she wraps her legs around me.

"Harder," she urges. God, this woman is perfect. My little bird. My angel. My everything. She saved me from my own demons, and now...I'll do whatever I can to banish hers.

Her fingers dig into my ass, and I slam into her, so hard and fast I'm scared I'll break her, but she holds my gaze, love reflected in her eyes. Grinding against her mound, I let myself go, her name tumbling from my lips like a prayer.

Wren follows me over the edge, her entire body quaking under me. "Ryker, oh God. Don't ever let go," she whispers as she wraps her arms around my waist and pulls me down on top of her.

"I won't, baby. Never."

Tears shimmer in her eyes, tumbling onto her cheeks. And now, her tremors aren't from her release, but little choking sobs.

My heart stutters, panic stiffening my limbs. "What's wrong, Wren? Talk to me. Did I hurt you?"

"No," she says firmly. "No. I...I feel so...broken. But maybe... we're all broken. Maybe...I didn't understand until now how beautiful broken can be."

37

Wren

I wake to a kiss and a light brush of knuckles against my bruised cheek.

Ryker smiles down at me, though I can tell the expression still feels foreign to him. "Sweetheart, I need to go check on West and Inara. See what the plan is. I...didn't want you to wake up alone."

"I don't know how to do this."

"Do what?"

"Care."

"You'll learn."

Our conversation from—was it only three days ago—plays in my head, and I cup the back of his neck. "Help me up? I want to come too."

"You should rest."

"Ryker." He frowns at my tone, but I don't care. "We've already had this discussion. More than once. Help me up or I'm going to do it myself and my knee still hurts."

Pulling back the sleeping bag, he runs his strong hands down my left leg until he finds the swelling. "What happened?"

"You." I grin but grab his arm when a mask of horror slides over his face. "When I jumped off the last balcony. I had to get to you. Stop worrying. It was either this or get shot. I think I got the better end of the deal."

With a shake of his head, he starts to knead just above the swelling. A sharp pain travels up my thigh. I hiss, and he pauses, his fingers warm against my skin. "Right there?"

"Uh huh."

Digging into the pocket of my discarded pants, he fishes out the tube of arnica and squeezes a dollop into his palm. "This won't be comfortable. But it'll help."

Gritting my teeth, I meet his gaze. "Do it."

His movements wouldn't be called a massage on any planet. It feels more like he's trying to dig deep into my thigh for buried treasure. But after a few minutes, the throbbing eases and it's like all the tension in my leg fades away. When he skims his hands down to my ankle, over the bruising and abrasions from the metal cuff, his fingers stiffen. "I should have been faster."

"I'm okay, Ry. For...right now, at least, I'm okay."

The intensity of his multi-colored eyes shocks me, and I scoot forward so I can wrap my arms around him and brush my lips to his ear. "There's so much I want to say to you. I...just need a little more time. But when it happens, I want you to remember...this was the moment I was sure."

<hr/>

Ryker

I follow Wren out to the living room, my hand on the small of her back. She almost said the words. At least...I think she did. I can't read her like she can read me.

West and Inara study his laptop, heads drawn together.

"Do we have a plan?" I ask. Wren heads for the kitchen, and I try not to watch her go, to worry about the slight limp, to call her back to my side because I don't want her out of my sight.

Inara stares at me like she doesn't recognize the man in front of her. "You okay, Ry?"

"No." West and Inara wear twin expressions of shock at my admission, and I run my hand over my scalp, feeling the rough stubble from too many days without a razor. "How did you deal with it? When Royce...?"

"Badly." Inara leans back against the table and her fingers close around the pendant at her throat. "I was a wreck. Shit. Every time he tried to get up, I was at his side. And he had a seizure the next day after dinner. I held it together until he'd recovered, but then I hid in the shower for ten minutes crying. And I do *not* cry."

If she's trying to reassure me, it's not working. "How'd you get through it?"

"I talked to him. Eventually. Took me a couple of days. But dealing with things on my own was what got us into that situation in the first place." Inara looks from me to West and back again. "I never apologized. I'm...sorry."

West rests a hand on her shoulder and squeezes. "We're a team, Inara. You didn't do anything Ryker and I haven't done before. In Ry's case...this week, even."

I don't miss the dig, but the understanding in his deep blue eyes tells me we're on mostly solid ground. "I don't *do* the whole talking thing. Don't know how."

"You're learning," Inara says with a pat to my forearm. "It takes time." Leaning closer, she lowers her voice. "If you love her, you try. Even if you mess it up half the time."

Wren pokes her head in from the kitchen. "Anyone else want tea?"

"I'll take some," Inara says. "West's coffee supply is running low and we're going to need all the caffeine we can get tomorrow night."

The former SEAL rolls his eyes. "You live in Seattle too, you know. Try packing some beans in *your* bag next time."

Inara laughs and jabs him in the side. "And risk you ridiculing my choices? No way."

West feigns offense, and all four of us laugh—though I think my rough attempt sounds more like a barking dog than a human. But the feeling of family fills the room, and as I meet Wren's gaze, light touches her green eyes for the first time since she was taken, and a piece of my soul settles.

Maybe...we'll all be okay.

WHEN WE HAVE mugs of strong tea in our hands, we gather around the table so West and Inara can go over the plan.

"Kolya's men found all of the cameras," Inara says. "And the battery in the thermal cam across the street went dead a few hours ago."

"Fuck. Why haven't you replaced it? He could be anywhere right now." Trying to contain my frustration, I clench my free hand so tightly the knuckles pop. Wren's fingers slide over mine, finding the beads around my wrist and tracing them slowly, and I force myself to breathe.

"Calm down," West orders. "We don't need to know where he is right now, because we know he's going to be at the mansion tomorrow night. And we're pretty sure Elena and half a dozen girls are going to be with him." West taps the keyboard, and an email thread pops up on the screen.

"This is an exchange between Kolya and a guy named Andrian Popov," Inara says. "Kolya's inviting Popov to an auction tomorrow night. And it's pretty clear from his wording that he's never met Popov before."

"The wording?" I ask.

Inara gestures vaguely, her hand in the air. "It's formal. Like Popov is someone Kolya respects. Given what I've seen in the rest of his correspondence, this isn't his usual MO. He's the alpha. The god among men. But in this thread, he's deferential, careful. Almost meticulous in his sentence structure. And he signs off with 'you honor me with your response.' The phrase doesn't translate directly, but that's basically what it means."

Understanding dawns. "You want to *impersonate* Popov?" I take a step back, regarding West with unease. "Do you even speak Russian?"

"Three, four words. Maybe? But my arm candy for the night is fluent." He nudges Inara's shoulder, and she glares at him. "You're going to have to work on that expression. You're supposed to be on my side."

"I'm playing your bodyguard, Sampson. Not your *date*." She snorts. "As if I could pull off the brainless bimbo in any universe. I'd kill someone before we got more than two steps inside the door."

"Hey, I was supposed to get married tomorrow. Cut a guy a little slack." West smiles, but his eyes reflect pain.

I can't repay them for this. Ever. I'll be in their debt for the rest of my life if we pull this off. Wren presses closer to my side, and her fingers graze my hip.

"I can encrypt a video channel," she says quietly. "So you can see each other without risking anyone intercepting the signal."

West meets my gaze. I have rules. No phones. No contact. Safer for everyone. But the idea of going four days without talking to Wren, seeing her, after what we've been through...I'd come out of my skin. At my single nod, West blows out a breath. "Thanks. I'd appreciate that."

"Inara and Royce too," I add. "And can you set that up for us every job? Anything more than an in-and-out, at least?"

"Yep. I can show you how to secure the connection." Wren

slides her computer closer with a quick glance up at me, and I press a kiss to the top of her head.

"Back to Popov." As much as I'd like to lose myself in Wren's body or spend the next few hours simply answering her questions—or maybe asking some of my own—we have a job to plan, and the sun's already gone down. "You know where he is? Because I don't think we want the real Popov showing up at the door while the two of you are inside."

"Yep." West pulls up a map. "He's an hour away, in a little town called Roshchino."

38

Wren

The tension in the room is about to send me fleeing back to the pile of sleeping bags in our little sanctuary, but Ryker has my hand clasped in a death grip.

"Promise me," he whispers with his forehead pressed to mine, "you'll stay close to Inara."

"I promise. I'll be fine. She brought almost as much firepower as you did." I try for a smile, but Ryker pulls me into a tight embrace, and I swear I feel him shaking against me. "Ry, you can't be at my side for the rest of my life."

"Watch me." His voice carries a rough edge, and suddenly I worry he's serious.

"Ryker McCabe. I'm not helpless." Jerking away, or trying to, I meet his gaze, and he releases me. "I love that you want to protect me. And most of the time, I'll let you. But Inara isn't going to let anything happen to me. And you and West will be back in a couple of hours."

"I don't know how to do this," he whispers.

"Care?" At his nod, I cup his cheek. "You're doing a good job. Just...relax a little, okay?"

He threads his fingers into my hair and pulls tight. The slight pinpricks of pain along my scalp make me feel alive, grounded, real, and I yield when his tongue traces the seam of my lips. The kiss is slow, sensual, and tender, so unlike the man he projects on the outside. I lose myself in the sensation, pleasure filling me all the way down to my toes. Until he sucks my bottom lip between his teeth, then pulls away.

"I have to gear up," he says, his voice rough. "Will you..." Pain fills his gaze, and he stammers as he tries to get the words out. "I mean...if you're here...I..."

"I'll be in the bedroom. You need to focus on the mission." I smile as relief washes over him. "I can read you, Ry. You don't have to worry about asking for what you need. Just don't shut me out." With a quick peck to his lips, I head for our little oasis, though I don't shut the door completely. I can still see him, his back to me, as he goes through his routine.

Patting down his pockets. Putting on his vest. Guns. Dart gun on the right, pistol on the left. Extra magazines. Knife. Compass. Earbud. With each item, he pauses, his head bowed, and touches its destination twice as if he's cementing its location in his mind.

West sits cross-legged on the floor a few feet away, his eyes closed. Inara's upside down in a headstand that would be the envy of yoga teachers everywhere. She'll run comms while West and Ryker do the dirty work.

Ryker whispers to himself, and I can't make out the words, but his hands move up and down his body as he goes, and I think he's confirming, yet again, that he has everything he needs.

"Ready, Sampson?" he says when he's done.

"Hooyah." West rises in one fluid motion, in direct opposition to Inara's descent from her headstand. "Comms check," he says.

"Roger," Inara replies as she moves to the table of computers. "Trackers on and transmitting. Romeo?"

"Check. Loud and clear. You see anything out of place on the satellite images—"

Inara snorts. "This isn't my first trip around the sun, boys. Come back alive. With the target."

As Ryker opens the door, and West heads for the car, he glances back and meets her gaze. "Hooah."

⬥

"You can come out now, Wren," Inara calls. "The boys are gone."

"I won't distract you?"

"Not right now. I'll let you know when they're getting close to Popov's home. At that point, just keep quiet." She offers me a tight smile and angles her head, indicating I should join her at the table. A few hours ago, Ryker found stools up in the attic, and I perch on one, my hands clasped in my lap.

"Why did West say 'hooyah' while Ryker said 'hooah'?"

Inara huffs out a laugh. "Because there's a long-standing rivalry between SEALs and Special Forces. 'Hooyah' is the battle-cry for the SEALs. 'Hooah' is for the army. Marines say 'oorah.'"

"What are you?" My cheeks heat as I hear myself. "I mean... what branch of the military did you serve in?"

"Army. Same as Royce and Cam. And Ryker, really. Even though he ended up a Green Beret. Graham, our new guy, was a marine. Still is, I guess, since he's in the reserves now. All we need is a Coast Guard alum and we'll have a complete set."

On the screen in front of us, the two red dots signifying Ryker and West's trackers travel along the route Inara mapped out for them. We fall silent for a while until we hear banging coming from the basement.

"Not now," Inara groans. "The little shit probably expects to eat again."

"I can bring him an MRE." Sliding off the stool, I start for the kitchen before Inara grabs my arm. Her fingers curl around my elbow where the needle marks still throb—though more from the memories than physical pain, and I hiss until she loosens her grip.

"Sorry. But...you should stay here."

Her gray eyes warn me she's serious, but I need to talk to the kid. Need to know why he thought Kolya would ever let Elena go.

"Ryker would murder me."

I straighten as much as my bruises will allow and try to force some strength into my tone. "Semyon was Zion's best friend. And I just...I need to talk to him. He's terrified of Ryker, and he doesn't know the guys are gone. This might be my only chance. Ryker doesn't need to know."

Inara sighs. "Leave the door open. If he makes a single move you don't like, you scream. Got it?"

"Got it." I reach out and grab her hand, giving it a quick squeeze. "Thank you."

Turning back to the computer, she shakes her head. "Don't make me regret it."

MRE IN HAND, I limp down the steps to the basement. It's actually kind of nice down here. Cool, but quiet. On a dusty old mattress, Semyon sits, his hands bound in front of him, resting with his back against the wall.

"I do not want trouble," he says, holding his hands up in surrender.

"Relax. I've...mostly forgiven you." With a jerk of my head back towards the stairs, I add, "Don't make me call for Ryker and you'll be fine. I brought you some food."

Like I've seen Ryker do a handful of times, I mix up the salt water that heats the meal, set the pouch inside until it's warm, then tear it open and slide it onto a plate.

"Here." Setting the dish next to him, I offer him a blunt spoon. This meal's a chicken pot pie, and while it looks more like a pale, beige brick than actual food, it smells pretty good. "Eat. And listen."

Semyon stiffens, but he picks up the meal and awkwardly tries to maneuver the spoon with his hands bound together. His quick hopeful glance up makes me snort.

"Don't even think about it," I say, and he nods quickly, his whole focus on the brick of pot pie. "When Zion came back to me, he didn't want to talk about what happened. Heck, until a couple of months ago, I didn't even know he'd been in Russia."

"He call you."

"From a blocked number." A ghost of a smile touches my lips. "He was a smart kid. Knew if I found out where he was, I'd come get him."

"I wish…" Semyon stares off into the corner of the basement, his meal largely forgotten. "I wish I had someone who cared for me like that."

"You do." At his disbelief, I risk patting his shoulder. "Zion. He left me pages and pages of emails. I guess he'd written them every couple of days during the years he spent with Kolya, but never sent them. He talked about you and Elena all the time. How you used to clean up his vomit when he'd take too much. How you took a beating for him once when he'd screwed up some delivery for Kolya. And the dumplings. That kid loved dumplings."

Semyon's lower lip wobbles.

"He loved you like a brother. Leaving you here…that was his biggest regret. If there'd been any other way…"

The boy's eyes turn glassy, and he sets the spoon down. "He abandoned us."

"No." I shake my head, then take him by the shoulders so he looks me in the eyes. "Elena got him out because Kolya was going to kill him. She made him *promise* not to come back. When Kolya found out what she'd done, he beat her so badly she couldn't even stand. And then he sent Zion a video *showing* him how he'd hurt her, threatening to kill him if he didn't come back. And *sell* you and Elena. Zion didn't think twice about it, Semyon. He told Elena he'd get you both out. But Kolya got to him first. Zion was a smart kid. And he made sure if anything happened to him, I'd find his messages—and I'd come get you."

Tears well in Semyon's pale blue eyes, and he sniffs loudly. "And then I betrayed him."

"You didn't know, kid. I...I wanted to blame you." I finger the abrasions around my wrist from the ropes Kolya used to tie me up. Anxiety tightens its icy fingers around my heart, and I draw in a deep, shuddering breath. "You're just as much Kolya's victim as Z. Or Elena. Or...me. Sit tight for a little longer, and then we'll all get out of here, okay?"

Choking back a sob, Semyon nods. "Thank you...Wren. Zion say always you were...how does it go...? In his angle?"

"In his corner?" I chuckle as Semyon offers me a weak smile. "For a long time, Z was the only family I had. And family always has each other's back."

39

Ryker

*T*he hour-long drive passes in a blur. A handful of cars on the motorway, yellowish cones of illumination from the occasional light posts breaking up the total and complete darkness, and a surprisingly comfortable silence between West and me.

As soon as Wren told him she could hook up a video chat for him, his entire demeanor changed. Well, no. It changed when I approved the call.

No unauthorized communications. One of my many rules. And while I won't go so far as to tell my team they can bring their personal mobile phones with them, I can't imagine how I'd feel if I couldn't talk to Wren—at least every day or two. Not now.

"That's some hard thinking you're doing, Ry," West says as he pulls off the motorway onto a side road and cuts the lights. We both flip on our night vision heads-up displays, and the lonely country road is painted in blues and greens and grays.

"Why'd you stay?"

"With Hidden Agenda?" He taps his earbud. "Fifteen minutes out, India."

"Roger that. Satellite images are clear. But they're on a ten-minute delay."

West clicks off comms and glances over at me, one brow arched.

"Yeah. With Hidden Agenda. Clearly, I've been an ass since I got out of Hell." I pat down my vest again, double and triple checking my equipment—as best I can in the cramped sedan. There aren't many cars big enough for my six-foot-eleven-inch frame.

West's laugh confirms that yes, I was a complete asshole. But he shrugs. "I needed the money at first. Insurance for the kids' program at the dojo is highway robbery. But," another turn, and he slows the car down to a crawl, "after I got shot, when you and Inara were practically holding vigil at that dirty veterinary office in Columbia, I realized what I'd been missing."

"You were missing bullet wounds and duct tape? Sweating your balls off in a tropical jungle? Wading through a river and then pulling leeches off your ass?" Snorting, I lean forward to peer out the windshield. Any unexpected movement could be a threat.

"Fuck no," he says with a chuckle. "The way a close-knit squad feels like a family. I saw it with you and Inara. And when I wasn't sure I was going to live, and the two of you took turns with the ice packs and blood transfusions...I felt it too. I love Cam. She's my heart and soul, and I'd die before I'd let anything happen to her. But I need you and Inara in my life too. I'm a SEAL. You know how it is. SEALs, Special Forces, Rangers. They burn it into you. 'Never leave a man behind.' You don't find that closeness, that total and complete loyalty anywhere else in life. I won't go back to the SEALs—even though there are some days I miss my old life more than anything—I can't do that to Cam. But I can do this."

"Thank you. I...don't say it enough. Or...at all." Running my gloved fingers over the beads around my wrist, I take a deep, centering breath. If we pull this off, we'll be one step closer to getting the fuck out of Russia. And I need Wren to be safe.

WEST PULLS the car off the road and parks behind an overgrown row of hedges five hundred yards from Popov's home. At 2:00 a.m., he should be asleep—and easy to capture. Except we have no idea what type of security he has around his estate.

"Going in," I say as we exit the vehicle. "No chatter."

"Roger that," Inara replies, as calm as ever. As the slight hiss of the static clicks off, I shut out everything except the mission. West gestures to the right with two fingers, then circles his wrist. After I repeat his motion as confirmation, I start creeping towards the house.

Fifteen minutes later, we're fifty yards from the back door. I flip on the thermal scanners on my heads-up display. A large patch of red on the top floor. A smaller orange glow downstairs is fading. Maybe a fireplace or heater. It's diffuse, larger than a body would be.

West pulls out the signal jammer and flips it on. If Popov has an alarm system, this should short it out. After a flurry of hand signals, we rush the house, West with his dart gun at the ready, me with my lock picks.

The tumblers click one after another, and then we're in. An overwhelming smell of onions makes my eyes water, and I signal to the left. Clear the downstairs before we approach what we hope is a bedroom.

Inara can see everything through the camera built into my display, and I find the source of the thermal reading—a massive cast iron stove in the kitchen that's still warm to the touch. Everything is meticulously clean, not a pot or knife out of place.

The living room whispers opulence, with rich velvet and thick carpets—perfect for muffling footsteps. After checking another three rooms, including what appears to be Popov's office, I meet West at the stairs.

I have a hundred pounds on the former SEAL, and though the stairs feature the same thick carpeting as the rest of the house, I hang back, letting West navigate the rise and check for creaks.

When he makes it to the top without a sound, I follow. Popov's bedroom door is cracked, and we angle glances inside. Two targets. Satin sheets pool around the woman's hips, and her obviously fake breasts point directly at the ceiling.

Popov sleeps on his side, loud snores shaking the walls. Blankets cover most of his body, making my shot that much harder.

Holding up my left hand, I start the countdown. Five...four... at three, I wrap both hands around the pistol grip and draw down on Popov. We keep the count and fire within a millisecond of one another. But my shot hits the edge of the blanket, and Popov jerks, coming alive with a roar as the woman screams. Before she can even untangle her legs, she slumps back against the pillows, unconscious.

My second shot grazes his arm. I'm too close, and he's too quick for me to hold my ground. I take a jab to the cheek, whirl away, and come back with an uppercut to his jaw as West hits him squarely in his bare—and heavily tattooed back. Popov grasps for the dart, spinning around, and for good measure, I send a second dart into his naked ass.

"And stay down," I mutter. "India, two targets down. Wrapping this shit up and heading to you."

"Roger. Everyone okay?"

"Fucker got one good lick in, but pretty boy here's just fine. He won't embarrass you tomorrow night."

Inara's throaty laugh carries over the feed. "Double-time it, Romeo. Night doesn't last forever."

WHEN I PUSH through the back door, Popov slung over my shoulders in a fireman's carry, Wren runs in from the main room. "Oh, thank God," she whispers, but then her eyes widen at the unconscious man on my back. "Popov?"

"Yep. Just be thankful West found track suits for these two." I head down the stairs to the basement, and Semyon scampers off the thin mattress and into the corner of the room.

"Wh-who...is that?" he asks.

Fixing him with a hard stare, I arch a brow. "The key to getting your sister back. Assuming you don't screw things up."

Semyon raises his still bound hands. "I no make trouble. I know truth now. Zion *zhertva* for us."

"*Zhertva?*" Letting Popov slide to the mattress, I step back and brush off my hands. West lays Popov's lover down next to him and checks their pulses.

"He...uh..."

"Sacrifice," Inara supplies as she joins us. "He knows Zion didn't abandon him."

She snaps pictures of Popov and his lover, then snags the duffel West packed with the man's wallet, phone, and laptop and heads back up the stairs where Wren's waiting, wringing her hands. "Come on, hacker-genius," Inara says as she hoists the computer. "Time to get to work."

40

Wren

The sun seeps around the drapes by the time Inara and I finish going through Popov's computer. The man's a brute—intimidating his competition, making them disappear on occasion, paying off government officials—and every new thing we learn adds to Ryker's tension. He's been surprisingly hands-off since he got back, with the exception of pulling me into our little bedroom for a kiss that rocked me down to my toes.

Now, he sits up against the wall, his eyes closed, his lips moving soundlessly.

"Is he okay?" I whisper to Inara.

She nods and draws me into the kitchen where she starts another pot of coffee. "You saw us before the men left for Popov's, yeah?"

I rinse four mugs while she leans against the counter. "Your rituals? Yes."

"This is one of Ry's. I don't know exactly what he does, but I think he's recounting memories. It's his way of staying motivated during downtime when he can't sleep."

"I'm surprised you don't read lips." Drying one of the mugs, I reach for another.

"I do. Just not Ry's." Inara's sad smile dims her gray eyes. "Our first missions, I caught a few words. Never tried again. The man went through...God. I can't imagine."

"He's never told you?"

She snorts. "No. He's changed, Wren. More than I thought possible. You found something in him I think he believed was dead."

I drop my voice to a whisper as I grab the last mug. "What?"

"Trust. Hope. Peace? Any or all of the above? He's...not the same man who left Seattle. I sure hope you're sticking around." The coffee pot sputters, and smoothly, not spilling a drop, Inara shifts one of the mugs in place of the pot to catch the precious nectar.

"I...don't want to lose him." My mind hasn't stopped racing since Ryker told me he loved me. How can we make this work when he lives in Seattle and I live in Boston? I can do my job from anywhere. But...I don't know if Dax would let me. Not with how he and Ryker feel about one another.

I can't take Ryker away from Seattle. Not when he's finally accepted Inara and West as family.

"You won't. Pretty sure he's head over heels for you," Inara says as she gathers two mugs and starts back for the main room. "Now...about that secure video connection you talked about?" She checks her watch. "Royce should be headed to bed in a few minutes. I miss him."

AFTER I CREATE the encrypted video channel and show both

Inara and West how to use it, Ryker and I disappear into our bedroom to give them some privacy.

Our bedroom.

There's nothing in this empty space but sleeping bags, our luggage, a few candles, and an open medical kit along one wall. It could be any room in any house. Belong to anyone or no one. But...over the past two days, it's become ours.

"Does it hurt?" I ask as I brush my knuckles along his jaw.

"A little." He doesn't shy away from my touch, and I run my hands down his thick, corded arms. So much pain. But...something's changed. His body no longer vibrates with tension every time he breathes. A piece of him has...settled, even here.

"The first thing I noticed about you were your eyes," I say as I trace the scar below his left lid. "The colors. The way you seemed to see right through me."

At my smile, his gaze turns sad. Almost wistful.

"I can't. See through you. Fuck, Wren, every time I look at you, I want to know what you're thinking. Because I can't...tell." His voice roughens, and he looks down at my hand splayed against his chest.

"You only think you can't tell. Try." Levering up on my toes, I wrap my arms around his neck and pull him in for a kiss. He tastes like coffee. Like strength and safety and a hint of toothpaste. And as I tease my tongue against the seam of his lips, I inhale his unique scent, stealing his breath as my own.

Ryker slides his hands under my ass and lifts me so I can wrap my legs around his waist. I can feel his heart thud against me, and he turns so he can press my back against the wall.

"What do I want, Ry?" I gasp, our lips so close, they're still touching. "What do I *need* that only you can give?"

He sets me gently on my feet and smooths a hand over my hair. "You want to know me."

"Yes," I breathe. "All of you."

Ryker steps back and strips off his shirt. His pants fall to the floor next, then his briefs, and he's naked in front of me. Despite the number of times we've been intimate in the past week, we've mostly been fused together. Or shrouded in darkness. I've seen glimpses of him. Of his massive chest, his eight-pack, his well-muscled thighs. His impressive, and already erect, cock.

Now, the soft glow from the candles illuminates his scars. The way one shoulder is a little lower than the other. He flexes his fingers, and a knuckle pops. The toes of his right foot are misshapen, and a thick scar runs down the outside of his ankle.

Fifty-four. Fifty-four bones.

I meet his multi-hued gaze, intensity turning his eyes a deep blend of blue and hazel. "You're the most beautiful, impressive man I've ever seen."

"We should get your eyes checked."

"Do you think I care about this?" Taking three steps forward, I trace one of the thicker, uglier scars along his ribs. "Or this?" My lips press to a rough, almost sandpaper like patch of skin along his collar bone. "You rebuilt yourself. Took the shattered pieces and put them back together. I want to know you. Yes. But I also want you to see yourself for who you are."

"Who am I?" Ryker asks, his voice so faint, I have to strain to hear it. Years of sadness and pain etch lines around his mouth, wrinkle his brow.

"You're one of only two Green Berets who survived Hell. You're a righter of wrongs. A leader. A protector. A good man. Someone who will sacrifice anything—everything—for those he cares about, but who doesn't feel like he's worthy of a single person caring about him."

With every word, the tidal wave of emotions churning in his eyes consumes more of him, until he grabs me in a fierce embrace and crushes me to his chest.

"I'm not...I don't deserve—"

I dig my fingers into his sides to shut him up. "And you're the man I love."

Several seconds pass, and I'm not sure he's even breathing. I peer up at him, and tears glisten on his stubbly cheeks.

"Ry?" I'm too short and held too securely to kiss the drops away, so I tighten my arms around him and feather my lips over his heart. "Talk to me, Ry."

He draws in a deep, shuddering breath before whispering in my ear. "You know me, Wren. You're...the only one."

Fingers sink into my hair, and then his mouth is on mine, claiming, taking, until I pull him down with me. My sweatshirt lands across the room, and Ryker's rough palm skims over my breast. "Did you mean it?" He meets my gaze, skating his thumb in a circle around my aching nipple. "What you said? Did you mean it?"

Arching my back, I afford him better access, and he scores his teeth over the other taut peak. "Yes."

"Say it again."

He holds himself over me, pinning me between his strong arms, promising—without words—to be the man I need. The man I want. The man I can't live without.

My lips curve. "I love you, Ryker McCabe. All of you."

41

Ryker

*T*he coffee's gone. Probably for the best, since I think West is vibrating. Semyon sits on the couch, his arms wrapped around his knees, rocking back and forth. If all goes well, we'll go directly from Kolya's mansion to the airfield and be on a transport plane back to the States by sunrise.

A part of me will miss this place. Not Russia. Not being this close to the man who almost destroyed my beautiful bird. My salvation. My love. But something changed in this house. In the room we packed up an hour ago. And I don't know what we're going to do once we land in Boston.

The day disappeared in a sea of slow, languid kisses, soft hands exploring every inch of me, and whispered "I love yous."

Now, Wren and I stand side-by-side, packing up what we'll need for the mission. "I wish you'd—no. Never mind. I don't." Shoving an extra clip into my bag with more force than necessary, I take back my words. I don't want her to stay here. I don't want her out of my sight.

Wren stops and stares at me, laughter in her pale green eyes. "Wait, we're not going to fight? Are you sure? Make-up sex is usually pretty hot."

"We can fight later. I'll pull your hair and you can steal the last MRE on the plane. The good one with the steak and potatoes."

"Ryker McCabe. Did you just...make a joke?" Inara asks as she emerges from the bathroom clutching her chest. "Zip me up, Wren?"

The black satin number clings to her curves, a sleeveless pantsuit of sorts, with wide legs that should allow her to move freely. To run. To fight.

"Cracker Jacks," Wren says, her eyes wide. "You look...like a movie star."

"Holy shit." With a whistle from the corner of the room, West fastens his cufflinks. He's already dressed in a black suit, black shirt, and black tie, and Inara spent the last hour with waterproof eyeliner copying Popov's neck tattoos onto his skin. "No one in the room's going to be looking at me."

"Let's hope not." Inara glances over her shoulder at him, concern drawing her brows together. "You say more than a few words, and we're blown."

With a snort, West checks his pistol and tucks it into his holster. "Whose plan is this?"

"Yours," she grumbles. "Now where are those damn earrings?"

As the two give each other shit, I head down to the basement to check on our "guests."

Popov and his wife, Katerina, sit on the mattress, hands bound behind their backs and secured to the cold water pipes running along the wall. I kneel down to check the zip ties, then offer them each a drink from a bottle fitted with a plastic straw. "As soon as we're done at the mansion, I'll send someone for you."

"Bastard American," Popov growls. "You expect me to give up? To stay here until we die?"

"I expect you to sit quietly while my team and I do your dirty work for you—and get a little payback of our own. If you do, my tech goddess will make sure Kolya's holdings find their way into *your* bank account. How much does he owe you?"

"Two hundred million rubles."

I stare into his steely blue eyes. For all his reputation—and his bravado—he broke in under five minutes when West threatened to cut his fingers off one at a time. He's never bought a woman in his life. His only purpose at tonight's auction was to deliver Kolya a message. Pay up or lose everything.

"You'll have it by morning. Along with an extra seven hundred thousand rubles from me. For the shitty accommodations."

Shock plays over his features, and his wife turns to him, questioning. He translates, as her English is barely passable, and she cocks her head. "*Ty yemu doveryayesh'?*"

Popov studies me. He's not much older than I am, but his skin shows the years in a way that tells me he's seen his share of death. "Yes. I trust him. Men like us...we understand each other."

I nod. "In six hours, this will be over. And you and I will never see one another again."

"Watch your back, big man. Kolya is spider. And he will catch you in his web if you are not careful."

SEMYON CURLS in the back seat of the SUV with strict instructions to keep his head down and his mouth shut. Wren hunches over her laptop, her fingers flying over the keys. We're six blocks from Kolya's mansion, but it's a straight shot into the square if we need to get to Inara and West quickly.

Inara's necklace and West's tie clip both sport small,

embedded cameras, and on the tablet mounted to the console, we can see everything they see, split screen.

The driver we hired for a ridiculous sum of money opens the back door of the town car. West gets out first, then turns and offers Inara his hand. She says something to the man in Russian, then leans in to whisper in West's ear. He looks vaguely uncomfortable. And then I remember it's his wedding day. Or...should have been.

"Andrian Popov," West says, his Russian accent passable after an hour of Inara's coaching. "And Natalya Volkova." A large, burly man swipes a metal detector up and down over both of them, but a month ago, Cam and Royce built us a short-range signal jammer small enough to fit in an evening bag, and our comms go quiet for a moment until the security guard waves the two of them inside, and Inara deactivates the little device.

The next few minutes pass in a flurry of Russian—Inara making what I hope is convincing small talk with several of Kolya's staff. Suited servers move through a grand ballroom with silver platters of canapés, and Inara never stops scanning the crowd until West snags two glasses of champagne from a passing girl who can't be much older than eighteen. They toast, and Inara leans closer.

"Kolya's in the far corner of the room. Two men by the stage wearing over-the-ear-comms units and packing. The auction is supposed to start in half an hour," she says quietly.

"Time to see if Popov was telling the truth." West clears his throat and straightens. "Kolya's headed right for us."

AT MY SIDE, Wren stifles a small sound as Kolya approaches West and Inara.

I reach over and cover her hand with mine. Her fingers are

icicles under my palm. "Relax, sweetheart. He can't hurt you anymore."

The hitch in her breath worries me, but I have to keep my focus. If I don't, all my reassurances might fly out the window.

"Nikolay Yegorovich," West says with a nod, his voice rough and stilted.

"Kolya. Please. May I call you Andrian?" Kolya holds out his hand, and Inara quickly intercepts him.

"Comrade Popov does not like to be touched, *Kolya*." Inara's sharp, authoritative tone demands respect, and she squeezes his hand hard enough Kolya's eyes widen. "I am his trusted advisor— and bodyguard, Natalya."

Here we go. He either buys this, or the entire operation is FUBAR.

Kolya's gaze roves up and down Inara's body, and I want to drive an ice pick into his pale blue eyes. To her credit, Inara doesn't look away, a serene smile on her face visible through West's tie camera.

"Natalya. You are not Russian."

"I *am* Russian." Pulling her shoulders back, she adopts an offended tone. "My grandmother immigrated from Iran when she was twelve. I am as Russian as my employer. Or you." Slipping into Russian effortlessly, she delivers what I can only assume is an expletive-laced verbal beat down, because Kolya steps back and bows his head.

"My apologies, Natalya. Please, may I offer you something stronger than Champagne?"

"Comrade Popov will take a scotch. Neat. I, however, am working. Will the auction begin soon?"

"In thirty minutes. The women are available ahead of the auction if Comrade Popov would like a private viewing."

"*Da. Spasibo.*"

After a suited staff member delivers three fingers of scotch, Kolya—and two of his goons—accompany West and Inara up a set of stairs to the second floor. He slips into Russian, and Inara laughs, West following a split second later. With Cam's help, Inara and Wren wrote a program to feed the English translation into West's ear and display it on screen.

"Your employer is a lucky man, Natalya. To have a trusted advisor so beautiful and so well-spoken. I am afraid the women I have to offer today are nowhere near as cultured. They are, however, obedient. And will never be missed."

"If they were otherwise, Kolya, we would not be interested in them," Inara says. *"My employer has earned his reputation through careful dealings with only the right people. If we suspected any of these women could be traced to him—or you—we would walk away immediately."*

An odd expression flits across Kolya's face, and my internal radar pings. Something's off. I tap my ear piece. "Watch your six. He's up to something."

Wren's brows furrow, and in the back seat, Semyon leans forward as Kolya enters a long passcode to unlock the door.

A single woman kneels on the floor, her head bowed. Her red dress clings to a too-thin frame, and Semyon cries, "Elena!"

Inara turns and glares at Kolya. "You said there would be women. Is this all you have to offer?"

"No, no. But this one...she is special. I believe she is perfect for Comrade Popov. I wanted him to have a few moments with her before the auction. Alone."

Inara leans in to whisper in West's ear in Pashto. *"You're supposed to fuck her. Put on a show and get her and the girls out. I'll distract Kolya."*

I don't like this. We knew they'd probably have to split up, but the plan was for West to excuse himself to the bathroom. Not be locked in a room with a girl he's supposed to fuck.

"Leave us," West grits out, striding over to the girl and grabbing a handful of her blond locks and forcing her head up to meet his gaze. He leans over, inhales deeply, and then turns around to glare at Kolya. "*Teper.*"

"Come, Natalya. I will show you to your seat for the auction. Sergei will wait outside for your employer." Kolya takes Inara's arm and guides her from the room as West wraps his hand around Elena's throat and hauls her to her feet.

As soon as the door closes, West leans in and whispers in Elena's ear. "Are there cameras in this room?"

Her eyes widen, but she doesn't answer.

With his hands roving down her body, he pretends to kiss her neck. "Elena. Listen to me. I'm here for you. To get you and the other girls out of here. Semyon is waiting. Along with Zion's sister. But you have to answer me. Are there cameras in this room?"

"*Da.* Behind you."

West roughly shoves Elena over to the settee in the corner as Wren's fingers fly over the keyboard. "Sixty seconds," she says. "Make it look good."

Grasping the strap of her dress, West glares down at the frightened girl. "Fight me, Elena." He climbs on top of her and pulls up her skirt with one hand, pinning her wrists with the other. She bucks, trying to throw him off, but he's twice her weight, if not more. "Just a little longer."

"You're good," Wren says and lets out a shuddering breath. "The cameras will be glitchy, but they'll mix static with a looped image."

"Thank fuck." West jumps off Elena and helps her to her feet. "I'm sorry, kid. I had to make it look real. Do you know where the other girls are?"

She nods, swiping at tears tumbling down her cheeks. "They are in basement."

"Any other way down there besides the stairs outside the ballroom?" West asks as he pulls his pistol from the holster.

Her eyes go wide, and she chokes back a sob. "Freight elevator. To the right, all the way down the hall."

"Let me guess. Cameras everywhere?"

"*Da.*"

West presses his back to the wall behind the door, motioning Elena out of the way. "We're going to move fast. Do you have shoes?"

"No. He take them." She shakes her head, staring down at her bare feet. Bruises cover her legs and her face has been used as a punching bag too many times. "I can run."

"Okay. Romeo, prepare for my signal. India, get the hell out."

On the left half of Wren's tablet screen, Inara laughs at something Kolya has to say, then lifts the glass of Champagne to her lips as she takes a step—directly into another guest's path. The glass tumbles from her hand, the liquid spilling onto her pants.

"*Der'mo! Imbecil,*" she mutters at the man she ran into, then turns back to Kolya. "Do you have a powder room? This will ruin my outfit."

"Show her," Kolya orders one of his men, and the beefy guard starts to lead her down the hall.

Back upstairs, West shouts, "Help! *Pomogite!*"

When the guard bursts into the room, West wraps an arm around his neck and squeezes, cutting off the man's air. "Shut the door," he hisses to Elena, and she rushes forward.

Fifteen agonizing seconds later, the Russian sinks to his knees, and West holds on for another four count before letting him drop. "Headed to the freight elevator."

"Roger that," I say, my eyes trained on Inara's camera as she reaches the ladies' room.

"Blondie," Wren whispers next to me. "I mean...I think his name is Victor. He...was one of the men who took me. He's... Kolya's favorite."

Her pale face is even whiter than usual, and her eyes glassy. I reach over and rest my hand on the back of her neck, squeezing gently until she blows out a breath.

But when I look back at the tablet, my blood runs cold. Blondie—Victor—and another man have Inara cornered in the opulent bathroom, guns drawn.

"Now, boys," she says, laying her Russian accent on even thicker. "I am certain there has been some mistake."

"No mistake. You and your boss are dead, *cyka*." Blondie rushes her, and after she throws a punch and tries to duck under his arm, the camera cuts out.

42

Ryker

"Fuck! Whiskey, report! Indigo is under fire." West's camera shows only the freight elevator doors, but the image still moves. Over comms, Inara grunts and glass shatters.

"Almost to the basement. India! Check in!" West snaps.

"A little...busy..." After a loud crack, a hiss sounds in my ear, and Wren checks the audio feed.

"Dead." She hunches closer to the screen, lines of code scrolling by faster than I can read them. "I'm trying to hack into Kolya's network. Shit. He discovered my back door. I can't *do* anything from here!"

"Hostiles," West says. "Stay behind me, kid."

Two shots, and I can't sit still any longer. Turning to Wren, I take her face in my hands. Fear churns in her eyes. "Baby, listen to me. Get behind the wheel. Engine running. I have to get them out of there. They don't have enough firepower."

"No, Ry. Please...don't—"

West's strained voice fills our ears. "Romeo, we're pinned down. One clip left. Switching to lethals."

"I have to, Wren. They're my family. Keep the engine running and, on my mark, you haul ass to the back of that fortress. Keep as low as you can, and if I tell you I'm blown, you go to Safehouse Bravo and get in touch with Graham. You hear me?"

Tears tumble onto her cheeks, but she nods. "I...I love you."

A vise squeezes my heart so hard I can't breathe. "I love you too, little bird." Pushing my door open, I shove to my feet, sprint to the back of the SUV, and grab an M-80 and extra magazines. I have two pistols and four clips tucked into my vest, and I'll kill every single one of them if I have to.

"Engine running, sweetheart. Be ready for my signal." Wren slides into the driver's seat, and I lean in, snake my hand around the back of her neck, and pull her into me for one passionate moment. The kiss is hard, desperate, and greedy, and I'd live right here if I could. For the rest of my life. But I won't ever leave a man —or woman—behind. I can't.

Without looking back, I take off at a run.

I REACH the backdoor of the mansion in record time and kick the deadbolt in. The hallway is utterly silent, and I race towards the ladies' room. Inara's my first priority. She was outnumbered and armed with only a knife and a small pistol in an ankle holster. West at least had extra magazines.

As I round the corner, a tall, dark-haired man with neck tattoos shouts something in Russian and takes aim. A single shot to his kneecap takes him down, and I kick his gun away, then slam the butt of my pistol against his head. I'll kill every single motherfucker in Kolya's employ if I have to—as long as my team and Wren are safe, but I'd rather not add more red to my ledger if I can avoid it.

At the ladies' room door, I pause and listen. Nothing. Pushing inside, I gawk. Water spews from a broken sink, the mirror is shattered into a thousand pieces, and the ornately carved wooden door to the toilet is off its hinges. Blood smears the fancy carpet, and one of Kolya's men lies dead, a gaping knife wound across his throat.

"India. Report." Nothing. A glint of light catches my eye as I reach for the knob. Her necklace.

"Base? Over."

Silence.

"Fuck." Yanking the burner phone from one of my many pockets, I check the bars. No signal. Kolya's got a jammer. I'm on my own. We all are.

Wren

The engine turns over with a rumble, and I struggle not to give in to the panic punching a hole in my chest. Semyon scrambles into the passenger seat and I shove my laptop at him.

"How good are you with tech?" I ask as I wrap my hands around the wheel.

"I can send email." His voice trembles. "Is…Elena…?"

"Whiskey? Status report?" I can't hear anything, and now both cameras are out. "Whiskey!"

Only silence answers me, and I take a deep breath. "Semyon, I'm trusting you with my life. With Elena's life. With everyone's lives." I hold his gaze, and in those pale, bloodshot eyes, I see a lifetime of pain. "I have to get in there. I can shut down the entire security system from inside the mansion. Turn off the power. The cameras. Everything. Give Ryker, Inara, and West a fighting chance. But you have to be me."

"Y-you?" He shoves the laptop at me. "No. I am not good with computers."

"All I need you to do is drive. Listen in on comms and be ready to bring the SUV to the back of the building when Ry tells you to. Can you do that?" My heart threatens to beat out of my chest, but if I don't go in there, they could all die.

Nodding vigorously, he says, "*Da*. I can drive."

After we switch seats, he peels out of our parking spot and heads for the mansion. Barreling through the square, he squeals to a stop at the side of the building, and I leap out of the passenger seat, tossing my earbud at him as I go. The tablet's already tucked into my pack—almost a clone of the one I broke in Kolya's bathroom—and I race to the building's back entrance, finding the door kicked in. Ryker. A fire alarm blares, and safety lights flash every few seconds.

I have to get up to Kolya's office.

As I pass the main stairway, men and women stream by me, some crying, others shouting. I try to blend in, but dressed all in black, my hair covered, my only hope lies in my short stature and confusion. I weave around four women huddled together, find the stairs, and force myself to climb them two at a time, ignoring the pain in my still-swollen knee.

A couple of teenage boys huddle in the stairwell on the second floor, whispering to one another, and I grab one of them by the arms. "Where is Kolya?"

"Up!" he squeaks, his voice in puberty's cruel grip.

"Anyone with him?"

"A big man go up too."

My eyes burn. Ryker. If he's with Kolya...he's either killing him or dead. With every blink, I see my brother's body. Ryker's stricken face as I fell off the balcony days ago. The tears tumbling down his cheek after I told him I loved him.

If Kolya's hurt him at all...I have to end this. I don't know where West and Inara are. Elena. The girls. If I fail…Zion's last wish…

Choking back a sob, I shove the boy up against the wall. "I need access to a computer. Away from Kolya. Where can I find his surveillance room? A server?"

The kid shakes his head. "I do not understand."

"Cameras. Computers. Security."

"Basement."

"Take me there. Now." Pulling a dart gun from a holster at my hip—Ryker forced me to take a tiny pistol too, but it's strapped to my ankle as I've never fired a shot in my life outside of video games—I aim it at the kid's head. Maybe he won't know it's just a tranquilizer.

"*Da.*" He hurries back down the stairs, turns right, and then motions me around a corner. A nondescript door at the end of the hall has a broken "Exit" sign over it, and I follow him down another flight until I hear the terrified whispers of at least five or six women and someone shushing them.

"Come out now and we will not kill you," a heavily accented voice says.

Holding up my hand, I stop the kid from going any further.

"Fuck you."

West. He's still alive. Thank God. Taking a quick peek around the corner, I see two of Kolya's men aiming at a bank of lockers.

Can I really do this? Tranq them? A warning shot ricochets off the wall, and one of the women screams. I have to. These girls…I could have been one of them. This…this is real. This is life and death. And I can fire a tranq gun to fulfill Zion's last wish. To save a man who flew halfway around the world to help me. And maybe…to save Ryker.

I slip around the corner. *One, two, three, four, five.* I imagine stroking my fingers over Zion's bracelet, centering myself. Focusing.

Releasing my breath on a sigh, I squeeze the trigger.

43

Wren

One of the goons goes down almost immediately, but the other turns and raises his pistol. I yelp and leap back around the corner, but two seconds later, there's a thud and a clatter, and then West's voice.

"Wren?"

I choke back another sob. "Fudgsicles. Yes. I'm here."

"Where's Ryker?"

Until he grabs my arms, I don't realize my eyes are closed. "I... I don't know," I whisper. "Inara?"

"No idea. Comms are down."

Forcing my eyes to focus, I count six girls behind him, including Elena. Her red dress is hanging half off her shoulder, and tears stain her cheeks. "I know. The security room's down here somewhere. I can disable Kolya's signal jammer. Heck, I can take down the cameras and probably control the lights too."

"Where?"

Turning back to the teenager, I arch my brows. "Well?"

"This way." He gestures to another door, and West stops me before I follow.

His deep blue eyes hold mine. "I'm going first. If I let anything happen to you, Ryker will kill me."

"Ry went upstairs. More than five minutes ago. Kolya's up there." The lump in my throat threatens to cut off my air, and I press my fist against my chest, rubbing in small circles, trying to calm myself down. I can't think about him now. Can't worry he might be dead already.

West swears under his breath and follows the kid through the door. "Clear. Come on," he says sharply, and the girls and I hurry to catch up. The security room is small—barely big enough for the nine of us, but unoccupied. "One of the guys you knocked out came from here. I guess he was the only one monitoring the cameras."

I slide into the chair and pull the tablet from my pack, along with a cable. After I patch myself into the system, I meet West's gaze. "Get the girls out of here. Semyon's waiting outside in the SUV."

"No. I'm not leaving without you." His hand clamps down on my shoulder, and for a second, I let his words comfort me. But then Zion's face flashes before my eyes.

"My brother promised he'd get Elena out. Please, West. Go. If I'm as good as everyone keeps telling me, we'll have comms again in five minutes and you can come back for me."

Indecision flashes across his face for a split second, but then he nods. "You do not leave this room until I come for you. Understand?"

"Roger." I can't give him my word. Can't promise. But he doesn't know that. With his arm around Elena's shoulders, he ushers the girls back out to the hall, along with the kid who led me here, and shuts the door behind him.

Ryker

A hard slap to my face rouses me, and I come to with a snarl, sitting bolt upright and lunging for whoever's hitting me.

"Green!" Inara hisses as her bare arms bruise under my grip. Green means friendly, and my addled brain registers the command seconds before I do real damage.

"What the fuck happened?" Lifting my hand to my head, I stifle a grunt as pain races down my arm. The coppery scent of blood fills my nostrils. There's a lead weight on my chest, and all around us, a fire alarm blares, its shrill screams disorienting.

"You took two. One in the chest plate and one in the shoulder. Not an artery." She helps me lean back against a wall, and I force a few deep breaths, trying to center myself. "You saved my life. Again."

The last few minutes come back to me. Inara, pressed to the wall not quite hidden by a bookcase, one of Kolya's men drawing down on her. I couldn't just shoot him. If I had, he could have squeezed off a round at point blank range. So I shouted, but as I fired, someone tackled me and the alarm started blaring. We both went down, but I managed to break the guy's neck before the first asshole shot me, twice.

Blinking hard to clear my vision, I scan the hallway. Asshole's dead, the thin slice from Inara's blade across his windpipe. "West?"

"I don't know. Comms are down. Your call, boss. Go find Kolya or get West and then get the fuck out of here?"

If we don't find the bastard, Wren will never be safe. "Split up. West was in the basement. I'm going after Kolya. Never leave a man behind, right?"

"Hooah." She pushes to her feet, and I reach into my holster for my backup piece.

"Take this. It's got a full mag."

"What's that leave you with?" Her brow arched, Inara accepts the gun, checks the safety, and waits for me to answer.

"Enough to put a bullet in that blond shithead's brain. Now go, soldier. That's a goddamn order."

By the time I manage to stand, she's gone. Every breath is agony. Rounds to body armor hurt like a motherfucker and leave one hell of a bruise, but my ribs aren't broken, and the wound in my arm is manageable. Compared to being burned with a blowtorch, almost anything is manageable.

Silently, I creep down the hall, weapon ready, listening for the slightest sound out of place between the alarm's ear-piercing clangs. A creak of a floorboard. Heavy breathing. Four quick cracks sound from the first floor, then shouts. God, I hope they make it out. I hope *I* make it out. Make it back to Wren.

Shut it down, Ry. Focus!

Directly under a metal speaker, the high-pitched wail makes me cringe, and I can't hear a fucking thing. I have to get to the fourth floor. If Kolya's anywhere, he's there.

With a quick check of the stairwell, I take off at a sprint, pausing only for a moment on the landing to check above me for any movement. Nothing.

Until I clear the last step to the third floor, and the barrel of a gun presses to my temple.

"You took my precious ruby away," a heavily accented voice says.

Kolya. Fuck.

"Drop the weapon, face the wall, and lace your hands behind your head. If you believe in God, big man, you should tell him you are coming to meet him."

44

Wren

*A*lmost there. I tune everything out, my focus on the screen in front of me. And the progress bar creeping along at a snail's pace. Eighty-five percent. Eighty-six. Eighty-seven.

"Please, please, please..." I'm a cliché again, but I don't care. Another few seconds and we'll have comms, and by then...maybe West will be back for me.

Ninety-eight. Ninety-nine.

Kolya's encryption falls away, and I scramble for a terminal window, starting the shut-down process. The machine throws up another password prompt, and my heart seizes in my chest. No.

Get it together, Firefly.

I can almost hear Z urging me on, and his voice in my head helps calm me down. Digging into my bag of tricks—all the data I stole from him over the course of the past two days—I let my password cracker go to work.

"*Cyka!*" The growl from behind me turns my blood to ice in

my veins. Blondie. His hand wraps around my hair, yanking me to my feet and hauling me against him. "Boss will be very happy to see you again."

"Let...me...go," I scream and try to elbow him in the ribs, but he spins me around and shoves me into the wall hard enough to daze me. I crumple to the ground, and before I can get my legs under me, he grabs my wrists in one beefy hand and slides a zip tie around them with the other. The plastic bites into my skin—hard, and I cry out, feeling my life slip away with every pulse of pain. I can't survive Kolya again.

Blondie grabs the tablet and thrusts it into my bag, loops the long strap over my head and around my neck, and uses it like a leash. "We go see boss now. You fight me, and maybe I do what he could not." His cold, blue eyes bore into me, and nausea churns in my belly.

If Kolya gets his hands on me, he'll do what he couldn't back in his bedroom. He'll destroy me. I'll never be...me again. I won't have Ryker. Won't care either. A sob wells in my throat, but the strap digs into my neck and burns, and the sound comes out closer to a squeak as Blondie yanks—hard—and I almost go down.

"You want me to teach you lesson now? I can do that."

"N-no...Kolya," I say, my voice barely audible, "can make me... feel good."

It'll be better...won't it? If he brings me back to Kolya rather than destroy everything I am here? Now? Kolya wants me docile. Wants me dependent. Maybe he'll take the pain away first. Blondie won't give me that.

Hold onto something real.

Ryker's real. But...is he even still alive? Wheezing breaths scrape over my throat, and the walls start to spin and tilt around me. Tears burn my cheeks as Blondie drags me into the elevator and punches the button for the fourth floor. Twisting my hands, I use the pain to keep me focused, try to feel my pulse under the plastic, count the beats.

We reach the top floor in what feels like record time, and then the strap around my neck tightens again as he drags me to Kolya's office. It's empty, and with a kick to the back of my knees, Blondie sends me to the floor. The tablet slides free from my bag, but the woven black strap is still tight around my neck. "Do not move," he orders me and presses his boot to my back, pinning me to the floor. My hands are trapped under my body, I can barely breathe, but the tablet flickers to life as Blondie reaches for something on the desk, and the fire alarm finally falls blessedly silent.

Da | Net | Otemy

Yes | No | Cancel

The password cracker finished. If I can tap yes, I can bring the whole system down.

I force my body to go slack. If Blondie doesn't think I'm a threat, maybe he'll take his foot off my back. No longer fighting the tears that threaten to consume me, I sob quietly as the crackle of a walkie-talkie pierces the air.

"Boss. I have the girl. The redhead. Zion's bitch sister. We are in your office."

"*Khorosho.*" Kolya's voice—full of self-satisfaction—sends a chill down my spine. "I think she will watch the big man die."

Ryker. Oh God. He has Ry.

"If I am not there in five minutes, kill her."

"*Da.*" Blondie's foot lifts off my spine, and he kneels down so his lips are close to my ear. "Anything happens to boss, we have a little fun before I snap your neck."

I cry harder and curl into a ball. My tears are real. Panic's cruel fingers snake around my heart, digging in, squeezing so hard, I'm terrified I won't be able to breathe—let alone move—much longer.

Just...hold it together...another...five...minutes.

Sneaking a glance at Blondie, leaning against the desk with

his gun in his hand, I inch my fingers forward. The tablet is half hidden by my bag, and I manage to touch the edge just as the office door opens.

"Wren!" Ryker's voice cracks, and Kolya slams the pistol against his head, driving him to his knees.

"Secure his hands," Kolya barks at Blondie, his gun pressed to Ryker's temple. Blood streams from Ryker's shoulder, and...oh God...drips down his left arm.

As Blondie crosses between us, I slide the tablet closer. I just need to see the screen for a second...long enough to touch the right answer. *Yes.* If I'm not careful, I'll hit no or cancel and then... my life, Ryker's life...they'll end right here. On plush carpet, surrounded by lavish walls and eighteenth-century antique furniture.

"I'm so...sorry..." I gasp as I hold Ry's gaze. True fear swims in the varied colors of his eyes. "I had to...try..."

"Wren, baby. Don't look. Close your eyes." With both Blondie and Kolya pointing guns at his head, he knows he doesn't have a chance. "Hold on...to something real. Us. We were real. I love you. Always. You saved me."

Kolya cocks his gun. "Say goodbye, sweet Red."

"You fucking bastard!" I scream, and my outburst startles everyone. Rearing up, I pray I don't miss as my finger comes down on the button that just might save our lives.

With a single beep from the tablet, all the lights go out.

45

Ryker

I see the tablet a second before everything goes dark, and I barrel roll into Blondie, sending him crumpling over me. With my hands bound, I have little leverage, but I grab his black jacket and try to throw him in Kolya's general direction. But the henchman lands just short, and Kolya sidesteps him with ease, springing for Wren.

"Move!" I yell, and in the diffuse glow from the French doors, I see Wren try to scramble up. And then Kolya reaches her side, twisting the strap of her bag around her neck and hauling her up against him. "Let her go, fuckwad."

He aims his gun at my head, Wren gasping for breath as she claws at the thick nylon choking her. "You lose, big man. She is mine."

"Not...yours," she wheezes and jerks, slamming her bound hands into Kolya's crotch. The Russian yelps and doubles over, and Wren's elbow connects with his nose. He jerks the strap around her neck, and her helpless choking sends pure rage flooding through my veins. With a roar, I yank my arms as hard as I can, the plastic digging into my skin, more blood slicking my hands until the zip tie snaps in two.

Behind me, Blondie staggers to his feet, but I have eyes only for Kolya. He'll die for hurting her. Tucking and rolling, I wrap my legs around his ankles and pull. A hoarse cry escapes Wren's lips, and then all hell breaks loose.

A door slams. Something crashes into my temple—the butt of Kolya's gun, I think—and I see stars. No. That's muzzle flare. Shouts in Russian don't make any sense, and then Kolya's under me, his fingers digging into the bullet wound in my shoulder as I wrap my hands around his neck and squeeze. He chokes, desperately clawing at my fingers, his eyes bulging. Lifting him two inches off the ground, I slam him back down again, his head landing with a satisfying—and sickening—crack.

"Ry!"

West.

"Let him go, Ry. It's over. He's bleeding out." Strong hands help me up, and West's concerned face swims in and out of focus for a few seconds until I get my bearings and shake off his hold. "You good?"

"Yeah."

Inara stands over a dead Blondie, her gun trained on Kolya as he tries to stop blood pouring from his stomach. It's hopeless. The stain on his white shirt is almost black. The shot caught him in the liver, and he has minutes at most.

West pulls his multi-tool from his belt and turns to Wren, sitting on the floor, still wheezing, frantically trying to unwind the strap from her neck and staring off into nothing. "She's panicking, Ry. Calm her down while I get this fucking thing off her."

"Wren, baby. Look at me." I cup her cheeks, brushing her tears away with my thumbs, then cursing under my breath as I smear blood across her pale skin. "Dammit." Wiping my hand on my pants, I lean closer, ghosting my lips over hers. "Wren. Take a deep breath for me."

"C-can't," she stutters. West unwinds the strap from her neck, and I stroke the bruised and abraded skin.

"Yes, you can." Gently, I press her fingers to my carotid artery. "Feel my heartbeat." I mirror her position, breathing slowly, audibly, until she stops shaking and her eyes start to focus. "There you are."

A quiet sob escapes her lips, and she tries to peer around me. "Is he..."

"Almost," Inara mutters. "He's going to have a very painful last few minutes." West snaps the zip tie around Wren's wrists, then heads for the French doors.

"Where are the girls?" I ask as I pull Wren into my arms, ignoring the burning pain shooting through my shoulder.

"In the car with Semyon." West angles a glance down at the square. "As soon as we got them to the vehicle, we headed back in. We were almost to the third floor when the lights went out. The police are on the way. If we don't want a whole lot of trouble, we need to get the fuck out of here."

I struggle to my feet, keeping Wren tucked against my side. "Can you walk, sweetheart?"

She nods vigorously, her red curls bouncing. She's still half-panicky, but her voice is stronger now, and her gaze doesn't leave Kolya as I guide her towards the door. "Y-yes."

I spare the Russian a quick look, and the truth registers in his eyes. He knows he's dead. His mouth opens and closes, but he can only gurgle weakly.

Returning my focus to Wren, I whisper, "He'll never hurt you again, baby. We're going home."

❤

I CALLED in a favor once we landed in Moscow, and two hours

later, a former Special Forces instructor met us at a private terminal with a van to take the girls somewhere safe. He'll arrange for new papers and good jobs once they have a few weeks to recover from being starved and beaten by Kolya and his men.

The sun is setting as we land at a military airfield outside Boston. The headsets protecting our hearing made it hard for me to be as close to Wren as I wanted on the flight, and the uncomfortable jump seats allowed only piss-poor rest, but we both fell asleep halfway over the Atlantic with my good arm slung around her shoulders. West dug out the bullet while we waited for my buddy, gave me a shot of antibiotics, and stitched me up. Thank God no one else was seriously hurt.

Inara and West deplane first, followed by Semyon and Elena. The brother and sister hold onto one another and blink up at the red and orange sky.

"Time to go, baby," I say as I help Wren to her feet. She's barely said ten words to me since we left Kolya's mansion, and I can't stand the silence between us. She moves stiffly—we all do—but as soon as she catches sight of our welcoming committee, she lets out a sob.

Dax and Ford stand with their backs to the setting sun, and Pixel bounces around at their feet, her little tail whipping around fast enough it's just a blur of white. Two SUVs idle nearby, one with a uniformed driver behind the wheel.

"Pixel. You brought Pixel," Wren whispers as she drops to her knees in front of the men. The little dog wriggles in her arms, and she buries her face in the soft fur.

Ford offers me a firm handshake and gestures for me to follow him—and Dax—while Inara wraps an arm around Wren's shoulders and murmurs to her quietly.

Out of earshot, Ford shoves his hands into his pockets. "You're all set up at the Fairmont again under a fresh ID and clean credit card. Figured you'd all need a couple of days, so we arranged for a flight to Seattle for you and your team on Thursday."

"Wren, too," Dax adds. "Until we can guarantee the Roxbury arm of Kolya's organization withers and dies without him, she's safer out of Boston."

I stare at her, Pixel in her arms, Inara leading her over to one of the SUVs. This is her home. Where her brother lived...and died. How can I ask her to leave? "It has to be her choice."

Raking a frustrated hand through his tousled locks, Dax half-growls, "There is no choice. She's not safe here right now, and you can protect her."

"I'd die for her." Both men wear twin expressions of shock. "I love her. I want a life with her. Fuck. I want *the rest* of my life with her. But you know her well enough to understand she's never going to let us tell her she *has* to do anything."

With a chuckle, Ford shakes his head. "You're right. But... maybe *strongly suggest* she at least go out to Seattle for a little vacation?"

"That I can do." We shake again, and he heads over to the driverless SUV. The one with Elena and Semyon in back.

Staring at Dax, I try to find the words to thank him for everything he did for us. All of our gear—except for Wren's laptop and tablet—he had delivered to the hotel. He handled all of the logistics for our return trip, coordinated with the proper border security agencies, and kept the shit at the mansion out of the papers. "I...owe you."

"You do. Maybe..." He takes off his tinted glasses and rubs his eyes. When he raises his head, I'd swear he can see into my soul. "Maybe you could give me a call sometime. To...uh...catch up."

If he lays me out flat, it'll still be worth it. I lean in and clasp him in a tight, quick hug. But he doesn't protest, instead returning the gesture and clearing his throat. Probably has a lump in it the size of mine, if I know him at all. And maybe...I still do a little.

"I promise." My voice cracks, and I release him.

"Those words...Wren's right. No one should ever say them if they don't mean them." Dax reaches into his jacket pocket for his cane, unfolds it, and concentrates for a moment before pointing himself directly at Ford's SUV.

Squeezing his shoulder before he can take a step, I force the lump away and blow out a breath. "I'll call. You're...family, Dax. And family keeps their promises."

He blinks hard, and I think I see a slight glisten to his pale, sightless eyes. "Hooah."

WAVING the keycard over the hotel room door, I try to calm my nerves. We're alone...finally. Except for the dog, who passed the forty-minute drive stretched across both of our laps. Wren only asked one question after I slid into the back seat of the SUV next to her.

"Are we going to my apartment?"

"No, baby. Tonight, we're going to the Fairmont."

She settled then, twining our fingers and resting her head against my arm.

"Are you hungry?" I drop my duffel and her bag in the corner, set the deadbolt, and wedge the desk chair under the knob. "I can order...whatever you want." Fuck. I don't even know what she likes to eat.

"I..." She stares down at her sweater, caked with dried blood, and wrinkles her nose. "I want a shower."

Settling Pixel on the little dog bed, she shuffles off to the bathroom, but doesn't shut the door. Am I supposed to go with her? I hope I am, because I need her like I need my next breath.

Stopping short when I reach the threshold, I find her staring into the mirror.

With morbid fascination, she touches the red burns around her neck. Next, she pulls up her sleeves, wincing when she brushes the zip tie welts on her wrists.

"Wren. Look at me." Her tiny gasp is barely audible, but I feel it as I press against her back. "You're okay. We're both...okay."

"Are we?" She pulls up my shirt, and once the bloodstained wool falls to the floor, she skims her fingers around the edges of the bandage over my latest bullet wound.

"I'll heal. Always do." Reaching into the shower, I twist the knob, and once steam starts filling the room, I carefully slide her sweater over her head, then unhook her bra.

"What do we do now?" Wren wriggles out of her pants and stares up at me. Her lower lip wobbles, but she doesn't cry.

"Shower. Eat. Sleep." I run my knuckles along her cheekbone. "Make love in an actual bed?"

Her laugh soothes all my rough edges. "Oh, come on. Those were awesome sleeping bags."

"Only the best for you, sweetheart."

The water runs red at our feet for too long, but I wash her hair, and she moans softly as I massage her scalp. "What...happened here?" she asks, pressing a kiss to the deep purple bruise just above my heart.

"That's what happens when you take a shot to body armor."

"Is this...are you...?"

Fuck. She was right. I know exactly what she's thinking, and fear takes over, sharpening my tone. "This is who I am, Wren. Running Hidden Agenda. Helping people. I don't know how to do anything else."

"I don't want you to stop." Pressing her naked body to mine, she slides her hands down to cup my ass. "Just...don't hide anything from me."

"Nothing. Ever. I pro—"

"Ry." She stops me with a finger to my lips. "You know what those words mean to me."

Cupping the back of her neck, I pull her in for a slow, deep kiss that sends my cock to attention and leaves her panting. "I do, sweetheart. And I promise. No secrets. Ever again."

Room service delivers burgers and fries, along with two icy cold bottles of beer. We eat in bed, wrapped in the hotel's plush robes, with Pixel racing between the two of us, begging shamelessly. Wren tears off a piece of fry every few minutes and indulges the dog. I want to ask her about Seattle. About coming home with me. But I'm afraid if I do, this warm, comfortable bubble we're in will burst.

And then she turns and smiles at me. I inhale sharply and tangle my fingers in her hair. "What changed?"

Her brows furrow. "I don't understand."

"Your eyes. I see *you*, Wren. It's like you're...back with me. After we left the safe house, you disappeared. Even earlier, in the shower..."

Her cheeks flush pink, and she stares down at my wrist where Zion's bracelet still rests. "I didn't realize I was hungry until the food showed up."

"It wasn't the food." Her eyes were so vacant after we left the mansion. And now, the copper flecks burn bright.

With a nod, she covers my hand with hers. "It kind of was." Her voice drops, and she pushes the tray aside, then snuggles against my chest. I can't see her eyes anymore, and she wears her shame like a mask. "When...Blondie found me in the security office, I was so scared. I didn't know where you were. Or if you were even still alive. He told me he was taking me back to Kolya, and I thought...for a minute...it'll be easier. I won't care about anything. I won't be scared. I won't hurt. I won't have to fight anymore."

"Wren—"

"Let me finish. Please?"

Pressing a kiss to the top of her head, I wait.

"And then...you were so scared. I've never seen you...scared." She waves her hand. "I know we've only known one another for two weeks, but come on." She peers up at me, the corners of her lips curving into a smile. "Pretty much our entire relationship has been one terrifying event after another."

"Not every event." Her nipple rises under the plush fabric when I skate my thumb over her breast.

Wren bats my hand away and links our fingers. "Hush. You know what I mean." After a sigh, she scoots up a little higher so we're eye-to-eye. "Nothing after the lights went out felt real. I remember everything. West cutting the zip tie. Kolya...gasping for air. How Semyon and Elena held onto each other the whole flight. Ford standing there with Pixel."

The dog yips, and I toss her another fry.

"As stupid as it sounds...this," she gestures to the remnants of our meal and then to the two of us tangled together, "is the first *real* moment I've had since we left the safe house. And...I want more of them. All of them." Running her fingers over Zion's bracelet, she meets my gaze. "With you. I love you. *We're* real."

Long seconds pass, and she touches my cheek, amusement dancing in her eyes. "You can talk now. I'm done."

My laugh still surprises me. The raspy tone. The way my entire body feels...warmer. Lighter. How I can't help smiling. "Just following orders, sweetheart." Several slow, tender kisses later, I draw back. "Come to Seattle with me. At least for a little while. We'll go to West's wedding. The future..."

"I can work from anywhere." Her words tumble out in a rush. "I'll need to fly back here once in a while...either for a job or just to see everyone. But...Boston stopped being home when Zion died. I want a fresh start, Ry. With you."

EPILOGUE

Wren

Two days later, Ryker eases the keys from my hand and unlocks my apartment door. So much has changed since I took Pixel out for what should have been an uneventful walk. He's tense, and I know he's hired someone to pack everything up for me, but I can't leave without a few essentials.

My favorite sweater. The photo of me and Z at the Sox game. My mother's jewelry box—where I store a collection of stones and crystals I've collected over the years. The green pendant Zion gave me. Pixel's toys, and the soft fleece blanket from my bed.

But there's one other reason I had to come back here. "Give me a minute?" I ask as I zip up the suitcase.

"I'll be right outside the door." He eases the bag's handle from my grip and brushes a light kiss to my lips.

Every day this man amazes me. He's still very much the same tough, hates-talking-about-his-feelings person he was when we met. But we don't always need words. He understands me, even when I don't understand myself.

Sinking down onto my bed, I let the pendant warm against my palm. I can't wear it. My neck is still raw and painful. But I need a touchstone.

"Z? Semyon and Elena are safe now. Ford is driving them to Maine this afternoon. Kolya...*donated* twenty thousand dollars to get them started, and we found them an in-patient recovery program that will let them stay together. New identities, jobs waiting for them when they get out..." I turn the green glass over in my hand, tracing the edges with my index finger. "I wish you could have met Ryker. You'd like him. Or...maybe he'd drive you crazy. But...I love him, so you'd find a way to get along." The image of the two of them facing off almost brings a smile to my face. "I...won't be back here again. Not in this room. So, come find me in Seattle, okay? I love you, kid. Always and forever." Heading out to the living room, I stop with my hand on the door knob.

"I promise."

One week later

Ryker

Wren leans back against me as we stand by the floor-to-ceiling windows in my—our—apartment. Pixel snores in the corner, a princess on the world's plushest dog bed. West and Cam's wedding was a quiet, small affair, thank God, and as we walked the few blocks home, Wren got me to admit it wasn't the torture I'd anticipated.

"What are you thinking, little bird?" Scoring my teeth along the shell of her ear, I relish the shiver that runs through her.

"Ten days ago, you stood in front of me, naked, and I told you I loved you for the first time."

"I remember." Every second of that night is burned into my brain. As she lay under the sleeping bags, sated and peaceful, I cataloged every word. Every feeling. Every emotion. Joy. Fear. Pride. Shame.

Turning to me, Wren slides her hands around my neck. "You said the words almost forty-eight hours before I did. How did you know?"

I scoop her up into my arms and carry her to bed.

"You're avoiding the question."

"Not...exactly." After I slide the green straps off her shoulders and her dress pools on the floor, I nudge her down onto the mattress, then kneel between her thighs. "Before I met you, I woke up every night screaming. Every fucking night for six years."

Wren unbuttons my black dress shirt, exposing the scars across my chest.

"I tried therapy. Sleeping pills. Alcohol. Nothing quieted my demons. And...I couldn't figure out why. Until you." I shrug out of the shirt, then take her hand and press her fingers to the scar below my left eye. "You asked me what happened. Back in Boston. That night...the demons didn't come."

"You...loved me before we went to Russia?" Her voice rises a few notes, and I chuckle.

"No, baby. Not then." I let her undo my belt, then step out of my pants and briefs. "Can I hold you?"

When we're nestled together, skin-to-skin, her nipples pressed to my chest and our legs entwined, I run my fingers through the soft curls of her hair. "I never wanted to talk to anyone. Even West and Inara...if it wasn't about the mission, I rarely said two words to them. But you... Every time you asked me a question, I *wanted* to answer. I needed to answer. Needed you to know what I was thinking. Feeling. I couldn't explain why. Pissed me off."

Now it's her turn to laugh. "I could tell."

"When you were taken, I knew. That night. West called me on it, and I tried to deny it, but...I couldn't." My eyes burn, and all I can see is Wren. Bruised. Bleeding. Afraid.

Warm fingers tighten on my hip. Over one of my many scars. "I'm *here*, Ry."

I can't tell her everything yet. If I could, I'd tell her being with her makes me feel like I matter. Like I'm more than my scars. My damage. My broken body and shattered mind.

I'd tell her how I hadn't smiled in months. Hadn't laughed—real laughter—in years.

Most of all, I'd tell her how she saved me.

"Kiss me, baby."

Her lips are warm, soft, and she tastes like rain. And tonight, a hint of wedding cake. Of sherry. And of need. I pinch her nipple, and she arches into my touch.

I skim my hand over her breast, down her stomach, all the way to her mound. Sliding a finger between her slick folds, I swallow her moan, tangling our tongues in a dance I never wanted to learn, but now can't live without.

"Ry," she whimpers. "More."

I trail kisses over every curve, adding a second finger when her eyelids start to flutter. The first gentle caress of my tongue has her hands fisting the sheets, and fuck. I inhale deeply, unable to get enough of her scent.

"I love you, little bird," I say against her clit.

"Need...you..." she gasps and grabs my arms. "I want to see you, Ry. Please."

One of those late night conversations I didn't want to have, but don't regret for a second? She's on birth control, and I'm clean. So when I slide home, there's nothing between us.

"God, Wren. You feel...so good." I suck my drenched fingers into my mouth, then lean down to kiss her. She moans again, and I thrust deep. Clutching my ass, she urges me on, and I raise my head just enough to look into her eyes.

"Come with me, baby."
Make me whole.
And she does.

HELLO,

Thank you for reading *On His Six*. This story is special to me for so many reasons, and I wanted to take a few minutes to tell you a little about me and *On His Six*. Books always seem to mean a little more to me when I know something about the author who wrote them, and I hope you'll agree.

I write characters I call "beautifully broken." Why? Because I think in some ways, every one of us is a little bit broken. But broken isn't always a bad thing.

Have you ever played with a glow stick? When you pull one out of the package, they're inert. Dull. Dark. Useless.

But once you *break* them, they start to glow. They're light in the darkness. They're useful. They're perfect.

We all go through dark times in our lives. Times that threaten to break us. Times that *do* break us. But that doesn't mean we're anything less than beautiful. Or capable. Or perfect. Just the way we are.

I'm broken in some ways. I have anxiety and ADHD. I'm short. I'm nearsighted. Yet, I'm beautiful. I'm beautiful because I'm me. I'm the person I'm meant to be. And I love that person.

You? You're beautiful too. Yes. You. No matter what. Because you exist. I hope you'll come on a journey with me through my books. See the Also by section for a list of the other books I have available or visit my website: http://patriciadeddy.com. I love talking to readers, so email me at patricia@patriciadeddy.com.

If you'd like, sign up for my newsletter or come find me on Facebook. You can also join my Facebook group, **Patricia's**

Unstoppable Forces, where we talk about books, life, and everything in between.

And above all, I hope you'll continue this journey with me. *Second Sight* is Dax's book, and he and Ryker...well, in some ways, they're two halves of a whole. Brothers in every way that counts.

Turn the page for a special sneak peek of *Second Sight*, and **ONE-CLICK it TODAY!**

Love, Patricia

SNEAK PEEK - SECOND SIGHT

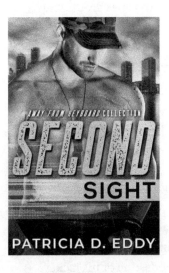

Six Years Ago

Dax

A dim halo seeps around the heavy canvas our captors tack over the cell doors. After so long here, I can almost see in the dark. Small variations in the rock walls. The flutter of air moving a corner of the shroud. My toes—if I wiggle them. Not that I've tried recently. The infection will take my leg soon. Or my life.

Let me fucking die already.

Ry's gone. Escaped. Hours ago. Killed at least four on his way out. We were supposed to go together. But I can't walk. He set my broken femur two weeks ago. One of the few times they let us stay in the same cell. But what should have been a minor burn festered, and now my whole leg is swollen and hot to the touch. At least they don't tie me up anymore.

Booted footsteps shuffle down the hall. I'm not as good as Ry. I can't always tell who's coming. The canvas is ripped away, and I blink rapidly, the dim lights of the hall searing my eyes after so long in the dark.

Rough hands close around my arms, someone throws a bag over my head, and I'm dragged from my cell. My leg screams in agony, the white-hot pain sending me barreling towards unconsciousness. Until they drop me.

Breathe. In and out. Focus.

"Get him up," Kahlid—the guy in charge—says, and I'm hauled onto a table. Before I can try to fight, they've tied my wrists together, then lashed me down with ropes around my torso, my hips, and my ankles.

Oh fuck. This is new.

"Sergeant Dash. How are you today?" As Kahlid pulls off the hood, I spit at him, but he's too far away.

"Fuck you."

The punch to my jaw isn't unexpected. Hell, that's how the fucker says hello. I taste blood, the metallic flavor turning my stomach.

His smile worries me. As does the glint in his eyes. "Would you like some water?"

This is some sort of trick. Say yes, and they'll waterboard me. I grind my teeth together, glaring at him, but in my current state, I doubt it's very effective. After Kahlid nods, one of his lackeys grabs my jaw and digs in, forcing me to open my mouth. A pill lands at the back of my throat, followed by half a bottle of water, and unprepared, I swallow before I can stop myself.

"Antibiotics only, Dash. Do not look so...frightened." Starting to pace with his fingers laced behind his back, he continues. "Your friend Ryker killed several of my men last night."

"Good for him." Another punch, more blood staining my lips.

"You gonna keep that up? You want me to talk, it ain't gonna happen if you break my jaw."

"I do not want to hurt you, Dash. I only want to know where your friend Ryker was going. He will not get far. We shot him many times. I am worried for him. Tell me his escape route, and I promise you, he will not be harmed when we find him. We will treat his wounds and send him to hospital."

"Yeah. And I'm Santa Claus." I don't have the energy to keep this up. My leg throbs with every beat of my heart, my split lip is swelling rapidly, and I'm nauseous from the water they forced down my throat.

Kahlid leans over me, and shit. The bastard's a good actor. He actually manages to look...concerned. "What I have to do, Dash... you will not heal from this."

Is he finally going to kill me? Fear snakes its cold, bony fingers around my heart, but I'm so far gone, so weak, in so much pain death would be a welcome relief. "That's not...my...fucking... name. Whatever you're...gonna do...just get it...over with."

Behind Kahlid, two of his lackeys pull on thick, rubber gloves, and my stomach churns. Not the blowtorch. Or a belt. Or even a metal rod. This...has to be something different. Kahlid grabs a fistful of my hair—it's longer now. Hangs into my eyes. "Where is he? Tell me and I will not have to do this."

"Go...to...hell," I grunt. "You'll never...find him."

Kahlid slams my head down on the wooden table, and the edges of my vision darken. His crooked smile is the last thing I see as a harsh, caustic liquid splashes into my eyes, and I start to scream.

♥

The metal tray lands on the stone floor with a crash, and I jerk awake, my heart racing. The cell door slams shut, and a weak glow of light dims as the canvas flops back down. I don't know how long it's been since they blinded me. Kahlid told me I screamed for half a day. Then he broke the last two fingers on my left hand when I still wouldn't talk. The one time they dragged me out of this cell since, my whole world was a muted sea of dull, washed out colors and agony every time I forced my swollen eyes open.

Crawling slowly, only able to use one arm and one leg without passing out from the pain, I feel along the filthy stone floor until I find the edge of the tray.

Fuck. I hope Ry made it.

I scoop up a bit of the rice slurry with my uninjured hand, then let it fall through my fingers. I can't. They've taken everything. Dax Holloway doesn't exist anymore. Hell killed him. I don't know when it happened. Every beating. Every scar. Every time they threw me in that goddamned hole. Left me there until I was out of my mind with hunger.

I can't walk. Can't make a fist with my dominant hand. Can't... see. Why keep fighting? Months ago, I was ready to give up. Starved myself for what I think was a week. Until they force fed me, then whipped Ry until his back was bloody. But he's gone. Safe. Or dead.

Forcing myself to sit up, I grab the tray and fling it against the bars. That'll earn me another beating. More broken bones. I don't give a shit. "You want me to talk? How's this? You're all a bunch of sadistic fucks. You can carve me into a thousand pieces, and I'll still never tell you what you want to know!"

I collapse, my head hitting the dirty floor. Shouts echo down the winding stone hall, and I try to scramble back, knowing they'll come for me. I don't care what they do, but I won't make it easy for them.

Despite all the months I've been here, I still can't understand much Pashto. But Kahlid's men sound panicked. Heavy footsteps race down the hall past my cell, and then...

Gunfire.

Not AKs. Not Taliban guns. Colt M4s. SEALs. Special Forces. Rangers.

"Go, go, go!" someone shouts, a hint of a Southern twang coloring their words.

"Four hostiles down," another voice responds. "Clear."

Wrapping my good hand around the bars, I try to pull myself up. "American," I call weakly. "Here."

"Get that goddamn door open. Now." Light flares, bright enough to penetrate my swollen lids, as the canvas is ripped away, and a dark shadow looms as someone breaks the lock. "Holloway?"

"Yes." I reach out a tentative hand and find a tactical vest as the man kneels next to me. "Who—?"

"West Sampson. SEAL Team Eight on a joint op with ODA. Can you—"

"Where is he?" Ryker roars from down the hall.

Oh God. He made it.

"Third cell," West calls. "I'm bringing him out."

Only a few feet away now, Ryker growls, "No one touches him but me. Dax?"

I jerk my head towards his voice, opening my eyes, desperate to see him. Except...I can't. Not after what those fuckers did to me. The pale reddish glow from the hall brightens as the heat of a flashlight paints my face.

"Fuck. Dax, what the hell...? Your eyes."

"Questions later," West says. "This place is coming down as soon as we're clear. Get him up and move."

"Where's Kahlid?" Ryker asks as he hauls me over his shoulders in a fireman's carry, his arm hooking under one knee as he grips my wrist tightly. Unable to see or tell up from down, I can't orient myself, and nausea crawls up from my stomach when he starts hustling down the hall.

Shouts, another three shots. "Blue Team Alpha approaching egress point. Need a location on Target Zulu," West says.

We start to climb. I'm...safe. I'm going home. The tears gathering in my burned and blistered eyes send shooting pain through my skull, but I don't care.

"Roger that. Kahlid's down. They've got him at the mouth of the cave. He'll be dead in five minutes."

"Then we've got time." Ryker's voice lowers, turns grave. "He's ours, Sampson. Give us sixty seconds alone with him, then we're gone."

West doesn't respond—at least not that I can hear. The first whiff of fresh, free air smells like heaven, and then West orders everyone to fall back. Somewhere below me, I hear raspy, rattling breathing.

"I told you I'd kill you," Ryker says as he bends and sets me on my feet. Keeping an arm around my waist so I don't collapse, he presses a pistol into my hand.

"I can't see, Ry," I whisper. "You have to—"

He shifts me. "Put your other arm around my shoulders and hang on. I'll aim for you. We fire together."

With a nod, I clutch the back of his tactical vest so I don't fall, and he supports my left arm with his. To my right, he cocks his pistol.

"Fifteen months, asshole. Every day, I pictured this moment. When your last sight would be the two men who took down Hell. Say your prayers, fucker." After a beat, Ryker snorts. "On second thought...don't."

We fire together, and as the gun falls from my shaking hand, Ryker says, "We're going home, brother."

Home. As Ryker half-carries me down the mountain and a series of explosions shakes the ground under our feet, I start to sob. We might be going home, but I'll never see Boston again.

ONE-CLICK SECOND SIGHT TODAY!

ALSO BY PATRICIA EDDY

Grab the rest of the *Away From Keyboard* series now!

Away From Keyboard

Dive into a steamy mix of geekery and military might with the men and women of Emerald City Security and Second Sight.

Breaking His Code

In Her Sights

On His Six

Second Sight

By Lethal Force

Fighting For Valor

Elemental Shifter

Hot werewolves and strong, powerful elementals. What's not to love?

A Shift in the Water

A Shift in the Air

By the Fates

Check out the By the Fates series if you love dark and steamy tales of witches, devils, and an epic battle between good and evil.

By the Fates, Freed

Destined: A By the Fates Story

By the Fates, Fought

By the Fates, Fulfilled

♥

In Blood

If you love hot Italian vampires and and a human who can hold her own against beings far stronger, then the In Blood series is for you.

Secrets in Blood

Revelations in Blood

♥

Contemporary and Erotic Romances

I don't just write paranormal. Whatever your flavor of romance, I've got you covered.

♥

Holidays and Heroes

Beauty isn't only skin deep and not all scars heal. Come swoon over sexy vets and the men and women who love them.

Mistletoe and Mochas

Love and Libations

♥

Restrained

Do you like to be tied up? Or read about characters who do? Enjoy a fresh BDSM series that will leave you begging for more.

In His Silks

Christmas Silks

All Tied Up For New Year's

In His Collar

ABOUT THE AUTHOR

Patricia D. Eddy lives in many worlds. Witches, vampires, and shifters inhabit one of them, military men and women fill another, with sexy Doms and strong subs carving out the final slice of her literary universe. She admits to twelve novels (though there are at least five unfinished drafts on her desk right now), all while working a full-time job, running half-marathons, and catering to the every whim of her three cats. Despite this whirl-wind, she still finds time to binge watch *Doctor Who,* all of the Netflix Marvel shows, and most recently, *The Handmaid's Tale*. Oh, and she hopes to one day be able to say that she plays the guitar. Right now, she mostly tortures the strings until they make noise.

If you made it this far and are still reading, you should be rewarded. Email Patricia at patricia@patriciadeddy.com with the code *Restrained Teaser* in the message body and she'll email you a deleted scene from *In His Silks*. Possibly even two.

You can reach Patricia all over the web...
patriciadeddy.com
patricia@patriciadeddy.com

f facebook.com/patriciadeddyauthor

𝕐 twitter.com/patriciadeddy

⧉ instagram.com/patriciadeddy

BB bookbub.com/profile/patricia-d-eddy